SHE ...
AS HE ...

. . . and her throat tightened at first sight of his broad, muscled chest with just a sprinkling of fine, blond hair. He held her gaze as he removed the rest of his clothing, and when he stood naked beside the bed, looking down at her, Julie felt only a moment's hesitation at the sight of his hard body.

And then he was beside her on the mattress, his hands moving over her flesh. He kissed her gently, then moved his lips to explore the body his hands knew so well . . .

Propping himself up on one arm, Micah looked down into her eyes, silently demanding that she not look away.

He lowered his mouth to hers, and after kissing her, pulled back only a breath and whispered against her mouth, "Feel it, darlin', let it take over now. Don't fight it . . ."

DIAMOND WILDFLOWER ROMANCE

A breathtaking line of
searing romance novels . . .
where destiny meets desire
in the untamed fury of the American West.

Diamond Books by Ann Carberry

RUNAWAY BRIDE

ANN CARBERRY

DIAMOND BOOKS, NEW YORK

This book is a Diamond original edition, and has never been previously published.

RUNAWAY BRIDE

A Diamond Book/published by arrangement with the author

PRINTING HISTORY
Diamond edition/April 1994

All rights reserved.
Copyright © 1994 by Maureen Child.
This book may not be reproduced in whole or in part, by mimeograph or any other means, without permission.
For information address: The Berkley Publishing Group, 200 Madison Avenue, New York, NY 10016.

ISBN: 0-7865-0002-6

Diamond Books are published by The Berkley Publishing Group, 200 Madison Avenue, New York, NY 10016.
DIAMOND and the "D" design are trademarks belonging to Charter Communications, Inc.

PRINTED IN THE UNITED STATES OF AMERICA

10 9 8 7 6 5 4 3 2 1

With thanks to Susan Macias, Jill Marie Landis,
and Justine Davis for the impromptu plotting
and the most fun I've ever had at a book signing

CHAPTER
···ONE···

"ALL RIGHT. LOSER gets Julietta."

"Shut up, Micah!" Tribulation Benteen snarled at his younger brother. "She'll hear ya, for God's sake!"

Micah snorted. "Hell, I'm past carin' *what* that female hears or don't hear! She's been nothin' but trouble since we first hooked up with her, and you damn well know it!" He waved one hand at Trib's splinted leg, propped up on bed pillows. "Jesus! She even broke your leg for ya, Trib!"

"That was an accident," Ritter Sloane tossed in and frowned at his brother-in-law.

"Accident, my eye." Micah glared at Ritter, then swept the others in the room. It was obvious even to him that Jericho, Shad, and even Trib himself sided with their sister's husband. "Look," he said hurriedly, "if she hadn't been tryin' to run off, she wouldn't've spooked Trib's horse the way she done, and the damnfool critter wouldn't've bolted, tossed Trib to the ground, and stepped on him to boot!"

Jericho chuckled softly, caught Trib's eye, and quieted immediately.

Micah swallowed, then sucked in a big gulp of air. Glancing at his oldest brother, he saw the angry flush

1

on the big man's face and guessed that it probably hadn't been the wisest thing to do ... reminding Trib about being thrown from a horse. Hell, besides the pain of a broken leg, the embarrassment alone was enough to kill a man.

"The durn horse *didn't* throw me," Trib grumbled. "I, uh ..." He paused for a long moment, then added, "It don't matter now anyway."

"Hell, yes, it matters!"

Shadrack gave Micah a shove, but he ignored it and continued, "Ever since me and Jericho caught up to you and that blasted woman, she's been nothin' but a burr under *all* our saddles! *I* say we let 'er do just what she wants to do. Go back to that friend of hers in Montana."

One long, silent moment passed. Wavering lamplight from the kerosene lamps on either side of the bed danced and dipped across the features of the five men. A cold mountain breeze slipped under the partially opened window and fluttered the starched, blue-and-white curtains.

Trib groaned and pushed himself higher up against the carved headboard of his massive, four-poster bed. His sharp, green eyes moved over the men clustered around him and finally, quietly, the head of the Benteen family spoke.

"Nobody *asked* you what you had to say, Micah."

"Trib—"

"No! It's finished. I already sent the wire to the girl's pa. Duffy's expectin' us to get his daughter back to Texas, and that's just what we're gonna do."

"Now you're talkin' about that," Jericho asked, "just

2

how the hell did the girl's pa, this Duffy fella, know you? And how to find ya?"

"And," Shadrack tossed in curiously, "why not just put her on a train? From what Micah tells me, you bunch already took care of those fellas that was givin' her trouble in Montana. Hell, she'd be all right on the train!"

"No." Trib glared at his brothers. He didn't want to waste any more time explaining himself. All he wanted was to get this job done and his indebtedness to Duffy finished. "No, she wouldn't be all right by herself. Those men were hired by the girl's grandma, down in Mexico. And from what I hear of the old bat, she ain't about to quit after only one try. There'll be more trouble, and it's up to *us* to get the girl past it."

The four men stared at him, obviously curious for more information. Trib rubbed his jaw viciously. He'd only been home a week or so, and in that time he'd found a newly married sister, a gunfighter for a brother-in-law, the tail end of a range war, and had his leg broken for him. He should've kept traveling.

Slowly he let his gaze move over the familiar bedroom. Once his parents' room, he'd moved in after they were gone. Now, save for their wedding portrait, still hanging on the far wall, there was little reminder left that the room had ever belonged to anyone else.

And that was as it should be. He was the head of the family now, and there was no escaping it. Even when being the head meant sometimes having to do things that went against everything inside him. It was his responsibility to see that the Benteen ranch *and* family survived. He pulled in a deep breath and unconsciously rubbed his propped-up thigh. If he had to pound that fact into his thickheaded brothers every day, then by thunder that's what he'd do.

Silently he studied the triplets, each of whom was leaning against either the wall or his bed. Jericho, the brother who saw something funny in everything. Shadrack, the quiet, thoughtful one. And Micah. Trib shook his head. Micah always *had* had more than enough temper for two men.

Glancing to his right, Trib watched Ritter Sloane for a moment and silently admitted to himself that so far he approved of his sister's new husband. True, the man had a past, but who the hell didn't? At least Sloane had a head that he used for more than a spot to hang his hat.

"Well?" Jericho prodded, snapping Trib back to the problem at hand. "How'd you meet this fella?"

"It's a long story," he said. And, he mentally added, he wasn't about to go into that! "It's enough for you boys to know that I met him in the war." He looked slowly from one to the other of them. "And I *owe* him."

Jericho met his brother's gaze evenly and nodded. Shad added his agreement, and Ritter gave the man one brief nod. With a telling glance at Micah, Trib waited. The man's wild red-brown hair and beard almost bristled with outrage, but finally the last remaining brother mumbled, "All right."

"Good." Trib raised his closed right fist. Three straws, seemingly equal in length, poked up.

"Why only three?" Ritter asked quietly and looked at the injured man through suddenly shuttered eyes.

"Don't get your back up," Trib countered. "First off, Hallie'd kill me if I sent her brand-new husband off on some trip with a pretty girl. . . ."

Ritter pushed away from the wall, but before he

4

could speak, Trib added, "*And* we can't hardly have you waltzin' around the countryside right when word's startin' to spread that you're *dead*!"

"He's got somethin' there, Sloane." Jericho nodded sagely and ignored Ritter's frown.

"Hell, all the trouble we went to, keepin' you alive, and you want to go on out and get yourself killed by some young yahoo lookin' for a reputation?" Shad shook his head and frowned.

Ritter sucked in a gulp of air and exhaled in a rush. His features tightened, and everyone in the room saw how much he wanted to argue with them. Obviously a man like Ritter Sloane didn't like being left out of something for his own safety. Finally, though, he nodded and stepped back to watch the other three draw.

"Now there's one short one in here," Trib said, jerking his head at his brothers. "Whoever gets it, goes."

"Why only one of us? Wouldn't it be better— *easier*—for two?" Jericho rubbed one hand over his bushy beard.

"Prob'ly. But we can't spare two of ya," Trib pointed out. "Ritter and Hallie here are gonna start in on buildin' their own sleepin' quarters right away, *and*," he said, loud enough to drown out Jericho's pleased chuckle, "it's gonna take at least two others workin' the ranch full time, now that it's spring." He jabbed a finger at his upraised leg. "I'm gonna be laid up about six weeks, Doc says, so that means two of you boys *have* to be here. 'Sides," he added, "the trip shouldn't take more'n a couple weeks goin' and a couple more comin' back."

"Let's do it then," Shad said. "The sooner we get it goin', the sooner it'll be done." He reached for his brother's outstretched fist and let his fingers move over the straws. Quickly he pulled one free and cupped it in his hand without looking at it. "You boys go on. We'll look at 'em together."

Jericho and Micah both reached for the same straw, but Micah grabbed it and his brother had to make do with the last remaining straw.

"All right then," Trib commanded, "let's see 'em."

Each of the triplets extended one hand, the straw lying across the palm.

Jericho began to laugh. Looking up at Micah, he said delightedly, "That's what you get for bein' greedy, Brother. You shoulda let *me* have that one!"

But Micah wasn't listening. Instead, he stared down at the tiny piece of straw he held. "Goddammit!"

In the main room the front door slammed with such a force it rattled the windowpanes.

Micah sighed. Wouldn't you just know it!

* * *

"*¡Santa Maria, Madre de Dios!*" Julietta muttered and stomped out into the empty yard. Wrapping her arms tightly around herself, she shook her head and started walking. She didn't care where, she just wanted to get away from that house—and him.

Micah Benteen. Hah! If her father had known that it would be a man such as Micah escorting her back to Texas, would the older man *still* have demanded she come home? She stopped dead, tilted her head back, and stared at the black sky overhead. Sighing, she admitted silently that yes, her father wouldn't care if the Devil himself were riding alongside her, as long as Julietta did as she was told.

Tears filled her eyes, and she pulled in a deep shud-

6

dering breath, trying to hold them at bay. She *wouldn't* cry. Not anymore. Not for something that had never existed and never would. Long ago she'd realized that her father didn't love her. Why was it, she wondered, that she still couldn't accept that one, undeniable fact? Why did she insist on *trying* to win the man's affections? His approval?

Rubbing her hands up and down her arms, she wished for a moment that she'd taken the time to grab a coat before rushing outside. Her long-sleeved white shirt was no match for the bone-chilling cold of a Wyoming night. She blew out a rush of air and watched it become a cloud of mist.

So different. It was all so very different from home. From Texas. She straightened abruptly and reminded herself that *different* was exactly what she wanted. What she'd *craved* since she was a child.

As far back as she could remember, she'd dreamed about leaving the rigid confines of the rancho. Julietta smiled as she recalled the wild daydreams and plans she'd made over the years. How she'd travel the country until she found the one man who would love her for who she was . . . *not* for what she could do for him. She sighed heavily. Though she'd finally packed away her foolish fantasies, she *had* managed to get away from the Duffy ranch. *And* her father.

Tossing a glance at the Benteen ranch house behind her, she muttered solemnly, "I *won't* go back. Not yet. Maybe not ever."

"Who ya talkin' to?"

Julietta spun back around, her hand at her throat, to face Hallie Benteen Sloane. Forcing a smile, she said quietly, "You frightened me."

"Sorry. Guess you were too busy thinkin' to hear me walk up." Or, she added silently, too busy cussing my brothers to be payin' attention.

Hallie's gaze moved over the young woman she'd known little more than a week. Julietta's night-black hair fell in a long, straight line to her narrow waist. Unshed tears shimmered in her deep, blue eyes, and her lips were clamped tightly together. Shaking her head, Hallie thought that it was a pure shame how her brothers could reduce a woman to talkin' to herself in only a few days.

"Somethin' wrong?" she asked, knowing good and well there was.

"Ah . . . ," Julietta paused, took a deep breath, then apparently decided to rid herself of her anger. "It is your brothers!"

"Naturally."

"They do not care that I have no wish to return to Texas. They won't even listen to me when I speak to them!"

"I know."

"All the big one—Trib—will say is that he has given his word to my father and it must be kept."

"Uh-huh."

"He treats me as if I have no say in any of what happens to me."

"Well," Hallie finally said, "accordin' to *him*, you don't."

Julietta snorted inelegantly, then raked her gaze up and down Hallie contemptuously. "You are no better than they are!"

"Now hold on one minute, lady." Hallie was more than willing to be sympathetic. After all, she'd spent her whole *life* trying to make those blockheaded brothers of hers listen to her. But she'd be damned if she was going to let this woman talk them down. Wagging one finger at her, Hallie went on, "You don't know us from Adam's aunt, and you're gonna stand there preachin' to *me* about my own brothers?"

Julietta's lips twisted and she started to speak, but Hallie cut her off.

"Now, I know the Benteens ain't never gonna win no prizes for good manners, but there's not one of them four that wouldn't do all he could for a body."

"But—"

"And you best learn right off that when a Benteen gives his word, it's as good as gold. The only thing that would keep a Benteen from keepin' his vow is death. And even *then* one of the others would make sure what needed doin', got done."

"Even when the one they are helping doesn't want the help?" One tear fell from the corner of her eye and trickled halfway down her cheek before Julietta swiped it away angrily.

Impulsively Hallie leaned toward the other woman and gave her a quick, hard hug. "Hell, I'm sorry I tore into you like that, Julietta." Their eyes met and Hallie continued. "*I* know better than *anybody* what it's like tryin' to deal with that bunch. But, hon, you got to realize. They ain't doin' this for you. They're doin' it cause Trib promised your pa to get you home safe."

"Hmmph!" Julietta shook her head slowly and gave Hallie a wan smile. "My *pa*, as you call him, only wants me back to anger my grandmother."

"What?"

"It's true." She sniffed and lifted her chin defiantly.

"But it doesn't matter. All that matters is that I have no wish to return to Texas. And I have decided not to go."

"Julietta—"

"No. It makes no difference to me what your brother Micah has to say about this. I will not go."

"Micah?"

Julietta frowned, narrowing her eyes. "I overheard them talking. Micah was the 'loser.' *He* is the one to escort me home."

"Micah?" Oh, Lord, Hallie thought wildly. Why not Shad for heaven's sake?

"Yes. *Him.*"

Her tone of voice, when she said that one word, held a whole worldful of anger. In an underbreath Julietta rattled off something in Spanish that sounded suspiciously like a curse. Switching to English in midsentence, she finished, "If they think to make me travel for more than two weeks with that foul-tempered, irritating man—" She stopped abruptly and looked uneasily at the sister of the man she'd just insulted.

"Oh, it's all right, Julietta." Hallie shook her head and smiled. "Can't hardly argue with the truth, can I?" Looking at the woman, Hallie didn't have the heart to say anything more. There would be time enough for Julietta to find out that she wasn't about to win this battle with Micah. The woman *would* be going to Texas.

And, knowing Micah, she'd be going real soon.

"Enough about the boys now," Hallie said suddenly, determined to make her guest's last days in Wyoming pleasant. "How'd you like me to show you the moon real close up?" Grabbing Julietta's arm, she started walking across the yard to the bench the boys had built her so long ago and the delicate instrument beside it.

10

"My husband Ritter? He sent for this here telescope all the way to Boston! Isn't that somethin'? Well, wait till you see the moon and all them stars through this thing. It'll curl your hair!"

* * *

Micah stepped out into the yard an hour later and paused to let his eyes become accustomed to the darkness. As he turned his head slowly, his gaze raked the open ground between the house and barn. He stopped when a sudden movement by Hallie's bench caught his eye.

Julietta. Had to be. Everyone else was inside, planning which route he should take to Texas. Sucking in a gulp of air, Micah rubbed his bearded jaw fiercely. How in the blue blazes had *he* got stuck with this damn job?

For God's sake, wasn't it enough he'd had to listen to her harpy's tongue all the way from Montana? Wasn't it only fair that somebody *else* should have to take her home? He took a step, then stopped again.

Maybe they could just hold her here at the ranch and send word to her father to come get her! He smiled suddenly at the thought and told himself it would be the perfect solution. Then he wouldn't have to be alone with her at all!

No, his mind sneered. You'd just have her around your house, under your feet, for who knows *how* long. Maybe her pa couldn't travel fast. Hell, maybe he *wouldn't* travel fast. Then what?

Though it pained him to admit it, he knew having the woman around the ranch would be too much for him to take. Despite her temper, her Spanish curses, and the disgust for him she didn't even bother to hide, Julietta Duffy stirred something in him he hadn't even known

11

existed. If she were to stay at the ranch for any length of time, he might be tempted to make a bigger fool of himself than he already had.

Micah frowned, grumbled a halfhearted curse under his breath, and started walking again. No. It was best he just did this and got it over with. If he hurried her along, they could prob'ly make Texas in two weeks. Sooner, with good horses and a hatful of luck.

Filled with new determination, he continued on toward the bench, where Julietta sat, staring up at the sky. He breathed deeply and tried to steel himself for what he was sure would be yet another of their stormy arguments. And he used to think *Hallie* was stubborn!

He heard her a heartbeat later. Sniffling and breathing rapidly, she tried to muffle the sound of her crying with one hand clapped over her mouth. But in the quiet night her hiccuping breaths couldn't be silenced.

For a moment he considered going back to the house. Pretending he hadn't heard her at all. He knew she wouldn't like knowing he'd seen her crying. Even in the short space of time he'd known her, Micah'd come to admire her pride and even, reluctantly, a hardheadedness to match his own. His mind worked quickly, searching for a way out of this latest muddle. But there wasn't one and he knew it. He couldn't just walk away and leave her there alone. Crying.

Micah forced his feet to move. Lord, he hated it when women cried. He was never sure what to do or say. And he hadn't had much practice dealing with a woman's tears, either. Most of the females he'd grown up around, including his mother and sister, would just as soon pitch a rock at a man as cry over him.

"You all right?" he asked quietly as he came up beside her.

Julietta jumped, wiped the tears from her cheeks frantically, then glared up at him. "Of course, I am not all right!" she snapped.

"Well, hey now," he countered and took a step back. "Ain't no call for you to go leapin' at *my* throat! This trip here ain't none of my doin'."

"Hah!" She pushed herself up from the bench, sniffed loudly, then went on. "I know. I heard you. 'Loser gets Julietta'!"

Shit. Micah swallowed, pulled in a deep breath, and blew it out again. She *had* heard him. Well, his mind countered, what did that matter? Hell, it ain't like it was any big surprise or anything. She knew as well as him that the two of them just didn't get along.

"Señor Micah,"

"Huh?" His eyes narrowed, he watched her warily. Her tone of voice had changed. All signs of anger gone, she took a step closer to him, with a forced smile curving her lips.

"If we try very hard, we may find a solution to both our problems," she whispered.

Micah licked his lips nervously. Moonlight flickered in her blue eyes and her honey-gold flesh almost seemed to glow. Something was wrong here. Very wrong. What had happened to the burst of temper he'd been expecting? Where were the Spanish curses he was getting much too used to?

Just what in hell was she up to?

"Will you listen to me for just one moment, Señor Micah?"

Sure, he told himself. He'd listen. Though he was

hard put to admit it, even to himself, he purely enjoyed how she sounded when she talked. Even when she was mad as spit, the hint of Spanish in her English made the words almost sound like music.

Besides, he was damn curious now.

"Before you came outside, I was thinking," she started.

"Yeah. I *heard* you."

A brief frown twisted her lips before she swallowed and forced a smile again. "That was nothing, I assure you. The tears, I mean. I was merely . . . *tired*."

"Uh-huh."

She cleared her throat. "Señor Micah . . ."

"Just Micah."

"Oh. All right then. Micah."

She smiled, and Micah felt like a virgin in a cathouse. He knew something was coming, wasn't sure whether he was gonna like it or not, but knew there was no way to escape it.

"You do not want to go to Texas, *sí*?"

"*Sí*. I mean, yeah." She took one step closer and Micah swallowed heavily. The soft, heady aroma of jasmine clung to her hair and drifted up to him. He breathed deeply, enjoying the scent even as he watched her nervously.

"*Bueno*. Good. I do not wish to go, either."

"So?"

"So," Julietta said on a deep breath, "I propose that we leave this place together, as the others expect us to. Then we each go our separate ways."

He knew it. Sure as anything, there *had* to be a reason for her to turn all sugar nice and soft talking. Micah shook his head slowly. Looking down into those big blue eyes of hers, he'd never guess that she could be that damn sneaky. She looked like such a *sweet* little thing!

"And what do I tell my brothers?" he asked, crossing his arms over his chest.

She waved one hand at him indifferently. "Tell them that I escaped from you. That I ran away and you couldn't find me."

The laugh exploded from him, startling a bird in a nearby pine into flight. Micah bent over, his hands on his knees, and let the chuckles shaking his body have free rein. After a few long moments, he straightened up again and wasn't the least bit surprised to find her eyes spitting daggers at him.

"I do not see what is so funny."

"No, ma'am, you surely don't." He grinned down at her. "I got to give you credit, ma'am. You don't have one bit of 'back-up' in you. But your plan just ain't gonna work."

"Why not?" She lifted her chin and straightened her shoulders.

"For one thing, a Benteen give his word that you'd get back to Texas safe, and that's just where you're goin'."

She opened her mouth but Micah cut her off.

"For another, nobody in this county would believe that you run off and I couldn't find you."

"And why is that?"

"Because, lady"—he shook his shaggy head and wiggled his eyebrows at her—"I'm the best damn tracker in the territory. I could follow one cow into a herd and *still* pick out that one cow's tracks from all the rest." Hands on hips, he leaned toward her, his self-satisfied smile still in place. "Now if I can do that, you really think one little female like you is gonna give me any trouble a'tall?"

Enjoying the game suddenly, Micah watched as a play of emotions darted across her features. Disappointment, then anger, filled her eyes. Her finely shaped lips clamped together into a grim line, and every inch of her shapely body trembled with frustration. Her gaze locked with his, Micah saw a glint of amusement flicker into life, and just for a moment he felt a hint of worry shoot through him.

"We will find out, won't we?"

"Huh?" His brow furrowed, he cocked his head at her. "What d'ya mean?"

"I *mean* that I am *not* going back to Texas. With you or anyone else."

"Oh yes, you are."

"We will see, *Señor* Micah. It is a long way to Texas. The journey can be filled with surprises." One black eyebrow lifted in a mocking salute before she whirled away from him and started for the house.

"That we will, *Hoo-lee-edda*!" Micah called, laughing at her blatant challenge.

Halfway across the yard, Julietta stopped, shuddered slightly, then stomped on toward the front door.

CHAPTER
···TWO···

"DAMMIT, MICAH," HALLIE ordered, poking her index finger at his chest, "you get ahold of your temper!"

He glared down at her. "I have got hold of it! If I didn't, so help me, I'd be in the house right now, tannin' her hide for her!"

Hallie's lips twitched, but she wisely swallowed the laughter bubbling in her throat. "*That* sure as hell wouldn't be a good way to start this little trip of yours."

"And this *is*?" He held up his hands, a stirrup clenched in each tight fist. "Damn her anyway! What the hell was she thinkin', slicin' up my saddle gear this way? And *when* did she do it?"

"Must've sneaked out here during the night." Hallie shrugged and let her gaze wander over Micah's mutilated saddle.

"What'd she think to fix by doin' this anyway? She must've known I'd just use one of the boys'."

"Yeah," she said, noting that the only saddle harmed was the one branded with an M. "Guess she just wanted to tell you something."

He glanced over his shoulder, through the open barn door toward the house where Julietta was still having breakfast. Then he looked back at the stirrups he held.

A clean knife cut slashed through the worn, brown leather straps and he cursed again just before he disgustedly threw them to the dirt. Through narrowed eyes, he watched his sister. "And just what in the *hell* d'ya s'pose it is that she's tellin' me?"

Hallie leaned one elbow on the top plank of the stall gate and propped her chin in her hand. "I don't know for sure, Micah. But I'm willin' to bet she ain't through tellin' ya yet."

He snorted and walked back to the tack room. Over his shoulder, he called out, "Tell Jericho I'll be usin' his saddle for this trip."

Hallie turned to leave, but her brother's voice stopped her again.

"*And* you can tell Miss Hoo-lee-edda Duffy for *me* that I got a few things to say to her, too!"

When the tack room door slammed, Hallie cringed and started for the house. Thank God, she thought, that she was safely married to Ritter. If she hadn't been, she suspected she'd have been dragged along to make sure Micah and Julietta didn't kill each other. Hallie shuddered. It was going to be the trip from Hell.

Julietta smiled at herself in the mirror and finished tucking the tail of her cream-colored shirt into her soft, brown leather split riding skirt. Even from inside the ranch house, she'd heard Micah's angry roar when he found his saddle.

Reaching for the mass of hair hanging down her back, she quickly began to braid it into one thick plait. Just because she was being forced to accompany him, that didn't mean she had to be pleasant about it. Her smile widened as she told herself that ruining his saddle was only the first step.

She wasn't a fool, by any means. In a house with this many people, she'd known he would have a replacement saddle handy. But slicing those stirrups free was only the warning bell. Julietta moved closer to the mirror, threw her braid over her shoulder, and stared at the reflection of her own blue eyes. Deliberately she straightened her spine and said softly, "I will *not* go back to Texas. He cannot make me go. Between here and the rancho will come many opportunities for escape—and I will need only one of them."

From outside, she heard Micah's shout and bit down on her bottom lip. Maybe she *had* made a mistake. Maybe taunting him with a ruined saddle *was* the wrong thing to do. But when he'd started ordering her about, just like her father did, she'd *had* to fight back. She wouldn't go back to living her life by someone else's rules. Not again. She was free now, and that was how she intended to stay.

She turned quickly, crossed the small bedroom, and looked out the window at the snow-capped mountains in the near distance. But instead of the towering, craggy peaks, Julietta saw herself as she'd been only three weeks before, at her friend Thea Moore's house.

Smiling, Julietta leaned her forehead on the cool, clear glass of the window and in her mind's eye watched herself dancing at the welcome party given in her honor. She saw the handsome young men who'd come to call on her. She heard the teasing note in Thea's father's voice when he accused his daughter and Julietta of trying to drive every unattached male in the territory wild. Bill Moore was everything Julietta had ever dreamed her own father would be. And how she'd loved being treated like a well-loved child.

Until Tribulation Benteen had shown up at the Moore house and ruined everything! If only Thea's father had been home that day instead of away on business. . . . Julietta *knew* that she'd never have been forced to leave.

Sudden movement caught her eye, ending her useless daydreaming. Across the yard, Micah stepped out of the barn, leading two horses. Her practiced eye raked over the animals in an instant. One of the horses, a magnificent black stallion, tossed his head proudly, while the other animal, a tired-looking bay, followed along humbly.

She frowned thoughtfully. Not a good omen, that. Julietta felt sure that Micah would expect her to trot behind him just as obediently as the spiritless horse he obviously intended for her. Even from a distance she saw his angry features and imagined she could hear him muttering. A slow smile curved her lips. Good. The damage she'd done to his saddle had accomplished her goal.

Now he knew what he could expect during this trip he and his brothers insisted on. She smiled slightly as an idea struck her. Maybe, if she made enough of a nuisance of herself, when she finally *did* escape, Micah wouldn't *want* to come after her.

Her fingers tightened over the edge of the windowsill. The smile on her face faded away as a grim determination filled her. She would find a way to get free of her "captor." Once on her own again, she'd ride to Montana. Julietta was positive that if she could only reach the Moore house, Thea's father would protect her from the Benteens and anyone else Patrick Michael Duffy, *or* her grandmother, sent after her.

She straightened up when Micah climbed the front steps and entered the house. The only problem with her plan was, she'd have to hurry. She couldn't delay in planning her escape. She *had* to grab her first opportunity.

Heavy bootsteps in the hall outside her room sounded especially loud in the silence. Unwillingly her mind still racing, she turned to face whoever was coming.

With every day of riding, she told herself, they would get farther and farther away from Montana . . . and sanctuary. And if Micah Benteen *did* manage to get her all the way back to Texas, it might be years before she had this chance again. Once her father got her back on the rancho, Julietta was sure he would find a way to bind her to the place for life.

The bootsteps in the hall stopped directly outside her door. She took one last, staggered breath and held it as someone knocked on the heavy, oak panel.

"Come in," she said.

The door swung wide, and the man called Shadrack smiled at her. "You about set, ma'am? Micah's fixin' to go now."

"*Sí.* Yes, I am ready." Julietta lifted her chin and forced an answering smile to her lips. Snatching up her bag from the bed, she marched across the room and into the hall without a backward glance.

It had begun.

* * *

"Dammit, woman." Micah looked over his shoulder and yelled at her. "That's a horse you're ridin', not a durn snail!"

Julietta didn't bother to comment. She had no intention of urging her horse into a trot. Ducking her head, she managed to hide her smile at Micah's obvious impatience. He'd spent the better part of the last two hours waiting for her to catch up.

Once, when she'd fallen so far behind him she couldn't see him for the surrounding trees, she'd considered making a break for freedom. Then, remembering what he'd told her about his abilities at tracking, Julietta had abandoned the idea. Her chance would come soon enough.

And by then, she told herself smugly, he would be so glad to be rid of her, he'd never *think* of following after!

As she came alongside him, Micah reached out and snatched the reins out of her hand.

"What are you doing?"

Wrapping the leather straps around his saddle horn, he merely glanced at her before grumbling, "I've waited all I'm gonna wait for you today, *Hoo-lee-edda*. If you can't figure out a way to make that dang horse move, then *I* will!"

He gave his own horse a quick kick in the ribs, and as they started moving, she heard him say, "Hell, I thought all you Mex girls could ride like you was born on a horse!"

"So I can."

"Hah! What I seen today, I'd say not."

"I have no problem riding, when I *wish* to ride, Señor Micah."

He tossed her a look over his shoulder then turned back to the trail. "I told you already. I ain't no señor. Just Micah."

"And I am not Hoo-lee-edda. It is Julietta." As well he knew, she told herself. There was no reason for the way he mutilated her name each time he said it. He did it purposely. To annoy her. It bothered her to admit how well he succeeded.

"Hell, I can't roll them letters out like you do," he complained, but she heard the smile in his voice.

"Very well," she countered. "Señor Micah, you may call me Julie."

"Julie?" He looked back again, his brow furrowed. "Don't sound very Mex to me!"

"It is how I was called when I was at school," she answered softly. Actually she thought, it was Thea Moore who'd christened her Julie. The other girl said at the time that Julietta was simply too big a mouthful to say when a person was in a hurry.

And along with a new name, Julietta had gained a friend and a new sense of confidence.

"School, huh?" Micah didn't look at her when he asked. "One of them big, fancy places, I'll wager?" Almost as an afterthought, he added, "Where was this school?"

"St. Louis," Julietta said on a sigh and immediately her mind was filled with memories of Mrs. Potts' Academy for Young Ladies. The two years she'd spent there, so far from home had given her her first taste of freedom. Though all the daughters of wealthy families had been cosseted and protected by the staff of the school, there *had* been opportunities for the more adventurous of the girls to get out and explore the city.

And Julietta had grabbed at each chance presented to her as a starving man would at a piece of bread. She and Thea, inseparable, had explored the city of St. Louis from the museums to the waterfront. From the docks they'd watched wistfully as the huge paddle wheelers set off upstream, bound for the gold camps along the Missouri and beyond. She smiled reluctantly as she recalled how the two of them had very nearly sneaked aboard one of the boats, only changing their minds at the thought of being caught as stowaways. Shaking her head, Julietta told herself that no doubt Mrs. Potts was much relieved that she and Thea Moore were no longer the old woman's responsibility.

"Julie, huh?" Micah said thoughtfully, and she was snapped back to her present situation. "Well, I'll admit it's a helluvalot easier on the tongue. Still don't sound Mex, though."

"As you have already said," she countered, wishing now that she'd jumped on that boat when she'd had the chance. "I am also half Irish."

"So you are."

A long minute passed, the only sounds their horses' hooves on the still winter-hard ground.

"All right," he finally said with a nod. "Julie." Then he glanced back over his shoulder and grinned wickedly. "Now hang on, *Julie*. We're gonna make up some time, here!"

She grabbed hold of the saddle horn with both hands as he urged the horses into a fast trot. Without holding the reins and controlling the animal herself though, she found it harder to keep a steady seat. Lifting her gaze to her companion, Julie noted Micah's easy posture in the saddle and how he seemed to be almost a part of the black beast he rode.

His rust brown hair curled over the collar of his buckskin shirt, and not for the first time she noticed how broad his shoulders were. He held his reins in a lax grip, his hand resting on his thigh. A shotgun lay easily in the crook of his arm, and she was suddenly aware that escaping from him would be no easy matter.

A quietly powerful man, he was clearly as at home in the saddle as he claimed to be in the forest. She'd already experienced his hardheaded determination and told herself that he would *never* simply give up searching for her should she manage to get away. Unless, of course, she'd made him so miserable he didn't even *try*.

Flopping unsteadily in the saddle, Julie told herself that it was best if she waited, however impatiently, until she could follow the plan she'd come up with back at the Benteen house. She groaned softly as her backside slammed down hard, but still a smile touched her lips. Tonight she thought grimly, *she* would offer to make coffee.

Micah laid another piece of wood across the dancing flames and averted his eyes from the light. Staring into a fire could serve to make you blind to the darkness. And that could get a man killed.

Warily he glanced at the woman not five feet away. He hated like hell to admit it, but she'd done all right for herself so far. He knew good and well that her behind had to be hurtin' something fierce from the pounding she'd taken all afternoon. But somehow he knew she'd never say so.

Shaking his head, he reached for the frying pan, sliced some bacon and started it cooking. Grabbing up his saddlebags, he tossed them to her and said, "Hallie packed some bread and such in there. Why don't you dig 'em out?"

From the corner of his eye, he watched her.

As she rooted through his saddlebags, Julie felt his eyes on her and forced herself to remain calm. He *had* to believe that she'd made up her mind to be cooperative. For her plan to work, he had to trust her. At least a bit.

With the towel-wrapped bread in one hand and the coffeepot in another, she dropped the saddlebags to the ground and walked to his side.

Reluctantly she thought that he'd chosen a good campsite with plenty of shelter from the night wind. Tall, ancient pines with gnarled limbs surrounded them. Huge boulders, crazily stacked atop each other as if dropped from a careless hand, completed the cavelike feel of the campsite. The swaying flames of the fire tossed eerily moving flashes of light over the darkness, and Julie shivered.

Suddenly aware of the total blackness of the night, she felt her already tenuous confidence about her escape waver. She was a stranger in this part of the country. She didn't know her way around. What if she got lost in her search for Thea's house? What if she simply wandered around in circles until Micah found her again?

She bit at her bottom lip nervously and stole a quick glance at the man by the fire. Completely at home, Micah appeared relaxed, easy. But if they were in Texas right now, Julie knew that *she* would be the one at ease.

Stop it, she told herself firmly. It would do no good at all to start doubting before her plan was even in motion! Besides, all she had to do was find the North Star in the wide expanse of sky. With that, she could find her way back to Thea's.

"Julie?"

She shook her head. "Hmmm?"

"You all right?"

"Sí." Cursing herself for a fool, she looked down at him and forced a reassuring smile. The last thing she needed right now was for him to be on his guard about anything. She met his gaze squarely and read the confusion in their green depths.

His brows lowered, his head cocked, he stared at her for another long minute before nodding slowly. "Supper's about ready."

For the first time, she noticed the scent and sizzle of the frying bacon. Her stomach growled in response, and Julie realized just how hungry she was. After all, they hadn't eaten since breakfast.

"You gonna hand me that bread there? Or just hold it all night?"

"Hmmm? Oh!" she started, then held out the loaf of sourdough bread. As he took it from her, she lifted the empty coffeepot and said, "I'll make some coffee."

His surprise was evident on his features. But just as quickly, a suspicious gleam shone in his eyes.

She turned, took a few steps, and stopped when he spoke.

"Where you goin'?"

Looking back at him, she pointed off to her right. "To the creek just below." She tilted her head slightly. "Even *I* will need water to make coffee."

"Uh-huh." His lips quirked, and he jerked a nod at his horse. "Well, there's two full canteens on my saddle yonder. You fill that pot with one of them."

"Señor Micah!" She hoped she sounded properly offended. "Did you think that I meant to make coffee only to steal away in the night?"

Firelight played on his face, illuminating his broad smile. "I figure that's *just* what you was plannin' on doin'."

"But that would be foolish!" She lifted her arms and shrugged. "Where would I go? Could I hope to escape you? On foot? In a country strange to me?"

He rubbed one big hand over his bearded jaw and studied her. Julie watched as he appeared to think over each of her statements. Maybe, if he believed that he had caught her up in a plan of escape, he would relax his guard just enough for her *real* plan to work.

"I reckon that's so," he finally said. "It wouldn't work, y'know."

"What?"

"You runnin' away."

"But I am not—"

"I figure you was thinkin' about it." He nodded his bushy head and continued, "But you best know right off, Julie. You ain't gonna catch me nappin'. You ain't goin' back to Montana. You're goin' to Texas."

She stiffened, but he went on.

"Once you're back with your pa, it ain't none of my business what you do. Hell, for all I care, you can take off again that same day! But until then, it's up to *me* to see you don't go nowhere I don't want you to."

Her grip on the coffeepot handle tightened so hard she was afraid she would snap the tin right in two.

"Now," he asked in a bantering tone, "you still want to make that coffee?"

She sucked in a gulp of air before answering, "Of course. That is all I *meant* to do."

He nodded, his lips quirked in a disbelieving smile. "Go ahead on, then. Use one of the canteens."

Julie spun about and stalked over to where the horses were picketed with ground ropes. She stepped around the stallion, cropping at the few blades of new grass, and bent down to take the canteen off Micah's saddle. With her back to the man and her body shielding her movements, she reached into her own carpetbag and pulled out a small brown bottle.

Thoughtfully, she stared at the laudanum she'd stolen from Trib's bedside. Briefly Julie hoped that the big man wouldn't be in too much pain before his family was able to get more of the medicine from the town doctor. After all, she reminded herself, it was only because of *her* that Trib had broken his leg in the first place.

Then she shook her head to rid herself of the pangs of guilt. She hadn't *asked* to be taken from her friend's home. Whatever befell the Benteen family from that point on was surely their *own* fault.

The bottle clenched in her left hand, she poured the canteen water into the pot with her right. Glancing over her shoulder quickly, she saw Micah, head bent, poking at the strips of bacon in the skillet. Setting the canteen down, she looked back at the small bottle in her hand and paused.

How much of the strong liquid should she put in the water? She certainly didn't want to kill him with too much! All she wanted was for him to sleep long enough for her to make her escape and hopefully get a head start back to Thea's house.

But could she really risk it?

"Yessir, Julie," Micah called out. "We keep makin'

good time like we done today, and I'll have you back home quicker'n scat!"

She stiffened. Home. The rancho. Her father. Grimly she pulled the cork stopper from the little bottle and dumped half the contents into the coffee water. Decision made, Julie shoved the cork home again and tucked the laudanum back into her carpetbag.

"Did ya find the coffee in my saddlebags?" he asked.

"¡Sí!" She rummaged quickly through his things, pulled out the canvas sack, and threw a handful of grounds into the water. Brushing her hand against her skirt, she stood up, turned, and walked back to the fire.

Micah relaxed slightly as she sat down opposite him. He watched her set the coffeepot on the rocks near the flames and told himself he was being much too jumpy. She hadn't tried anything. Oh, that halfhearted attempt to get down to the creek and out of his sight didn't even count. He'd expected her to be a helluvalot trickier than *that*!

With a woman who sliced up a man's saddle for no good reason ... Hell, there was no tellin' *what* she might do.

His gaze moved over her features, and he warned himself sternly to keep his eyes to himself. It would do no good at all for him to keep on studyin' the way her blue eyes tilted up just a bit at the corners. Or how she chewed at her lip when she was nervous. Or how the way she held the long, slender length of her neck made her look like a queen out of some fairy story.

He had to force himself to keep his gaze from straying to her narrow waist and nicely rounded hips. And he'd already noticed far too often how the buttons of her shirt pulled against the swell of her breasts.

Groaning inwardly, Micah shifted position and deliberately lowered his gaze to their supper, sizzling in the cast-iron skillet.

His heart pounding, mouth dry, he called himself all kinds of a fool for letting his imagination take him where he'd never dare go on his own.

Lord Almighty! Micah rubbed his jaw viciously. No matter what Julietta Duffy did to his insides, he had no business even thinkin' about the likes of her! She had a fine education, and he could hardly write his own name! Her pa probably had more money than God, and he didn't own much more than that damn horse and his saddle . . . which, he reminded himself with a wry smile, now had to be fixed.

Besides, he thought firmly as he speared the strips of bacon with his knife and dropped them onto plates, the one thing he *didn't* need in his life was another hard-headed woman. Hell, he'd seen enough stubborn, willful females over the years to know that they sure as shootin' didn't make for a peaceful time. He'd always planned on findin' him a nice, quiet woman. Someone gentle, soft-spoken.

He snorted. That sure as hell was *not* Julietta Duffy!

To get his mind off her curves and back to business, Micah asked suddenly, "So how come you don't want to go back to your pa?"

Startled, Julie jumped slightly, then reached for the tin plate he held out to her. After taking a bite of bacon, she said offhandedly, "He doesn't want me there any more than I want to be there."

He squinted a look at her. At the mention of her father, her features had stiffened. Now he watched as she pushed her food around on her plate disinterestedly.

"What's that mean?" he prodded. "He's your pa, ain't he?"

"Oh, *sí*. Yes, he is my father. But beyond the connection of blood, we share little."

"I don't know about that," Micah countered. "He went to a lot of trouble findin' my brother and gettin' him to take you home."

She lifted one small hand and smoothed a stray lock of raven black hair back from her face. The smile curving her lips was a sad one, and when she spoke, her voice was so low Micah had to strain to hear her.

"My father would do much to anger my grandmother."

"What?"

When she raised her eyes to his, Micah noticed the unshed tears shining in the firelight. He squirmed uncomfortably.

"Do you remember those men you fought with in Montana?"

"Hell yes, I remember. If they'da been a heartbeat quicker with those guns of theirs, I doubt me and Jericho would've lived to tell the tale."

She nodded. "They were sent by my grandmother."

"Trib said something about that. But he didn't tell us why."

"It is very simple. My grandmother, Doña Ana, has sold me to one of her neighbors."

Micah's jaw dropped.

"Would you like some coffee?"

CHAPTER
···**THREE**···

MICAH SHOOK HIMSELF all over, like a big dog after its bath. Leaning forward, eyes narrowed, he finally ground out, "No, I don't want any coffee, and what in hell are you talkin' about? Your granny *sold* you?"

"*Sí.*" With her fingertips, Julie tested the side of the coffeepot. "It is not ready yet anyway." She sighed and looked him squarely in the eye. "Doña Ana, my mother's mother, is a very powerful woman."

"Yeah?"

"She wishes to be even more so."

"That still don't explain . . ."

Julie leaned back against one of the surrounding rocks. Though she didn't really *want* to talk about her family, she told herself that she might as well. The drugged coffee wasn't drinkable yet anyway. Besides, she thought with a sudden burst of hope, if she could make Micah understand exactly *why* she had no wish to return to her family . . . well, when he woke up from his laudanum-induced sleep, he might be more sympathetic.

He shoved one big hand through his hair, pushing the wavy mass off his forehead. When their gazes met, Julie's breath caught. Firelight glinted in his green eyes, revealing a shadow of fierceness that she hadn't noticed before.

"Well?" he prodded.

She swallowed heavily and told herself to be calm. "*Sí.* I received a letter several weeks ago from"—she paused, glanced at him, and said softly—"a *friend* in Mexico. He, this friend, I mean, thought I should know that my grandmother, Doña Ana, had arranged a betrothal between me and her neighbor Don Vicente Alvarez."

Micah's tension-filled body relaxed somewhat. "You mean she picked out a husband for you?"

"*Sí.* Yes."

"That's a far cry from *sellin'* ya," he said softly, his eyes never leaving her face.

A wry smile touched Julie's lips, and she shook her head gently. "The only difference is in the words, Micah." Idly her fingers smoothed the material of her skirt as she went on. "Doña Ana wants the title to a huge tract of land bordering her own rancho. She has worked for years to acquire it."

"So?"

"So. The land belongs to Don Vicente."

"Oh." He rubbed one hand along his jaw thoughtfully.

"*Sí.* My 'friend' tells me that Don Vicente has at last agreed to sell the land to Doña Ana." She shrugged and smiled sadly. "*I* am the price she must pay."

"And you don't want to marry up with this *Don* fella?"

"No." Julie shuddered. "He is as old as my grandmother. His eyes, when he looks at me, tear my clothes from my body like a wild dog." She glanced at the man across from her and saw that the hand draped across his upraised knee was curled into a fist. Quietly she added, "Also, he is fat and his hands are always wet."

For a long moment, neither of them spoke. The fire snapped and spit its flames into the darkness. In the distance a lone wolf howled.

Julie wrapped her arms around her and inched closer to the warmth of the fire. She didn't blame Micah for being silent. She knew what he must be thinking. What *anyone* who didn't know her family would think.

Though she'd had to accept that her family was like no other, it was still humiliating to admit to anyone how little her own grandmother and father thought of her.

"What?" she said quickly when she realized Micah had been speaking to her.

"I said," he repeated, frowning, "what's your pa got to say about your granny's plan?"

Her lips twisted, but she fought back the spasm of regret. There was no point in lying about her father. If Micah *did* succeed in getting her back to Texas, he would meet Patrick Michael Duffy for himself. "My *pa*, as you call him, is frantic to prevent the marriage."

"I guess so." Micah nodded, a half smile on his face.

She shook her head, leaned forward to touch the coffeepot gently, then satisfied that the coffee was ready, reached for two cups. As she poured the inky liquid, she countered, "It is not for love of me that my father is doing all that he can to keep me from my grandmother."

"What d'ya mean?" He took the proffered cup and sat back again.

"It is only that he cares less for Doña Ana than me.

He enjoys doing battle with her. He takes great pleasure in ruining her plans." Julie held her cup to her lips, then pretending it was too hot to drink, set it down nearby.

Micah shook his shaggy head. "Don't make much sense, Julie. None of it." He took one sip of coffee and screwed his face up.

She held her breath. Worry coiled in the pit of her stomach. Was the laudanum taste strong enough to notice? With great effort, she managed to keep her voice calm when she asked, "What is wrong? Is my coffee so foul tasting?"

"Hmmm?" His eyebrows arched. He stared down into his cup for a long moment before looking at her again. "No. No, it's just the way I like it. Strong enough to peel the hide off a buffalo."

Julie sighed and hid a smile.

He took another sip and nodded at her still full cup. "Ain't you gonna have any?"

"Uh . . ." She glanced down at her cup and thought frantically for a moment. "No," she finally said in a rush. "I am ready for some sleep, and it would only keep me awake." As he nodded, Julie told herself that she should be worried about her character. Lying was becoming much too easy.

"S'pose so," Micah agreed, then leaned back against the rocks. "Speakin' of tired," he added on a long sigh, "I'm so beat out I can hardly move myself. Hallie tucked some of her fresh cookies into my pack yonder. Would you mind gettin' 'em for me?"

Already his eyelids looked heavy. It was truly miraculous how quickly the drug took effect. One eye on him, Julie pushed herself to her feet. It took only a minute or two to find the cookies, and when she returned, she was pleased to see that Micah was pouring himself another cup of coffee.

He took the package she held out to him and asked quietly, "What makes ya think your pa don't care for ya?"

She cocked her head. "Would a man who loved his child allow such a woman as Doña Ana to sell her in marriage?"

"Well, no. But you said yourself, he's hired us Benteens to keep your granny's coyotes away."

"True. But for his own reasons."

"He always been like this?"

She kept her gaze lowered. It was too humiliating to look him in the eye and tell him about her father.

"Since the year I was six, my father has had little to do with me."

"What happened when you were six?"

Her lips clamped together, and she took several deep breaths, fighting down the rising tide of emotions threatening to swamp her. "My mother died."

"Oh."

From the corner of her eye, she saw him refill his cup again and felt a new tingle of worry spread through her body. Was he drinking too much? For heaven's sake. Who would have thought a man would drink so much coffee at such a late hour?

"Well, it don't make sense, I say," Micah mumbled, and Julie noticed his words were a bit slurred.

"Why," he went on as he stretched out on his bedroll, "if somebody tried somethin' like that with our Hallie, we boys'd teach 'em some manners real quick."

He shifted around on the hard ground until he was comfortable, then dropped his hat over his eyes.

"Yes, ma'am. Wouldn't let *nobody* do dirt to Hallie." He muttered something unintelligible and then whispered. " 'Night, Julie."

"Good night," she said softly, then held her breath, watching him. Tears pricked at the backs of her eyes as she let herself think about what he'd said.

No, she was sure that no one would attempt to hurt Hallie or anyone else the Benteens cared about. How lovely it must be, she thought, to know that you are loved that much. How wonderful to be able to be the kind of person you wished and at the same time be certain that you would be loved no matter what.

She blinked rapidly and swallowed the knot in her throat. For the first time in her life, Julietta Duffy was jealous. Jealous of the kind of loyalty and caring the Benteen family shared. She wondered if they knew how rare and precious a thing it was. She wondered if Hallie Benteen Sloane knew what a very lucky woman she was.

Micah grumbled and stirred on his blankets. Julie deliberately pushed all other thoughts aside and concentrated on him. Though his hat covered his eyes, the rest of his face was visible, and she found herself wondering what he would look like without the reddish brown beard that covered most of his features.

She told herself she was being foolish, but still she couldn't keep her eyes from straying to his broad chest, now rising and falling with his deep, regular breaths. Deliberately, she inhaled sharply and fought to control the fluttering feelings swarming in her stomach. Instead, she tried to concentrate on the ride ahead of her.

Tilting her head up, she let her gaze wander over the clear night sky. The stars seemed to shine especially brilliantly, as if trying to share as much of their light with her as possible. When she finally located the North Star, she mentally mapped out the route she would take on her flight to Montana and safety.

Lowering her gaze, Julie looked around her at the surrounding darkness. Even with the combined light from the stars and the sliver of moon, the shadows under the pines remained dark, forbidding. A flicker of unease sparked to life inside her as she told herself that she would have more than simply Micah Benteen to worry about on her trip.

Somewhere out there, maybe closer than she dared imagine, were men hired by Doña Ana to kidnap her and carry her forcibly to Mexico. Julie wasn't foolish enough to think that the two men Micah and his brothers had taken care of in Montana were the *only* men her grandmother had sent. Doña Ana was not merely a powerful woman. She was a careful woman as well. She would leave nothing to chance.

And now that she was so close to acquiring the land she had lusted after for years, the old woman wouldn't risk losing it.

In the quiet, Julie listened to her own raging heartbeat. The night sounds of the forest rustled around her. Wind rattled the limbs of the pines, scattering dry needles, and when the horses stamped their hooves against the ground, it sounded unnaturally loud.

Julie shuddered, swallowed, and glanced at Micah again. He hadn't moved. As she watched, a low rumble erupted from him and slowly built until it became a snore resembling the deep-throated growl of a mountain lion.

Leaning forward, she peered into his coffee cup and

saw that it was still half full. But he *had* drunk at least two cups. Apparently, she told herself with a half smile, it was more than enough.

She pushed herself to her feet and cautiously stepped around the dying campfire. Her nerves were stretched to the point of shattering and still she moved slowly, terrified she would wake him up and ruin everything.

But he didn't stir. Not a muscle. Only his massive chest moved up and down regularly. His snoring had become even louder, and Julie bit at her bottom lip.

What is he'd had too much laudanum? What if he was sleeping so soundly he never woke up? Immediately she told herself she was being foolish. He'd only had two cups. Besides, she thought with a wry grin, if his snores were any proof at all, he would most certainly live.

And yet . . . With her moccasined foot, she gave his shoulder a hard nudge. Micah stirred restively, mumbled under his breath, and after a moment quieted again. Julie held perfectly still until another reverberating snore shook the silence.

Smiling, she nodded. He would be fine. And who knows, she thought with a muffled chuckle. Maybe after such a good night's sleep, he wouldn't even be angry about her escaping him. With one last glance at the sleeping man, she crept across the campsite to the two tethered horses.

Micah's black stallion sidestepped nervously as she approached, but Julie whispered a sharp rebuke and he settled down. Quickly she snatched up the saddle blanket and threw it across his sleek back. Then, as she struggled to lift the weight of Micah's saddle up to the stallion's back, she told herself that she had no choice but to take his horse. The black was such a superior animal, she would be able to travel much faster.

Besides, if Micah was forced to follow her astride the less spirited bay mare, she would gain even more time. When the cinch strap was tightened, she bent to grab up the one full canteen. Slipping the rawhide strap over her saddle horn, Julie grabbed the reins and paused one last time.

She looked back at Micah Benteen and for a moment felt a pang of conscience. But just as quickly, it faded again. She'd made no secret of the fact that she would try to escape him. It was his own fault if he found himself in an embarrassing situation now. He shouldn't have been so smug about his tracking abilities.

Pulling in a deep breath, she turned back around, stepped into the stirrup and swung aboard the stallion. Urging the huge black animal into a quiet walk, she ducked to avoid a low-hanging tree limb and moved off into the thick stand of pines.

Silently she congratulated herself on such a well-thought-out plan. It had worked even better than she'd hoped. When she was no more than twenty feet from camp, a loud, insistent whistle shattered the quiet.

The stallion suddenly reared up onto its hind legs.

Julie scrambled to keep her seat. Leaning forward, her knees pressed tight against the huge animal's sides, she clutched at the reins desperately. Frantic, she glanced around her, still not sure what she'd heard. What was affecting the horse so?

A second whistle sounded out. This one was longer, sharper, louder than the first. And it came from behind her. From the campsite.

The huge black seemed to leave the ground entirely.

His forehooves slashing through the air, he snorted, shook his great head and answered the whistle with a shrill whinny. Just when Julie was sure she had the beast under control, he reared up again and at the same time jumped forward, then did a sharp turn.

Her already precarious seat dissolved completely, and Julie felt herself falling. Somehow she tumbled around when she fell and landed facedown with a solid thump on the hard ground.

She lifted her head from the dirt, gritted her teeth, and watched the blasted horse trot back to camp like a well-trained dog! As if from a great distance, she heard Micah speaking to the animal in a low, soothing voice.

A roaring filled her ears as completely as the anger rushing through her bruised body.

He was awake.

He'd tricked her.

Her fingers curled into the hard earth, and as she pushed herself up, she fed the fires of her anger by calling down on Micah Benteen's head every curse she'd ever heard.

Once on her feet again, she paused long enough in her muttering to listen. Something moving through the trees. He was coming for her.

Without another thought, she turned and began to run. Heedlessly, frantically, she ran through the dense woods. Ignoring the slap and sting of pine needles against her face and arms, Julie ran. Even knowing that it was a useless flight, that he would probably catch her in moments, she went on.

Her breath ragged, she heard him as he got closer. She didn't look behind her. She didn't want to know how close he was.

Through the soft soles of her moccasins, she felt every stone and stick in her path. Tears of frustration filled her eyes. She'd done her best. Why hadn't it worked? Why hadn't he drunk the damned coffee? Why wasn't she even now astride that black beast on her way to Montana?

Was the small taste of freedom she'd been given at Thea's house all that she would ever know?

"No!" she shouted and gulped in air as she fought back the tears. No. It wouldn't end here. If not tonight, then some other night. She *would* escape both her grandmother and her father!

Strong arms snaked out, wrapped around her waist and lifted her free of the ground. With very little effort, Micah swung her around to face him.

Bracing her hands on his muscled forearms, Julie looked down at him. Instead of the anger she'd expected, though, all she saw on his face was a tired amusement.

"I told you, Hoo-lee-edda," he said quietly. "*You're* goin' to Texas."

She swung her right leg back and kicked him hard, her foot smashing against his thigh.

He grunted and winced slightly.

"And as I told you, Señor Micah. I will not go easily."

The big man stared at her for a long moment. She matched his steady gaze with her own, unwilling to be cowed into submission. But slowly she began to see something else in his eyes. Something beyond the anger and amusement she was becoming used to.

His hands at her waist suddenly felt rock hard. The

warmth from his flesh seeped into hers and breathing became difficult.

Just as quickly as it had begun, it was over. A shutter fell over Micah's eyes and he looked away.

"Easy or hard," he said, his voice rough. "You choose." Effortlessly he tossed her over his shoulder, her head and arms hanging down his back. He clamped one ironlike arm across her legs to hold her still.

Her palms against his broad back, Julie pushed herself halfway up. "Put me down!"

"No, ma'am. I'm too damn tired to go traipsin' off into the forest every time you get a itch to run."

"All right," she yelled and slammed her fist into his back. "I give you my word. I will do no more this night."

He stopped dead, then gave her a good, hard swat on her backside.

Julie flailed uselessly in his grip. *"¡Bruto barbudo!"*

"Well now, I don't know if I wanta know what you just called me. . . ."

A long, flowing stream of Spanish flew around him, but Micah ignored it. "It ain't gonna do you no good at all, y'know. Gettin' yourself all worked up like this. I caught you and that's that."

"You struck me!"

"Yes, ma'am, I reckon I did." He started to walk back toward camp. "But then you did some strikin' of your own. Now," he said, hunching his shoulders to adjust her weight more comfortably. "I promise I won't spank you again if you quit hittin' me. It ain't ladylike."

"Ladylike!" She wriggled about, desperately trying to free her legs from his grip. "You speak to me of ladylike? You think it is ladylike to be carried like a sack of corn?"

He snorted. "Maybe not. But then, I don't believe *most* ladies go about druggin' up a man's coffee and stealin' his horse!"

When she didn't say anything, Micah too fell silent. This was his own fault anyhow. He never should've pretended to drink that coffee. Shaking his head, he fought down a reluctant smile.

Hell, one sip of the damned stuff and he'd known there was *something* in it. It hadn't taken much thinkin' to figure out what. The only thing it could've been was the laudanum Doc left for Trib. She hadn't had time to find anything else.

Oh, she was pretty slick about it. Dosin' that coffee. Pretendin' to have a cup herself, then sittin' there pretty as you please, chattin' away like he was a Sunday supper guest. Guess she didn't mind at all that he might've had too much. She might have killed him!

And it would have served him right, too. Imagine, him—Micah Benteen—gettin' so caught up in a girl's pretty blue eyes that she can drug his coffee and he don't notice till it's almost too late! For God's sake. If the boys ever found out about this, they'd never let him hear the end of it.

He stepped into the circle of their campsite and dropped her none too gently onto the ground.

She glared at him while rubbing her backside gingerly.

"You just set there while I unsaddle my horse."

When he was finished, he crossed back to the fire and sat down opposite her.

"You tricked me," she finally whispered.

"Yes, ma'am, I surely did."

"You are *proud* of it?"

Micah glanced at her. She sounded astonished. He tried not to look into those eyes of hers when he answered, "Hell yes."

She sucked in a gulp of air and opened her mouth to speak, but he cut her off.

"Look here, Hoo-lee-edda. What in hell was I s'posed to do? Go ahead and drink that gawdawful stuff you give me, even *knowin'* somethin' was wrong?"

"But I—"

"So I poured it out when you wasn't lookin' and let you think I had a couple of cups of the stuff."

"You tricked me."

"Yeah. But you tricked me first."

"Hah!" Julie crossed her arms over her chest and lifted her chin defiantly. "I did not trick you. I *told* you that I would try to escape." She shrugged her shoulders and cocked her head. "It is not my fault if you did not believe me."

His eyes narrowed. "Yeah, well, I believe you now."

"What do you mean?"

"I *mean* you won't be gettin' any more chances at escape, ma'am. You and me are goin' to Texas, and it's best you just accept that right off."

"But—"

"No buts about it, lady. That's just the way it has to be."

"And how do you plan on stopping me from running away?" She leaned toward him and quirked her lips in a derisive smile. "Are you going to tie me up?"

Micah took a deep breath and studied her for a long minute. No matter how mad she made him, he had to admire her guts. But admirin' and trustin' were two different things. And he wasn't fool enough to trust her again!

"Ma'am, don't you think I ain't thought about it."

Her eyes widened and her jaw dropped. "You wouldn't!"

"It's right temptin', I'll admit." He grinned at her and got up. Two long strides brought him to her side and he dropped to his knees before her.

"What are you doing?" she asked, scooting back from him warily.

Micah gave her a slow smile. "I'm gonna fix it so's you can't go a step without me knowin' about it."

CHAPTER
···FOUR···

JULIE SCOOTED BACK from him, clearly nervous. He could almost feel her fear, and suddenly he was disgusted with himself *and* her. Hell, no woman had *ever* had cause to be afraid of him. And after all the time they'd spent together over the last few weeks, a body would think she'd *know* that!

No matter how mad she'd made him, he'd never once given her a reason to act as skittish as she was now. 'Course, he told himself, maybe she was worried about him gettin . . . familiar. A glance into her anxious eyes was enough to tell him that's exactly what she was thinkin'. He reached up and scratched his jawline thoughtfully. Though he'd like to be able to say he hadn't even *considered* such things, he knew damn well it'd be a lie.

And so would she, probably.

Still and all, he wasn't the man to *force* a woman, for God's sake! Least of all, *her*!

Micah sat on his heels and shook his head.

"Don't look so damn trembly," he snapped, determined to rid himself of any lingering fancies. "You don't have a durn thing to worry about from me! Last thing *I* want is to get even more mixed up with you than I already am!"

Immediately she sat stock-still. Lips pursed, she cocked her head and stared at him. Now she's insulted! he told himself wearily. The woman had a way of wearin' on a man's nerves.

"What do you mean?" she asked finally, her blue eyes narrowed.

Tired, frustrated, and so mad he could hardly see straight, Micah shot back, "I mean, you're a evil-tempered woman. Before I come across you, I always figured Hallie to be the most rock-headed female in the country. But lady . . . you beat *everybody*!"

"Evil-tempered!"

"Yes, ma'am. You don't listen to nobody but yourself. You can't see any further than your own ideas, and you don't give a good goddamn about what you got to do to make sure you get what you want!" He pulled in a quick breath and finished, "And somethin' else while we're at it . . . you talk too damn much!"

He watched his words take their toll. A short burst of anger flared up and died away just as quickly. Her full lips clamped shut as though she was bitin' down on her tongue to keep from answering him back. She folded her legs up Indian style and stiffened her back so that it looked like she was nailed to a board.

But those big blue eyes of hers looked deep into him. He felt her stare as surely as he did the rocks under his knees. He squirmed a bit guiltily. If he hadn't known better than to be taken in by that haunted look in her eyes, Micah'd swear that he'd hurt her feelings. But he *did* know better. He'd found out the hard way. Ignoring the small stabs of shame, he held his tongue and waited her out.

Julie finally laid her hands in her lap and cleared her throat. Tilting her chin up, she sniffed and said, "Since you obviously care little for being around me, it would be best for both of us if we went our separate ways. Don't you think?"

Micah's jaw dropped. He couldn't believe it. She *still* didn't understand. "See there? What'd I just say? Lady"—he snaked one hand out and grabbed her left foot—"*we* are goin' to Texas. Then *I* am gonna go home and apologize to my sister for ever'thing I ever said to her!"

He ran his hand up her calf to the rawhide strings lacing up her knee-high moccasins.

"What are you doing?" she yelled and tried to slap his hand away. She twisted violently in his grip, trying to work herself free. It was useless, though. In seconds he had the laces undone and was pulling her moccasin off. Then he reached for her other foot. "Micah! What are you doing, I said!"

He didn't speak until both her shoes were off. Cradling her bare feet in his hands, Micah tried desperately not to notice how small and dainty her feet were. How soft. His thumbs moved over her flesh and slipped up to the fragile bone of her ankle. She jumped slightly in response. It was enough to remind him just what he was doing.

Swallowing heavily, Micah cleared his throat, released her, and said, "I'm fixin' it so's you won't be runnin' off again anytime soon."

She pulled her knees up to her chest and drew the

hem of her riding skirt down over her bare legs. "I will, though. I will run anyway and you can't stop me."

Micah nodded slowly, tiredly. He wasn't surprised. There was no reason to expect her to give up just because her first attempt had failed. Hell, she'd already tried to drug him and had stolen his horse. Why should she stop now? Dammit.

His mind racing, his lips parted in a wicked grin as he allowed himself the pleasure of thinking just what he'd do to his brothers to pay them back for forcing him on this bloody trip!

"Micah?" Her voice was soft, hesitant.

"What?"

"Why are you smiling so?"

"Hmmm?" He tossed a glance at her. "Oh. Nothin' to do with you." Drawing in a deep gulp of the cold night air, Micah exhaled on a sigh. "Julie ... I'm dead tired. But the minute I fall asleep, you're gonna try to hightail it again, aren't ya?"

She met his gaze squarely, lifted her chin, and jerked him a nod.

"That's what I thought," he mumbled. He picked up one of her moccasins and tugged at the rawhide thong until it came free.

"What are you doing now?" She made a grab for her moccasin. "Those are the only shoes I brought with me."

"You can have the string back in the morning." On his knees, he moved toward her. Ignoring her watchful looks, he ordered sharply, "Lay down!"

"I will not." Her eyes flashed a warning at him. Hands curled into fists at her sides, she went on, "You cannot tie me up, Micah. I won't let you. It is not right." When he paid no attention to her, she demanded, "What kind of man are you?"

"A *tired* one, Julie. A tired one." In a lower tone he added, *"Jesus*, don't your mouth never quit?" Before she could react, he reached over and laid her out on her blanket. He grabbed her left foot and quickly, before she could pull away, tied one end of the rawhide strip around her ankle. Then, sitting down beside her, he tied the other end of the string to his right ankle.

"There." He gave her a satisfied smile. "That ought to do it."

Stretching out beside her, Micah sighed, crossed his arms over his chest, and closed his eyes.

Julie sat up and stared at the string binding them together. Slowly she let her gaze slide up to the relaxed features of her captor. Deliberately she jerked her leg to one side and smiled when he grunted.

"Cut it out," he warned, his eyes never opening. "Ya might's well get used to it. We'll be sleepin' together till I get you back home."

"I cannot sleep like this," she said softly, wincing at the throbbing pain in her ankle. Yanking on the rawhide had only hurt her. His booted ankle wasn't bothered in the least. "Did you hear me?" she said and gave him a poke in the ribs. "I said I cannot sleep like this!"

He chuckled. "Have some coffee, Hoo-lee-edda. I'll wager you'd sleep just fine, then."

Julie glared at the man beside her for a long moment before she reluctantly lay back down. Carefully she made sure there was at least a couple of inches of empty space between them. Eyes wide open, she stared at the sky, mentally saying everything she wanted to scream at the tall, scruffy . . . *disturbing* man.

He mumbled something unintelligible, then crossed his feet at the ankles, tugging at her leg. In retaliation, she crossed her own feet, pulling the rawhide string taut.

Glancing at him, she noticed the half smile on his face and the almost overpowering urge to smack him filled her. Knowing that he would probably keep his promise and spank her again was all that stopped her.

She turned her head away slowly. In the silence her mind ran free. For the first time since leaving the Moore house in Montana, Julie realized that she might *not* escape. Micah Benteen was proving to be a far more worthy adversary than she'd first thought. And if she *didn't* get away, what then?

Moisture crept into her eyes, and she squeezed her eyelids shut against the threatening tears. The night seemed to crowd around her. The air seemed suddenly thick, heavy. A knot formed in her throat, and she struggled to breathe past it, gulping reflexively. Shivering, she wrapped her arms around herself and tried to recapture the confidence she'd felt when she began this journey.

But it was gone. That illusive brush with freedom looked to be over, and there wasn't a thing she could do about it.

"Cold?" Micah mumbled.

"Sí," she managed to answer, then bit down hard on her bottom lip. She couldn't bring herself to tell him that her shivering had nothing to do with the cold.

He turned onto his side, curled one strong arm around her middle and drew her up against him, her back to his front. Then he released her long enough to reach back and pull the edge of the bedroll over the two of them.

Julie held perfectly still for a long moment. She'd never been held that close to a man before. In truth, she couldn't remember meeting any man she'd *wanted* to hold her closely. But now, with Micah's arm draped across her and his thighs just beneath hers, his heart beating under hers, she felt almost . . . *safe*.

But that didn't make any sense at all. He was the man taking her, against her will, back to her father. He was the one who'd called her evil-tempered. He acted as though he didn't even *like* her.

And yet . . . his warmth and strength encircled her, and she instinctively snuggled in closer. A strange, fluttery feeling blossomed in her stomach and snaked out through her body, leaving her calm and at the same time more alive than she'd ever been.

Closing her eyes, Julie told herself that it surely wouldn't hurt to pretend, just for this one night, that all was well. To let herself believe that Micah's strength and warmth were hers for the taking. That they were tied to each other by more than a rawhide thong.

She smiled, sighed, and for the first time in years fell instantly, dreamlessly, to sleep.

*   *   *

"In jail!"

"*Sí, Señora*. That is what Diego read in the telegram."

Doña Ana Santos y Cervantes glared at the little man in the arched doorway. His gnarled brown hands crushed the brim of his battered straw hat, and beneath his sandaled feet, she noticed with a frown, was a pale, soft layer of dirt sifting over the polished red tile floor.

His gaze dropped to follow hers, and he shifted position nervously. He dipped his graying head and held his arms close to his sides in an impossible effort to turn in on himself.

Her lips curled in distaste, Doña Ana took small, measured steps across the room until she stood directly in front of the old man. Clenching her long-fingered, elegant hands into fists hidden by the flare of her maroon silk gown, she waited for him to look at her again.

Esteban wished desperately to be anywhere but in the same room with the coldly furious woman. Though they were of the same age, they had little else in common. As he was raised to serve *el Patron*, Doña Ana was raised expecting to be served. But it was more than that, Esteban knew.

There was something in the woman that craved more. More of everything. He had never known her to be happy. Or content. Always there was the hunger driving her. Pushing her. It was whispered around the rancho that her unending quest for power was what had killed her husband, the Patron. A kind, gentle man, Ricardo Santos had finally lost all desire to continue living with such a *bruja*.

Instantly the old man wiped his mind clean, as if in fear that the woman standing in front of him knew he'd called her a witch.

Esteban told himself fleetingly that if only Don Ricardo were still alive, Julietta would not now be running from a marriage that only Doña Ana wanted. But there was nothing to be done about that now. He certainly could not help the girl. It would be all he could do to stay out of *la Patrona*'s way.

When he finally looked up into her face, strangely

unmarked by the years or her own viciousness, he barely managed to hide a shudder. Doña Ana's black eyes sparkled dangerously with an icy glint he recognized all too well. He held onto the brim of his hat even tighter to prevent himself from making the sign of the cross.

"You say they are both in jail?" she asked again, her soft voice giving no hint of the rage coursing through her.

"*Sí, Señora.*" And, Esteban thought, if the two men were smart, they would never return to Mexico when they were released from the gringo jail.

"It was so simple," she muttered thickly. "To bring the girl here. That was all they had to do." She spun about, took several steps, and stopped again. "Fools! I am surrounded by fools!"

Esteban swallowed and tried to back out of the grand room.

She turned quickly, and the old man silently cursed his sandals for the noise they made.

"Wait!" she ordered, and he stopped dead.

Doña Ana moved quickly to a small walnut table along the far wall. Picking up a pen, she wrote a few lines in a crisp, clean hand, blew on the ink to dry it, then folded the paper in half. Waving the paper at the old man, she urged him forward.

"Take this to Ramon. Tell him to ride to El Paso and send this wire to Enrique in Montana."

Esteban's callused fingers closed over the thick, cream-colored paper. As if he had already left, Doña Ana began speaking to herself. "It will fall to Enrique. He and Carlos will have to find her now." She inhaled sharply. "How difficult can it be?" she asked of no one before she made a quick turn and walked to the wide window overlooking the dark yard of the rancho. "Damn that girl!"

Esteban moved quickly while her back was turned to him and while she was too busy bringing down curses on her granddaughter's head to notice him leaving. When he was safely outside, he breathed deeply, pushed his hat down onto his head, and opened the folded paper.

He squinted in the soft moonlight. His watery brown eyes moved over the ink scratches, and he frowned. Though the cursive lines meant nothing to him, he knew very well what they would mean to Julietta.

Merely the thought of men like Enrique and Carlos being *alone* with Julietta was enough to bring a shudder to the old man's body. Surely though, they would do no . . . *harm* to the girl. Even Doña Ana would expect a virginal bride to present to Don Vicente.

Quickly Esteban crossed himself. He turned his gaze on heaven and murmured a prayer. There was little else he could do to prevent Julietta from being turned over to such a *malvado*, evil one, as Don Vicente Alvarez.

If he was a brave man, he told himself, he would "lose" this paper before he found Ramon. But he was not a brave man. He was an old man. With little time left and nowhere else to go. And he didn't doubt for a moment that *la Patrona* would have him thrown off the rancho for his defiance. Maybe she would do more. Besides, if he did not deliver this paper to Ramon, Doña Ana would only find another way to send her message. Nothing would be gained by his action except that he would lose his home.

His shoulders hunched, Esteban tucked the paper inside his shirt and walked toward the stables.

La Patrona, Ana Santos, turned around as soon as the old fool had gone. Disgusted, she stared at the trail of dust he'd left behind and made a mental note to have the maids in to scrub the tiles again.

So close, she told herself. She was so close to finally getting her hands on that corner section of land. Thoughtfully she turned to face the massive stone fireplace that took up fully one half of the far wall. She let her gaze slide up over the blaze in the hearth to the conspicuously blank space above the carved, oak mantel.

Doña Ana stared at the spot where her husband's portrait used to hang and as always took strength in its absence. She straightened her already ramrod-straight spine and lifted her chin in triumph.

From the day Ricardo died and she'd burned his likeness in the wide hearth, the Santos rancho had been hers. Oh, he'd tried to leave his land to Julietta ... but, Ana smiled, the *jurista* carrying the new will back to El Paso had met with an unfortunate accident.

"You will *not* thwart me from the grave, Ricardo," she promised in a venomous whisper. "I will have that corner section of land again. It will be a part of this rancho as it was always meant to be." She took another step toward the blank space, her black gaze boring into the whitewashed adobe. "As it still *would* be if you had not sold it to Alvarez deliberately, for a few miserable pesos just to spite me!"

A cold desert wind rushed through the open patio doors. The night slipped into the room. Long tendrils of

Doña Ana's silver hair were plucked free and flew about her grim features. Flames on the beeswax candles in the wall sconces dipped, swayed, and sputtered before they died. Tapestry drapes billowed into the long room, and windowpanes rattled as if they were the bones of the dead.

* * *

Micah groaned when the woman moved against his hardened body. His left arm across her middle, he held her still and tried not to think about her gently curved behind nestled up close to him. Slowly he opened his eyes to slits.

The day was already beginning to lighten with the coming dawn. Slashes of pink and deep orange filled the sky, and he knew he should move. Get up. Get to traveling.

And yet . . . he was reluctant to leave her side. Even if staying locked together meant more delicious torture. Julietta sighed, mumbled something, and wiggled her hips, looking for a comfortable position. Micah's jaw clenched and he screwed his eyes tightly shut.

Mentally he tried to *will* his body to relax although he knew it was useless. He'd never spent a more miserable night. Nor had he ever spent an entire night with a woman only to wake up so painfully aware of unfinished business. With every move she made, his body screamed at him in frustration. And as much as he knew he should stay away from her soft curves and jasmine scent, Micah realized dismally that he wouldn't trade those hours in the dark for all the sleep in the world.

Once, during the long night, she'd turned in his arms and he'd watched her sleep. Her warm breath on his cheeks, her palm resting on his chest, Micah'd felt a swell of something even more potent than the desire racking his body. He'd even let himself pretend that they were together because they wanted to be. That she was his woman and that it was his right to hold her close and protect her. Love her.

Love her? Where the hell did *that* come from? He'd have laughed out loud at his own stupidity if he hadn't been afraid he'd wake her. Jesus, Micah told himself. His thoughts were gettin' way out of hand! Why, he had no more business thinkin' about her like that than he did ... tryin' to be President of the United States!

Hell, the two of them were as alike as dirt and water. Lace and buckskin. Whiskey and lemonade.

She shifted again and he groaned silently. He wanted her like he'd never wanted another thing in his life.

It had taken every ounce of his willpower to keep from kissing her, touching her. He wanted nothing more than to let his fingers caress her until she was crying out for him to ease the ache he'd created. And then he wanted to fill her body with his own and hear her whisper his name as the first tremors of delight shook her.

His eyes flew open. Pulling in a deep breath, he pushed the maddening thoughts aside and told himself he'd have to apologize to Ritter Sloane when he got back home. *Now* Micah understood exactly what had happened between the gunfighter and Hallie Benteen. *Now* Micah's sympathies lay entirely with his brother-in-law.

Julietta sighed, stretched slightly, and turned in his arms to face him. He curled his fingers to keep from brushing a stray lock of hair out of her eyes.

"Buenos dias, Señor Micah."

"'Mornin', Julie."

She smiled and tried to inch back from him. "I am sorry for lying so close to you. You must have been uncomfortable."

"No," Micah forced an answering smile and lied, "not a bit. Slept like a log."

"Good." For just a moment, Micah thought he saw disappointment in her shining blue eyes. Then she looked away hastily. She turned and sat up, pushing her hair back from her face. "It is a beautiful morning, is it not?"

"Yeah." He kept the edge of the blanket over his hips. The throbbing of his hardened body reminded him that he hadn't recovered enough yet to be ready for polite company. "Yeah, it is." He had to get her away from him. At least for a few minutes. "But we got to get movin' real quick here. How 'bout you go make us some coffee, Julie?"

Glancing at him over her shoulder, she said, "The canteens are empty. Will you go down to the creek and fill them?"

Lord! He couldn't get up. At least not yet. If he did, there wasn't a chance in hell that she'd miss the very obvious evidence of his frustration. "Uh, no. You go on. I'll, uh . . ." He tried to think. "Get some biscuits cookin'." He nodded briefly. "Yeah. That's it. I'll make up some biscuits while you fetch the water."

She narrowed her eyes thoughtfully. "You would let me go away from camp? Alone?"

"Sure. Hell, even *you* wouldn't run before coffee. 'Sides," he added, "thought you might need to be by yourself to, uh . . . uh . . ."

Julie's cheeks reddened, and she looked away quickly. *"Sí.* Yes, that is a good idea."

"Well then, you go on. Just don't make the same kind of coffee you did last night, all right?"

She gave him a quick look and grinned before jumping up. After one short step, though, she fell back and dropped onto his lap.

His breath left him in a rush before Micah groaned aloud and screwed his eyes shut in pain. "What the hell are you doin', woman?" Even his voice sounded strangled.

"It was not my fault, Micah." Still seated on his lap, she scooted around, ignored his obvious discomfort, and held up her left leg for his inspection. The rawhide thong tying the two of them together was still in place.

"Oh, Lordie," Micah whispered plaintively.

Julie lowered her leg and quickly untied the leather strip. She rubbed at her ankle and ground her hips against him as she turned to look at him. "Did I hurt you, Micah?"

"No." He shook his head and swallowed heavily. "No, I'm all right."

"You do not sound at all well. And why do you not open your eyes?"

"Unhhh," Micah moaned again and bit his lip. Everything would be fine if she'd just get her behind off his lap. "I said I'm fine, Julie! Now dammit, will ya go get the blasted water?"

She pushed herself up and Micah sighed.

"Very well." She sniffed haughtily before adding in a stiff tone. "I was only trying to help."

He watched her as she pulled on her moccasins, strode across the camp, and snatched up the two canteens and the coffeepot. Her angry mutterings drifted back to him long after she disappeared into the trees.

Micah's head dropped back onto the ground, and he stared up at the wide expanse of sky overhead. "Help? She was tryin' to *help*?" He shifted his hips tentatively and winced. "I think she *broke* somethin' I've gotten almighty fond of over the years, Lord."

CHAPTER
···FIVE···

THEY RODE ALL day in virtual silence. Beyond an occasional word of warning or a muttered curse at her to hurry up, Micah'd hardly opened his mouth.

And after a few halfhearted tries at making conversation, Julie'd given up, resigning herself to the relative quiet of the surrounding countryside. Though they'd ridden what seemed like hundreds of miles, the landscape hadn't changed much. Except for the few patches of open meadow she'd glimpsed from the trail, they were still encompassed by trees.

Pines, birch, and aspen huddled together as spring began its march across the countryside. Everywhere she looked, Julie noticed fresh buds, new leaves, and even infrequent splotches of color as wildflowers burst into life in the shadow of the woods.

Truth to tell, if she hadn't been on her way to the rancho, she would have been enjoying her journey very much, despite her silent companion. So many new things to see and appreciate. The countryside was wild, open . . . *free*.

Though she'd enjoyed the ride, it felt good to sit still. Shaking her head, Julie sighed, poured herself another cup of coffee and stared at Micah, opposite her. He'd hardly said a word the whole time they'd been setting up camp. Beyond a grunt or a one-word answer to her questions, he'd completely ignored her.

She reminded herself that he hadn't felt that way in the morning.

Following that thought, another rushed into her mind for the hundredth time.

Immediately a flush of heat swept up her neck and colored her cheeks. She looked away and tried to keep her head turned from him so he wouldn't see her embarrassment. She closed her eyes and sucked in a breath of cool, pine-scented evening air. But closing her eyes didn't shut out the memory. Instead, she saw it all again.

Waking in his arms, feeling his heartbeat beneath her palm, looking into his green eyes and seeing his open hunger for her.

Julie swallowed nervously and tried to stop thinking. But she couldn't. Again, she remembered falling onto his lap. She remembered the feel of his hard body beneath her and the realization that Micah Benteen wanted her as a man wants a woman.

Her heartbeat quickened and her breath came in shallow gasps as she let herself recall how she'd *enjoyed* that moment. How the knowledge of his desire had fed the embers in her own blood. Julie *forced* herself to admit that she'd lingered on his lap far longer than necessary. That she hadn't wanted to move away. That his swollen body pressed against her behind had awakened a pulsing response that had built into a throbbing ache deep in the core of her.

How had this happened? she wondered wildly. *Why*

had this happened? Why was it *this* man whose touch moved through her body like fire?

Even now, after a day's riding, her flesh still tingled. Clamping her legs tightly together, she drew her knees up to her chest and tried to ignore the irritating feeling between her thighs.

Rubbing her eyes with her fingertips, Julie thought dismally that perhaps she *should* have been traveling with a duenna.

Who would have thought she'd need a chaperon around Micah Benteen?

"You all right?" Micah's voice was gruff, and it seemed to rub raw on her already sensitive nerves.

"I am fine."

"No need to snap."

"I did not 'snap.' I only answered your question in the same way you asked it." She looked at him. Even though she heard the strident tone in her voice, Julie was helpless to stop it.

"Fine."

"Fine." She jerked a nod at him, but he didn't see it. He was staring into his coffee cup with deliberate concentration. Obviously he wasn't going to speak to her again.

Her lips twitched angrily. Hmmph! she thought, more disgusted with him than she'd even been before. He desired her body, but refused to *talk* to her? Did he think her of so little importance? Well, she would not be ignored. It was bad enough that she was being forced to make this trip to somewhere she didn't want to go. It was bad enough that he had awakened feelings in her that she didn't want. The *least* he could do was speak to her.

Besides, something had been bothering her since her ill-fated attempt at escape the night before.

"How did you do that?" she challenged.

"Huh?" He looked up at her as if surprised to see her. "Do what?"

"That trick. With your horse." She waved one hand at the beast. "Last night you made him return to you as if he was nothing more than a puppy!"

"Oh, that." Micah glanced at the stallion, whose ears had pricked at the sound of his master's voice. "I raised him since he was just a baby. Taught him a couple tricks, is all."

"More than coming when whistled at?"

"Yeah." His gaze turned back to her, and he shrugged. "Satan's a real smart animal."

"Hmmph!" she snorted inelegantly. "Satan. An appropriate name."

Micah cocked his head at her. "You mean for the horse? Or for me?"

She met his gaze squarely. "For either of you, I suppose." He didn't say anything, so she continued. "That black beast of yours is not responsible for what he does. He is an animal. He does as he is trained to do. But you . . ."

"Yeah?" His fingers were tight on the handle of his tin cup as he waited for her to finish.

"You do as you please." Julie blinked frantically. The sting of tears in her eyes warned her that she was dangerously close to embarrassing herself. Too much had happened to her too quickly.

Tired from two days of hard riding, she was also beginning to think that she'd *never* get a chance at escape.

The coffee in her cup slapped against the sides with

the shaking of her hand. Trying to steady herself, she breathed deeply before blurting out, "How can you do this? How can you take me to what will only be a life as a prisoner with my father . . . or as a wife in an unwanted marriage?"

Setting her cup down hurriedly, she clasped her fingers together and repeated, "How can you do it?" in a small voice.

Micah bit down on his bottom lip and let his head fall back on his neck. He couldn't bring himself to look at her. The beaten look that had sprung into her eyes was just too hard to face.

He wished she hadn't said anything, but he could hardly blame her for asking. Hell, hadn't he been asking himself the same thing for the last hour? It surely went against the grain, forcing *anybody* to do something they had no mind for. And pushin' a woman into something was downright *wrong*. Especially, he admitted, *this* woman. He chanced a glance at her.

A solitary tear rolled down her smooth cheek before she hurriedly wiped it away. As if a lance had penetrated his chest, Micah groaned softly. Dammit, it wasn't right. No matter how you sliced it, it came out wrong.

But what was he to do? He'd given his word to Trib and the boys. Duffy was expectin' his daughter to be returned to him. No Benteen that he knew of had *ever* broken his word—and he wasn't about to be the first! There just wasn't no way outta this mess, he told himself.

Then it occurred to him that he knew next to nothing about this girl's situation and what she was facin' at home. Maybe, he told himself hopefully, maybe things at her pa's place wasn't really as bad as she thought. Maybe she's made more out of it than was there.

If he could just get her to tell him a little somethin' about her pa and this granny of hers. . . . Well, dammit, he might think of *somethin'*!

"What's so damn terrible about goin' *home* for God's sake?" He winced slightly at the edge in his voice.

Julie looked up at him, and it was all he could do to meet her gaze. Unshed tears still glimmered in her eyes, making the deep blue color shine and sparkle like a lake with the sun and wind teasing the surface.

"Home?" she whispered with a sad smile. "My father's rancho is not 'home.' It is merely a house."

Confused, Micah rubbed his jaw for a moment then asked, "Well, where's home then? Your granny's?"

She snorted a laugh, then let her forehead drop to her upraised knees. "Doña Ana? *Home?*" Shaking her head slowly, she looked up at him. "Señor . . . I mean, Micah. You do not know how funny you are."

It wasn't the first time he'd been laughed at, Lord knew. But dammit all, he at least liked to know *why* folks was laughin'. He shifted position a bit and snapped, "Supposin' you *tell* me."

She inhaled, and Micah kept his gaze firmly away from the swell of her breasts.

"What do you want to know?" she asked quietly.

"Tell me about your pa."

"Bueno." She nodded thoughtfully. "My 'pa', as you call him, has no love for me." Her mouth worked feverishly and he could see what it cost her to admit such a thing out loud. "But it has not always been so." Her eyes closed and a half smile touched her lips briefly. "When I was a child, my father would take me with

him on his horse to ride out over the rancho. And at night"—she sighed softly—"I would sit with him in his big leather chair, and he would read stories to me for hours. Sometimes I think I can still smell the peppermint on his breath when he kissed me good night."

Micah felt as though he was intruding, but he had to say, "That don't sound so bad."

"No." She straightened up quickly and kept her gaze locked on the surrounding pines. "But those times ended long ago."

"We all got to grow up. Put the storybooks away."

"*Sí*. But it was more than that." She wrapped her arms around her legs and held herself tightly. "When my mother died, it was as if he died also."

"Grief can do—"

"No!" Julie shot out, interrupting him in midsentence. "It was not *grief*." She turned her head to look at him. "By the time she died, I believe my father hated my mother more than he had ever loved her."

"What?"

"He hated her." She pulled in another shaky breath. "And when she died, he hated me, instead."

"That don't make any sense a'tall!" Surely she was wrong. She'd been just a child. And losing a mother and all, hell, it was enough to make *anyone* see things that wasn't there. "Maybe he was just so broke up that he . . ."

"You do not understand, Micah." Her eyes bored into his. "I saw all of you Benteens together. There is a . . . *thread* that binds you all closely. You are separate people, yet you are *one*. How can someone like you understand what it is to grow up in a house that is so alive with hatred, the very air chokes you with each breath?"

A cold chill crept up his spine. He studied her tortured features in the uncertain firelight. Micah saw the truth in her face and knew that *no one* could just make up something like that. Unless you'd lived it, you just wouldn't expect such a thing. She was right. He couldn't understand.

All his life he'd grown up surrounded by family. Knowing he was a part of something. He'd had parents who loved him. An older brother to teach him, a younger sister to torture and tease. And more than that, he was a triplet. Jericho and Shad were more than just brothers. It was almost as if the three of them were . . . *connected* somehow. There had even been a few times in their lives when one triplet was in trouble and the other two knew it, felt it, without being told.

Micah could no more imagine life without his family than he could imagine the beautiful woman across from him growing up unloved. Surely she'd had *somebody*.

He cleared his throat and forced himself to ask, "What about your granny?"

"Ah, Doña Ana." Clearly trying to push thoughts of her father aside, Julie smiled and reached for a cold biscuit. As she tore off small bits and put them in her mouth, she said, "My grandmother is a very *different* woman."

"As 'different' as your pa?" he grumbled before he could stop himself.

"*Sí.* But for other reasons."

She put a tiny piece of bread in her mouth and licked her fingertip. Micah swallowed and tried to concentrate on her voice.

"Doña Ana does not hate anyone in particular."

"Well, that's *somethin'* at least."

71

"She hates *everyone*."

"Jesus! Ain't there *one* person in your family that's nice?"

She cocked her head and gave him an unexpected smile. "There is me."

He snorted.

Obviously insulted, Julie snapped, "I am very nice. You just have not seen me at my best."

"You were tellin' me about Granny?"

"Oh, *sí*. Doña Ana." She pulled in a long breath. "Doña Ana disowned my mother when she married my father."

"Jesus!"

"And it is said that she drove my grandfather to his grave with her mad cravings for wealth and power."

"Lordy . . ."

"And now she wants to marry me to one of her neighbors so that she can get control of a piece of land that my grandfather sold years ago."

"This fella"—Micah swallowed—"she wants to marry ya to . . . what's he like? S'pose he's young and rich, huh?"

"No. He is old and rich." Julietta's blue eyes met his with complete honesty. "He has been married twice before, you know."

"Somehow," Micah groaned, "I ain't surprised. What happened to 'em? S'pose he *killed* 'em?"

"Hmmm." She cocked her head and tapped one finger against her chin. "No one has ever said *that*."

Micah knew he was going to be sorry he asked, but he just *had* to. "What exactly have they hinted at?"

For the first time since speaking about her grandmother and the man she'd picked out for her, Julietta looked worried. "They say that screams have been heard in the night."

"Could be anything," Micah said, though a finger of doubt worked its way through his body.

"And," she went on, "when the servants mention the screaming, they are fired. Removed from the rancho." She chewed at her lip. "So after the first wife's passing, no one ever remarked on the screaming in the night again. But I have always wondered what was the cause of the screams." Her gaze slipped up to his. "Can you guess why a woman would behave so?"

Micah looked deeply into her eyes and managed to keep from shuddering. Somehow he kept his voice steady, even. "No. No, Julie, I got no idea," he lied. But it wasn't really a lie. He didn't *know* for sure. And he didn't *want* to know.

His gaze moved over her slowly. She was so small. Fragile, almost. He couldn't meet her gaze. His gut twisted painfully and his tongue was suddenly thick in a too dry mouth. He had to look away. Hideous images of an evil old man doing unspeakable things to her rushed through his mind. For a split second, he imagined her screaming in pain, her eyes wild, looking in vain for *someone* to help her.

Micah ground his teeth together and thrust the visions from his brain. Gettin' all worked up and thinkin' the worst wasn't goin' to do a damn thing except drive him crazy!

Dammit. After all the talking she'd done, he still had no idea what to do. The only thing he was absolutely *sure* of was that he would do *anything* to keep her safely away from her grandmother. Even her father seemed a better bet. At least the man wasn't plannin' on marryin' her off to some damned filthy bastard who'd do God knows what to her!

He glanced at her as she stood to unroll her bedroll. How had she managed to come from such people and not be as hateful and twisted as the rest of her family?

And why was *he* the one chosen to see to it that her dreams of independence, freedom, remained only dreams? As she bent to smooth out the blanket, Micah's gaze followed the line of her body.

She lay down close to the fire and was asleep almost the moment her cheek touched the old, worn blanket. He smiled wistfully. There'd be no reason to sleep tied together tonight, he told himself. She was far too tuckered out to be plannin' on runnin' anywhere.

He stretched out himself, but instead of sleeping, he lay quietly, watching her. As much as he wanted her, he knew damn well that was just another fancy ... like one of those stories her pa used to read to her. It would never happen. She was just not for the likes of him.

Though it pained him to acknowledge that fact, he could live with it. Because he *had* to. But at the same time Micah swore silently that he would keep her safe. No matter what. And when they finally reached Texas, he would look her old man over for himself.

This Patrick Michael Duffy better treat her right, he told himself. 'Cause if he didn't ... Micah's jaw clenched tight at the thought. If Duffy didn't strike the right note, Micah knew he'd grab Julie, throw her on a horse, and trot her right back to her friend's house in Montana. He couldn't have her—but he could damn well make sure she had the *chance* to be happy.

Even if he *did* become the first Benteen to go back on his word.

Deliberately closing his eyes, Micah fell into a restless, dream-filled sleep that had him tossing and turning all night.

* * *

He was never going to stop.

Julietta sighed, tightened her grip on the saddle horn, and hung on. Her eyes bored a hole in Micah's broad back as his horse set the pace for them. Seemingly oblivious to her discomfort, the big man was apparently able to stay in the saddle for hours without complaint.

Disappointment swelled in her. Somehow she'd hoped that telling Micah about her family would be enough to convince him to let her go. She frowned and tightened her grip on the saddle horn reflexively. So far he hadn't even shown any sign of slowing down, let alone quitting this journey altogether.

Julie gritted her teeth and tasted the dust from the road. Every bone and muscle in her body ached with the constant jostling. Despite the chill in the air, she felt beads of perspiration roll down her back beneath her dirty white shirt. Mumbling a curse, she told herself that even the grime and misery of such a ride would be acceptable if only they were headed in the other direction. And as soon as the man in front of her called a halt for the day, she'd do all she could to make him turn around.

Heaven knew, she'd *already* done everything she could think of to try to slow him down. Determined to annoy him enough so that he'd be eager to let her go, she'd even allowed herself to fall off her horse!

Embarrassment flooded her cheeks as she recalled the graceless thud she'd made on the hard ground. She hadn't fallen off a horse since she was five years old! And the indignity of the fall hadn't been the worst part. Micah'd barely glanced at her before telling her to climb back aboard and get moving. When that ploy didn't work, she'd forced him to stop for so many "nature" calls, Julie was sure he must think she was dying of some strange disease.

And still he didn't give up. Didn't slow down. After every stop, he'd merely urged the horses into a mile-eating trot to make up the time lost. He wouldn't even let her hold her own reins anymore!

Instinctively she dipped her head to avoid a low-hanging pine branch and realized she'd hardly noticed the country she was passing through. Fool, she groaned silently. She *had* to pay attention. On the off chance she did get away from Micah, she'd better have some notion of how to get back to Thea's house in Montana.

She flicked a quick glance at Micah again. How strange it was, Julie thought, that she resented his single-minded determination and admired him for it at the same time. He truly was a man seemingly unbothered by the doubts that plagued everyone else. He simply did what he thought best, no matter the cost to others.

Like herself.

Julie shook her head slowly and told herself that if only he were on *her* side, together they could accomplish anything.

Micah pulled back on his reins, bringing his horse to an abrupt halt. She drew in a quick breath, intending to ask him what he was doing, but he held one hand up, silencing her before she could speak.

Something was wrong. She watched him let his gaze move slowly over the narrow path and the surrounding trees. Nervous, Julie looked around uneasily. She squinted and tried desperately to see beyond the thickly wooded tree line, but she saw nothing.

A cold spiral of fear began to build in the pit of her stomach. The irregular, undetermined path they sat on suddenly seemed too open and exposed. She imagined watchful eyes focused on her from the safety of the trees.

Was it her grandmother's men? Already?

When a hand fell softly on her calf, Julie jumped and gasped before she saw Micah. He stood beside her horse, his index finger across his lips, a frown in his eyes. His arms reached up for her, and she slid off the mare into his strong embrace.

For all too brief a moment, he squeezed her tightly and Julie heard his heartbeat pounding frantically. She looked up at him and whispered, "Micah . . ."

Immediately his fingers covered her mouth. He shook his head, staring only at the path ahead and beyond. After a long moment, he finally lowered his gaze to hers.

In a whisper no stronger than a sigh, he said, "Go into the trees, Julie. Stay there."

Staring into his eyes, Julie saw . . . not fear, she told herself, but worry. Concern. For her. He was trying to push her to safety at the expense of his own.

Her mouth suddenly dry, Julie's mind worked furiously. She couldn't let him stand alone to face whatever was headed toward them. Besides, she knew herself to be a fine shot. She could help.

Her decision made, she shook her head firmly and met his unwavering stare. In the depths of his eyes she watched his concern for her replaced by a growing anger. She sensed his urgency and shared it. They didn't have time to argue. In a barely audible voice she said, "I won't go, Micah." When he didn't agree, she went on hurriedly, "If something happens to you, I'd be alone with whoever is out there."

She watched him anxiously for an eternity-filled moment before she saw the reluctant acceptance in his eyes.

Quickly he pulled the rifle from his saddle scabbard and thrust it at her. Keeping a firm grip on his own shotgun, Micah pulled at the horses to get them as far off the trail as possible.

The coming hoofbeats were louder now and Julie held her breath, her fingers curling over the rifle stock. In seconds, Micah was beside her again. She felt the tension in his body as if it were a live thing, reaching out for her. He sidled closer to her, gave her a quick glance, then looked back toward the oncoming rider for an instant before turning to look into her face again.

A dozen different emotions flashed across his bearded features in a heartbeat. As the approaching hoofbeats came even nearer, he sucked in a gulp of air, then reached out and pulled her to him.

Pressed close to his chest, Julie tilted her head back to look up at him just as his lips came down on hers in a quick, hard kiss.

Almost before it began, it was over and Micah was

78

pushing her behind him. She staggered back a pace and swallowed heavily. Julie struggled to catch her breath as he positioned himself between her and the coming trouble. Legs spread wide apart, shotgun held at the ready, Micah faced the lone horseman just coming into view at the curve of the path.

CHAPTER
···SIX···

THE MOUSE-COLORED HORSE stepped tiredly around the bend, and Julie heard Micah's breath leave him in a relieved sigh. As she studied the rider, she wasn't sure she shared Micah's opinion.

A man who looked as old as the mountain sat ramrod straight atop his horse. A moth-bitten bearskin cape hung around his narrow shoulders and fell to below his buckskin-clad knees. Over his wild, iron gray hair, he wore a wolf's head and pelt for a cap, the fur blending in to his full, straggly beard. In one hand, he held the reins to his horse, in the other, a gleaming, like-new rifle. Ammunition belts crossed his thin chest, and his leathery features were creased in a frown.

"Who the hell are you?" he called out, bringing his horse to a stop several feet away and leveling his rifle at them.

"Name's Benteen," Micha offered, making no move to step into the open.

"Who else you got there, Benteen?" the trapper asked. "Step on out here where I can get a look at ya!"

Cautiously Micah took a half step forward, motioning with one hand for Julie to stay where she was.

"What'cha doin' there, boy?"

"Nothin', old man. I'm comin'." Out of the corner of his mouth, he whispered, "You stay put, y'hear?"

"Ain't nothin' wrong with my ears, boy. Who you keepin' hid back there?" He cocked his head warily. "You wouldn't be thinkin' about harmin' a innocent old coot like me, would ya?"

Julie pushed past Micah's restraining arm and stepped into the open, her own rifle pointed at the unpleasant man.

"Dammit, Julie—"

"I will not stay hidden behind a tree!"

"Haw, haw, haw!" The old man's wheezing laugh slashed through the air. "Hell, mister. Shoulda told me you had a fe-male tucked away in yonder!" He shook his grizzled head and gave them a lopsided grin. "Now just settle down there, little lady. Don't you get to feelin' fretful and pull that trigger there."

"Dammit, Julie," Michah snapped, his voice low, furious. He walked to her side and stood in front of her deliberately. "Do what I tell ya."

"I will not. You cannot make me hide behind a tree while *he*"—she waved her rifle barrel at the old trapper—"decides if he wants to shoot you or not."

The other man's laughter rang out again, and Micah watched with wary eyes as the stranger slowly lowered his gun. "Hell, son! Save your breath! Never did know a wife to mind her man—"

"Wife?" Julie said.

Micah reached behind him, grabbed her elbow, and squeezed it briefly. Keeping his attention on the other man, he said, "Well, I never quit tryin' to remind her just who the husband is around here."

"Can't say as I blame ya, boy." The trapper let his

gaze move over Julie appreciatively. "She's a looker all right, but she appears to be a handful of trouble, too."

Julie swung her head back and forth, following the conversation in stunned surprise.

Micah took advantage of her momentary silence to ask, "You seen anyone else on this road, old man?"

The trapper leaned forward in his saddle and studied the young couple for a long minute before answering. "No. No, I ain't. Why you so curious?"

"My wife here," Micah said and spoke louder to cover Julie's gasp, "her pa wasn't too set on us gettin' hitched. Figured he might just send out a couple of his boys to chase us down." He risked a quick glance at his 'wife.' Her eyes wide, mouth open, she stared at him like he'd lost his mind.

Deliberately he threw one arm around her shoulder and pressed her close. Looking back at the other man, he added, "See, we just up and run off together."

Julie stiffened, but he kept a tight hold on her.

"Yep"—Micah grinned—"she just keep botherin' me somethin' fierce, till I couldn't take it no more. Finally I give in and married her."

Julie wrapped her arm around his waist and under the cover of his coat gave the flesh of his waist a vicious pinch.

The old man gave them a wide smile, displaying wide spaces between his tobacco stained teeth. "Don't blame ya a bit, boy. Why, a woman *that* good-lookin' might could talk *me* into a hitch up, too!" As his smile faded, he went on. "I ain't seen nobody on the trail, but that don't mean a damn thing anyhow." He waved one arm, encompassing the surrounding woods. "Hell, you could prob'ly hide a army in there and not know it. Best if you keep a sharp lookout yourself."

"Plan to," Micah answered and released Julie.

"Well, happy life to ya," the grizzled old man called out as he started on his way again. "And don't you two get so caught up in frolickin' that ya forget it's springtime."

"Huh?"

"Springtime, boy! Bears!" He looked over his shoulder at them. "The grizz is startin' to cut loose about now, and, mister, after a long winter nap, them bears is *hungry*! Believe you me, you don't want to run afoul one of 'em."

"I'll remember," Micah yelled back as the man disappeared down the path.

Of all the damn fool, stupid, foolish men, he had to take top prize. Micah spun around, stomped past Julie, and walked to the horses. He hadn't even been thinkin' about the damn grizzlies. Jesus! The woods're prob'ly *crawlin'* with 'em, and *he* hadn't given 'em a passin' thought.

With both horses standing docilely on the path, Micah immediately checked the cinch straps on the saddles, more out of habit than anything else. While he completed the familiar task, his brain railed on.

He was endangering both him and Julie because he wasn't keepin' his mind on the job at hand. Hell, he might've stumbled right into a bear and then what? Get himself killed? Or *her*? He glanced over at her and suppressed a shudder at the thought of a grizzly's claws ripping through her flesh.

For God's sake! He'd been actin' like some moonstruck kid. He hadn't even heard that fool trapper until the old coot was right on top of 'em! Micah ran the flat of his hand down the length of Satan's neck. The big stallion shook his head, obviously glad for the attention.

Micah snorted. Keepin' his mind too much on Julietta Duffy could get 'em both killed.

"Why did you tell that man we are married?" Julie said as she quietly stepped up beside him.

Micah jumped and moved back a pace. She followed him quickly. She'd been waiting for some sort of explanation, but it seemed that he wasn't going to say anything unless she asked. Even now she could tell by the hard set of his jaw that he had no wish to speak to her. In fact, he looked furious.

He hardly spared her a glance before saying gruffly, "Climb aboard, Julie. We best get goin'."

"No."

His head dropped to his chest. "What?"

"I said no."

"Julie—"

"I want to know," she prodded, "why you told that man we are married."

He sighed, ran one hand through his too long hair, and locked his eyes with hers. "Because, your granny's men ain't lookin' for a married couple. If that ol' hide hunter runs across anybody askin' after us, he'll say we're a couple. Maybe throw Granny's men off the chase for a bit."

She nodded slowly. It made sense. Then she asked, "Hide hunter?"

"Hide hunter. Used to be just for buffalo hunters, but I figure it could go for trappers just as easy." He jabbed his thumb at the horse behind him. "*Now* will ya climb aboard and let's get goin'?"

"Not yet."

"Lord Almighty, woman ..." Micah groaned, glanced back at the trail where the old man had gone, then turned again to face her. "What is it now?"

Julie took another step closer to him and laid one hand on his arm. Looking up into his eyes, she asked quietly, "Why did you kiss me?"

He frowned and stared down at her hand, lying on the sleeve of his buckskin shirt.

She held her breath. Maybe she shouldn't have asked. Maybe she should have pretended that nothing had happened. But how could she? Somewhere deep inside her, the fluttering reaction to his lips on hers still stirred.

In an instant Julie remembered it all. The feel of his hands on her arms, drawing her close. The confusion and desire shining in his eyes just before he lowered his mouth to hers. The tickling sensation of his beard against her skin as his lips slanted across hers.

Then, before she was fully recovered from his kiss, he'd claimed her as his wife.

She studied his features, trying to read his expression beneath the rust-brown beard and his wild mass of wavy hair. But it was impossible. And suddenly Julie thought that perhaps he was *hiding* behind that beard of his. Using it to mask feelings that otherwise would be written plainly on his features.

Finally he raised his gaze to hers, seemed about to speak, then changed his mind. Taking the rifle from her hands, he turned and slid it into the scabbard on her saddle.

"I think you ought to keep this weapon with ya. Just in case." He snorted a weak laugh and added, "I'm trustin' ya not to shoot me just to run off."

"Why, Micah?"

" 'Cause it could get dangerous from here on. And I sure as hell hope you can shoot as good as you talk."

"No." She came up behind him, held his upper arm, and turned him around to face her. "I am not asking about the rifle, and I think you know that."

"Julie . . . just let it go."

"Why did you kiss me?"

Everything stopped. Even the sounds of the horses' breathing faded into the background. Late morning sun poked through the branches of the pines and threw dappled shadows across his face. He seemed to be considering her question—trying to decide if he should answer or not. Julie waited, not sure of what she would hear. Not even sure she would *like* his answer. But she *had* to know.

Finally Micah looked directly at her. Beneath his beard, she thought she saw a smile. Slowly, hesitantly, he raised one hand, touched her cheek gently, then let his arm drop back to his side. He gave her a crooked, nervous grin and shrugged. "For luck," he said and looked past her, over her head into the trees.

Julie began to breathe again. She was still no closer to the truth, she was certain. At the same time, she realized that he would not admit to anything else. His agitation plain in his rigid stance, Julie felt sure that he was desperately hoping to end this. Now.

But she couldn't. It seemed that so much had changed in the last few minutes. At least as far as *she* was concerned. She forgot the fact that he was only with her to take her to her father. She told herself that it didn't matter that only hours ago she was plotting to escape his watchful eye.

Instead, she remembered what he'd done when he thought she was in danger. Julie realized that for the first time in her life, someone had come to her aid not for what he could get from her . . . but simply because *she*, Julietta Duffy, was in trouble. He hadn't been acting for her father. Certainly not for her grandmother. In fact, she admitted with a start, Micah Benteen was the first man *ever* to look at her and see only Julie, the woman.

In a vivid flash of memory she saw him again as he stood between her and danger. He'd placed himself directly in that old man's line of fire to protect her. She recalled how he'd tried to keep her in the trees, out of sight. How he'd claimed her so easily for his wife, and most especially, she remembered the feel of his lips on hers. The warmth of his breath against her face and the pounding of his heart.

Just in remembrance, her own heart began a quick beat that throbbed throughout her body. She swallowed heavily, lifted one hand and laid it against his broad chest.

As if stung, Micah jerked unsteadily and looked down at her through shuttered eyes. "What is it, Julie?"

She read his embarrassment easily, but chose to ignore it. "There is still a long journey ahead of us, Micah . . ."

"Yeah?" He shifted uneasily, but didn't look away.

"I only thought . . . ," she said, with a sharp intake of breath.

"What?" His voice dropped to a low, husky rumble that shuddered through her.

She moved both hands to his shoulders hesitantly. "Perhaps . . ."—she looked into his eyes and saw herself reflected in the forest green depths—"perhaps we might need a bit more luck. . . ."

Micah sucked in a gulp of air, and she felt him tremble beneath her hands. For one, awful moment she thought he might refuse her. Turn away. But in the next instant he lowered his head and touched his mouth to hers in an almost reverent caress.

Julie sighed and leaned into him.

At her surrender Micah's lips pressed more firmly against hers. She groaned softly when his tongue parted her lips and slipped inside her mouth. In a silent dance his tongue moved over hers, enticing, teasing. And with every touch Julie's heartbeat quickened until it became nothing more than a constant roar in her ears.

She couldn't breathe and she didn't care. His strong arms closed around her and lifted her feet from the ground. Julie's fingers clasped at his back desperately as she struggled to hold on despite the suddenly spinning world.

An incredible heat rushed through her body and filled her with a need for more. One of his big hands moved over her back, slid over the curve of her hip, and cupped her behind, pulling her fast against him. She felt the hard, swollen proof of his desire rub against the already throbbing juncture of her thighs and moaned gently in response.

As if awakened from a trance, Micah pulled away from her mouth abruptly and buried his face in the hollow of her neck. Julie stared blankly up at the sky, drawing short, quick breaths that did nothing to calm her racing heart.

Tantalizingly slowly, Micah skimmed her body along his as he lowered her back to the ground. Her knees folded up and he held her steady. She leaned her forehead against his chest, felt the rise and fall of his rapid breathing, and knew he was as affected as she.

"Mount up, Julie," he whispered into her hair.

She blinked and shook her head. Looking up, she found him staring down at her. "What?"

"I said"—he licked his lips and inhaled deeply—"mount up. We gotta get movin'."

"That is all you have to say?"

"Ain't nothin' else *to* say." He ran one finger down the length of her face, then reluctantly turned away.

"*I* think there is *much* to say!"

He snorted. "Not surprised." A forced smile curved his lips. "You *always* got more than enough to say."

"Micah," she whispered, a catch in her voice that she couldn't quite contain, "don't do this. You cannot pretend that nothing—"

"Yeah, I can." He cut her off and handed her the reins to her mount. "And that's just what I'm gonna do. So I'd appreciate it if you didn't go lookin' at me like that."

"But why?" Julie took the reins and kept talking, despite the fact that he was turned from her and already stepping into his saddle. "Why would you forget this?"

"Jesus, woman!" His shout rang out and settled over her like a cold fog. He pulled his foot out of the stirrup again and turned to face her. There was no tenderness in his eyes now. Only pain. And anger.

"What the hell kind of man do ya think I am? I ain't

made of stone, Julie." He pulled in another great gulp of air. "I can't kiss you like that knowin' I got no right."

"But if I give you the right . . ."

"You can't." The anger gone, he looked down at her and said sadly, "No one can, Hoo-lee-edda. Not even you. Maybe *'specially* not you." Micah swallowed and added through gritted teeth, "Now *please*. Mount up."

She could argue with him, she knew. But it would do no good. Whatever it was between them that had flared so briefly to life, was gone now. She couldn't hold onto that magic alone, and Micah had closed himself off to it.

And maybe it was best. Perhaps this was a sign that she should remember her first plan. Escape. God willing, she would be able to manage it soon. She held that hope tightly. The sooner she was away, the sooner she could build her *own* life. And she would find a man who would love her and find the magic they shared as important as she did.

Julie looked up at Micah and wanted to scream at him. To kick him. But she didn't. Deliberately she pushed what was left of her bruised feelings down deep inside her and wordlessly snatched the reins from his hand.

"Julie—" he started softly.

"No." She cut him off, stepped into the stirrup, and swung herself into the saddle. From her safe height she let her gaze slide over him before speaking in a flat, expressionless voice. "You were right, Micah. And I will do as you say. After all, I *am* your prisoner."

He winced slightly, but after a moment he gave her

a brief nod and mounted his animal. He urged the horse into a slow walk, and Julie obediently followed behind.

* * *

Patrick Michael Duffy propped his feet up on the arm of the hide-covered chair in front of him. The spikes of his spurs dug gouges in the wood, but he was beyond caring.

Deliberately he tilted his head back and tossed a jiggerful of *aguardiente* down his throat. The raw liquid burned all the way down to his stomach, and he welcomed the fire. Soon he knew he would be too numb to feel even that much.

Lifting his pale blue eyes to the portrait he kept on his desk, Patrick suddenly reached for the ornate silver frame. Holding it in his lap, he stared down at the lovely face gazing back at him serenely.

The woman in the portrait was dark. Black eyes, black hair . . . black heart.

"Damn your soul, Elena," he muttered in an underbreath. "Damn it for all time." His eyes narrowed, and he jerked his head back. She was laughing at him. Just like before. Just like always.

With a sudden burst of energy he threw the framed picture with all the strength he could summon up. It sailed across the narrow room and hit the far wall, its glass splintering and raining down on the polished oak floor.

He smiled and grabbed the bottle of liquor off the edge of his desk. From the corner of his eye he saw the letter he'd received only that morning from some lunatic female fall to the floor. Deliberately he kicked it into the middle of the floor.

With the neck of the bottle between his lips, he

pulled a long drink, then wiped his mouth with the back of his hand. He let his feet drop to the floor and stood up unsteadily. Snorting a half chuckle, he purposefully stepped on the crazy woman's letter.

Just what he needed, he told himself. Yet *another* female to give him fits. Well, it would be a cold day in summer before he'd get himself mixed up with another woman. And a *crazy* one to boot!

For a moment he hesitated, then crossed the room with shaky steps. Bending down, he picked up the portrait, shook the broken glass out, and stuffed the framed image under his arm. Carefully he walked to the doorway and stepped into the darkened hall.

Weaving his way to the big bedroom at the other end of the long, low house, Patrick bumped his shoulder against first one wall, then another. His feet stumbled, his spurs making a soft, chinking sound in the silence.

If there was anyone else awake in the great house, they knew enough to stay clear of the drunken man. Oh, they'd all tried, years ago, to make him stop. They'd even hidden his bottles of whiskey. But sometime in the last few years they'd finally quit trying.

Now Patrick Duffy's routine was uninterrupted. Every evening he sat in the rancho office for as long as it took to get thoroughly, completely, drunk. The splintered glass in the picture frame was always quietly replaced. His shouts and curses went unnoticed. Then, in the middle of the night, he made his way to his bedroom and fell asleep, fully clothed across his bed.

Now, as he slumped down onto the feather mattress, he thought he heard pounding in the distance. Patrick snorted and a sloppy half grin curved his lips. Probably just the pounding in his own brain. He sighed, moved his head around lazily until he was comfortable then, let his eyes slide shut.

"Santa Maria, Madre de Dios," Juana Lopez whispered minutes later as she looked in the open door to *el Patron*'s bedroom. The man was spread-eagled across the pale blue coverlet, his long legs hanging over the edge of the bed, his spurs snagged on the expensive fabric.

He had gotten worse in the last few weeks.

Since finding out about the marriage Doña Ana had planned for Julietta, Patrick Duffy had been as one possessed.

Juana stepped softly into the room and looked down at the master of the Duffy ranch. His mouth open, eyes shut, his gray-streaked black hair fanned out around his head, he clutched the portrait in his arms tight against his chest. A once-handsome man, he seldom made any effort at his appearance anymore.

"Ah, Elena," Juana whispered. Gingerly she pulled the portrait free and looked into the flat, emotionless eyes staring back at her. Shaking her head at the young woman in the silver frame, she asked, "Did you know what hell you caused before you died? Did you care that Julietta would have to pay for your sins?"

Muttering under her breath, the older woman lifted one corner of the quilt and tossed it over her drunken employer. "All of this pain, Patron. For what?" Her whispered questions went unanswered, as she'd known they would. "Is it so important for you to best Doña

Ana? Must you make Julietta pay for what you and Elena did to each other?"

His sonorous breathing sounded overloud in the still room. Pity, anger, and disgust warred within her. He'd thrown so much away over the years. Carelessly, heedlessly, he squandered the passing days as if they would never end. Closing off parts of his heart like unused rooms in an abandoned house, Patrick Duffy had shut out the world.

She sighed and crossed the wide floor to the patio doors. Throwing them wide, she stepped out onto the cool stones and let the music of the falling water in the central fountain soothe her.

Under the stars she wrapped her arms around herself and stared up at the night sky. Somewhere in the darkness, miles from the rancho, Julietta was on her way home. *Home!* Juana's features twisted into a frown. A hushed prayer left her lips, not for the first time since coming to this house of sadness. Twenty years she had worked for the Patron. And the last sixteen, she had stayed only for the sake of Julietta. Was it not for the girl, Juana would have turned her back on the misery of this place long ago.

If it was in her power, she would send a miracle to Julietta. To protect her. To keep her safe from those who should have loved her best.

"No time like the present, sir!"

Juana spun about, searching the shadows for the source of the strange, stilted voice. Unbelievably it came again. Loud this time. Closer. A woman.

"I realize, of course, that I am a bit late, but the delay was unavoidable, I assure you."

Raul's worried, answering voice was pitched too low

for Juana to hear, and the housekeeper wondered who it was the boy had allowed into the house.

The sharp tapping of her heels on the tile floor heralded the strange woman's approach. Juana listened, fascinated by the unusual accent. She waited for her first glimpse of the newcomer.

"Mr. Patrick Duffy is expecting me. I do not intend to be put off another moment, young man." She stepped into the open doorway of the master bedroom and paused, silhouetted against the light from the hallway behind her. "Good heavens!" she finally breathed as she looked at the master of the house.

Juana watched the other woman walk slowly into the room, her gaze locked on the snoring, sloppy figure of Patrick Duffy.

The stranger was tall, angular. She stood in a small halo of light cast by the oil lamp on a nearby table. Her features were sharp, and her pale brown hair was pulled back from her face and hidden beneath the brim of a wide, lavender hat. She was not young. And, Juana told herself, not pretty. Not even in the soft glow of moonlight. But still there was *something* in the woman's carriage, in her brown eyes, now narrowed in disgust, that made *pretty* seem like a small word.

"Of all the insulting, insufferable . . . ," the woman's voice droned off, and Juana stepped into the room from the patio. Immediately the woman looked up. "Who are you?" she demanded.

"Juana, Señora. I keep the house for *el Patrón*."

The tall gringa smiled and nodded. "I have already noticed the care given this magnificent house. I am sure that in daylight it will only shine more beautifully. *I* am—" A loud, reverberating snore interrupted her, and she shot the drunken man a malevolent look. "I am Penelope Butterworth. I have an appointment with Mr. Duffy."

Juana hurried forward. "Ah, Señora. Perhaps you should return tomorrow? When he is awake?"

"Sober, you mean?" Penelope's eyebrows shot straight up. "No. Juana, is it?"

"Sí, Señora."

"Well, Juana, I don't believe coming back tomorrow is the answer to this particular problem." She turned this way and that, casting anxious glances around the room. Finally she spied what she'd been looking for. A half smile on her face, she walked to the bureau and lifted a tall vase filled with early wildflowers.

She pulled her cream-colored gloves off and laid both them and the purse dangling from her wrist on the bureau top. Lifting the rose-patterned vase easily, she walked back to Juana's side.

"Simply lovely, Juana," she said, admiring the delicate blossoms for a moment. "I do so enjoy fresh-cut flowers," she added before taking them from the water and handing the loose bouquet to the older woman. Smiling grimly, she pointed out, "No sense casting pearls before swine."

Juana frowned in confusion, but held the dripping wet flowers tightly, expectantly. In all her years of service, *nothing* had prepared her for *this*! The woman was so calm, so sure of herself. . . . Juana didn't know what she should do. It was unusual, to be sure, for anyone to visit the rancho these days. And *never* had a woman been in *el Patron*'s bedroom.

Not since Elena died.

Perhaps, though, *el Patron* was expecting this woman. If so, he would be angry indeed if his housekeeper were to dismiss a guest.

Besides, the older woman admitted silently, she was eager to see what the uncommon *gringa* would do next.

CHAPTER
···SEVEN···

PENELOPE HELD THE heavy, water-filled vase easily. A strong woman, she was no stranger to hard work. And now, looking down on the man she'd come so far to see, a strength born of rage filled her.

She stood beside the bed, deliberately upended the vase, and smiled as the used, flower water splashed down onto Patrick Duffy's face.

He sat up sputtering and coughing. Patrick shook his head violently and rubbed the water from his eyes with the backs of his hands. Glaring at the woman towering over him, he yelled, "Who the hell are you?"

She swung her right hand back and slapped him resoundingly across his face.

Patrick and his housekeeper gasped.

In the stunned silence Penelope ordered, "I'll thank you to keep a civil tongue in your head, *Mr.* Duffy!"

"What?" His hand cupping his cheek, he blinked frantically, trying to focus his gaze.

Penelope sneered, then turned her back on him. "We shall need coffee please, Juana. Black. *Oceans* of it."

"*Sí, Señora,*" the older woman replied, but showed no signs of moving.

"*I* am Penelope Butterworth," she said and turned a

glare on Patrick Duffy. "You received my letter this morning, did you not?"

"Letter?"

"Yes. Letter. Words written on fine paper?" Good Lord. That her hopes for justice should rest on *this* pitiful excuse for a man! If his mind was as blank as his eyes, Penelope thought, there'd be no help coming from *this* quarter. Hands on hips, her foot tapping angrily, she said, "How *dare* you become intoxicated when expecting a *lady*!"

Duffy and the woman stared at each other, an arc of anger rippling between them. Juana looked from one to the other, then smothered a chuckle, and hurried from the room.

There was coffee to be made. As she hustled down the long hall, headed for the kitchen, she spared a quick glance for heaven.

Perhaps the miracle she'd prayed for had finally arrived.

"My head's gonna explode."

"It most certainly is not," Penelope countered briskly. She held a cup and saucer under his nose and waited until he'd smelled the strong black coffee before adding, "Your condition is merely a penance the Good Lord gives to miserable drunkards like yourself to teach them the error of their ways."

He slid one look at her and wasn't in the least surprised to see a grimace of distaste on her pursed lips. His cheek still throbbed from the smack she'd given him, his head pounded in time with his heartbeat and the inside of his mouth felt like a river bottom. The female demon hadn't even allowed him time to don a dry shirt and the soaking one he wore clung to his chest like a clammy hand.

Covertly he glanced at her again. Perched on the edge of a deep red velvet armchair, she held her spine rigid and her fingers laced tightly together in her lap. She looked like a damn queen forced to entertain one of her lesser subjects.

"Just who the he—heck are you, Penelope Butterforce, and why are you here botherin' an innocent man in his own home?"

"Butterworth."

"What?" Hell, she was as crazy in person as she'd sounded in her letter!

"My name. Penelope Butter*worth*, not force."

"Oh." If she only knew how *little* he cared what her name was! He attempted one swallow of coffee and shuddered slightly. Maybe if he added a shot of brandy ... He got up unsteadily.

"And," she tossed in, "I would hardly refer to *you* as 'innocent.'"

"Fine. *Worth*." He nodded and walked to the sideboard. "And I'm a no-account. Now why are you here in the middle of the night?"

"It is nowhere near the middle of the night, Mr. Duffy."

"Pat."

"I beg your pardon?"

"As well you should, lady," he mumbled and bent to pull open the cabinet door. He could hardly stand up. Jesus, Mary, and Joseph! Patrick squinted against the throbbing pain in his skull as he leaned down to find the brandy. When his fingers curled around the neck of the bottle, he sighed gratefully. He'd need all the liquid help he could find to deal with the lunatic staring at him.

Straightening up, he pulled the cork from the bottle with his teeth and began to pour.

Before one drop of the fine, amber liquid had so much as reached the top of the bottle, the damned interfering woman snatched it from his fingers.

Damn, she was fast! He hadn't even heard her get up. He spun about and immediately regretted the action. The room seemed to tilt, and his stomach flopped dangerously. It was a long moment before he could lock his gaze on the interloper. Then, what he saw had him shouting again, despite the ache behind his eyes.

"Stop it!" A few stumbling steps brought him to her side, but she held the bottle out of reach, just outside a window. Patrick watched the Napoleon brandy spill onto a freshly weeded flower bed. "Goddammit! You give me that bloody liquor and you give it to me now."

Penelope Butterworth drew herself up to her considerable height and looked him squarely in the eye. "I have already shown you what I think of profanity, Mr. Duffy. If need be, I shall show you again."

Patrick looked into her brown eyes and knew without a doubt that the formidable woman would do just as she promised. Then what? Even *he* wasn't drunk enough to actually strike a woman . . . even in justified retaliation!

Just find out what she wants, he told himself. That's the easiest way. Let her talk, then get her the hell out of his life.

"What do you want from me, lady?"

She dropped the empty bottle to the dirt outside and Patrick winced at the soft thud. He fell onto the nearest seat and sat looking up at her. She held her hands firmly clasped beneath her abundant bosom, squared her shoulders, and lifted her chin.

"I've come to you for one reason, Mr. Duffy. *You*, I believe, are the one man who might be willing to help me in my quest."

"Quest? For what?" Absently he took another sip of black coffee and grimaced before setting the cup down on the nearby table.

"Justice."

He snorted. "Justice? Me?" Pushing himself to his feet, Patrick straightened up until he and the woman were at eye level. He'd never cared much for tall women, and now he knew why. They made him feel smaller, somehow. Less important. Less intimidating.

His gaze moved over her rather plain features quickly. Not a pretty woman by any stretch of the imagination, he had to admit that she carried herself well and appeared to have a fine figure. From the swell of her bosom to her not too narrow waist and gently rounded hips, Penelope Butterworth's body more than made up for what her face lacked.

And yet there was something in her plain, open face that shone more brightly than mere beauty. She was at least thirty-five years old, and since she wore no ring on her hand, he was willing to assume she was a spinster. Besides, she had that "old maid" air about her. That untouched, unsullied quality that always scared the hell out of a man.

He met her gaze again and finally was able to put his finger on the one, unmistakable quality shining on her features.

Honesty.

Good Lord.

"Yes, you, Mr. Duffy. I need your help, and I think that once you have heard why, you will be more than happy to lend your assistance."

She obviously didn't know him as well as she thought she did. "Lady," he sighed and turned to walk away, "it's been years since I helped anybody but me. And right now, I think I'll go help myself to some *aguardiente* and go back to bed." He glanced at her over his shoulder. "You can find your own way out, surely?"

"Mr. Duffy," she called out, undeterred by his attitude. "I am not interested in trying to have an intelligent conversation with an intoxicated man."

"Then you'd best go somewhere else, lady." He kept moving. " 'Cause in about ten minutes, that's exactly what I plan on being!"

"I have every intention of accomplishing my goal with or without *your* help."

He waved one hand and kept walking. "I'm sure, Miss Buttercurdle. And good luck to you."

"Aren't you the slightest bit curious as to what my goal might be? After all," she spoke louder as he neared the door, "I *have* come all the way from England. Halfway around the world, just to see my task done."

Patrick stopped. It had been a long time since he'd run into a woman as hardheaded as *this* one. His chin on his chest, he said just loud enough to be heard, "Fine, Miss Buttertaster. Why don't you tell me your little goal and then take yourself back to jolly old England?"

"Very well." She paused. He heard her take a deep breath. "I intend to see Doña Ana Santos *hanged* for the murder of my brother."

His heart stopped. Patrick did a slow turn. His eyes narrowed, he looked at the surprising woman across the room from him. There it was again. That damned honesty. But he had to admit, she'd gotten his attention. Tilting his head, he asked, "Who was your brother?"

She held her chin up higher. "Eustace Butter*worth*. Solicitor to Don Ricardo Santos before he died." Her lips trembled slightly. "I believe the old woman had Eustace killed to prevent him from filing the Don's new will. The one he'd made disinheriting Doña Ana."

A sudden roaring filled his ears. His heart began beating again, and his foul headache miraculously disappeared. Patrick walked back across the room and stopped just a foot or less from Penelope. Nodding, he said quietly, "Have a seat, Miss Butterworth. We need to talk."

*　　*　　*

"Why won't you talk, dammit?"

Julie's gaze flicked to Micah, then back to the empty trail ahead of them.

"You ain't makin' the least bit of sense, Julie."

She sat her horse stiffly, refusing to even look at him again. The anger in his voice was plain, but she didn't care. Tired, hungry, and still a bit hurt at the way he'd brushed aside her kiss, Julie wasn't about to make any part of this trip easier on him.

She'd lost count now of how many days had passed since leaving the Benteen ranch. The days had slipped together until they'd become no more than a long nightmare of discomfort and crushed pride. They hadn't even seen another living soul since leaving the trapper behind who knows *how* long ago!

Every time he heard the slightest bit of noise, Micah

was bustling them off the trail into the surrounding woods. And that was something else, she reminded herself hotly. Even the countryside hadn't changed! The same trees, the same trail—why, for all she knew, they'd been going in circles for days!

But finally their supplies were running low. Now Micah was *forced* to stop at the next town for more, and he actually wanted her to promise not to try to escape. Hah!

"Dammit, Julie," he tried again, his tone strained. "If you don't give me your promise, I'll have to—"

She jerked her head around to look at him. "What? What would you have to do?"

One of his huge hands rubbed at his bearded jaw. He didn't quite meet her gaze as he said, "Only thing I *could* do. Tie ya up and leave ya someplace safe till I get back."

Her jaw dropped. "You would *do* that? Leave me in the forest where the wild animals could get me?"

"I said, someplace safe."

"And where would that be, Señor Micah? A cave? A tree? What would happen to me if something should happen to you?"

"I didn't say I *wanted* to do it, Julie!" What she could see of his features turned splotchy red with anger. "But goddammit, I don't see no other way. I can't go on into a town with a lot of folks—keepin' one eye out for your granny's men and the other eye locked on you!"

She sniffed and lifted her chin. "I did not ask to be taken on this trip, Micah. You knew that from the beginning."

He inhaled slowly, deeply. When he spoke again, he

seemed a bit calmer. "Yeah. I knew. But I thought we
... well ... you know ... back there—" He jerked his
head at the trail behind them—"When we ... uh ...
Hell. I thought we'd kinda reached a truce, is all."

Julietta's fingers tightened on the reins. He had not
mentioned the kiss they'd shared since it happened.
He'd kept his promise about forgetting it entirely. At
least, it had seemed so. Until now. *Now* he talks about
it and even throws it up to her as a reason for her to be
cooperative!

She fought against her rising temper. Being angry
wouldn't do her the slightest bit of good. And if she
didn't give him her promise, she wouldn't go to town.
She knew that. Oh, she didn't for a minute believe that
he would simply leave her tied up, alone in the woods.
But he *would* find some other way of getting supplies.

Julie bit down on her bottom lip and weighed her op-
tions. She could continue to fight him and not see another soul until they'd reached Texas or she managed to
escape. *Or* she could promise to be a "good girl" and
thereby enter a real town. See people again. Maybe
even get a bath.

From the corner of her eye she saw him watching
her, waiting for her decision.

Though she longed to say no and challenge him to
carry out his threat, Julie knew she wouldn't. She was
tired of the trail. Tired of the never-ending jostling of
her horse. Tired of campfire cooking and the layer of
dust she wore beneath her clothes.

For a change of scenery and the chance at a bath, she
was even willing to forgo thoughts of escape. *Tempo-
rarily.*

"Well, Julie," he said, "what's it to be?"

"Very well. I give you my promise, Micah. I will not try to escape while we are in town."

His eyes narrowed as he looked at her, obviously trying to gauge her trustworthiness.

She met his gaze squarely. "I have given you my word, Micah. And *you* are not the only one to whom honor means something."

He had the grace to look embarrassed. "All right then. Town it is."

Turning his horse toward the right fork of the trail, Micah led the way, Julie close behind him.

*　　*　　*

Bent Pine, Colorado, was not exactly San Francisco. A mismatched collection of buildings, it squatted on a relatively flat piece of ground, ringed by towering pine trees and mammoth boulders. It look less than one minute to ride the length of the one and only main street.

Eager for even this tiny snatch of civilization, Julie turned this way and that in her saddle, looking at everything.

One general store, four saloons, a blacksmith shop and livery, a tiny restaurant, and a sheriff's office were all that Bent Pine had to offer.

But Julie was so pleased to be among people again, even the tiny hotel looked like a palace. Standing at the second-story window of their hotel room, she looked down on the street below and tried to forget the embarrassing scene she'd just lived through.

And everything had gone so well up until then, too. Julie shook her head slowly. After purchasing their supplies, they'd had supper at the town's restaurant. It was such a treat, eating something they hadn't had to cook, Julie forgot herself enough to make another suggestion.

For heaven's sake! She hadn't *meant* to insult the man! Fingers at her temples, she rubbed her aching head, wishing she could rub away the look on Micah's face when she offered to pay for a hotel room.

Her only reason for offering was that she hungered after a night's sleep on a real mattress again. And it was only fair that *she* pay for something that wasn't a necessity.

She groaned and rested her forehead on the cool windowpane. From the look on his face, one would have thought she'd just confessed to killing his mother! His green eyes frosty, his strong jawline rigid beneath his beard, he stared at her as though she'd grown another head.

"What's that s'posed to mean?"

"Micah, I don't know—"

"You beat all, you know that?"

"If you don't want to stay at the hotel, I'll—"

"I didn't say that." He swallowed the last of his coffee and slammed the cup down on the table. "I think that's a fine idea. We'll get a good night's rest, the horses can get some grain over to the livery. . . ."

"Wonderful," Julie agreed, so pleased at the prospect of a hot bath and a bed she was willing to forget about her earlier anger with him.

"But I don't need your money to do it."

"Micah, I only—"

"Never mind." He stood up abruptly and looked down at her. "You ready?"

He hadn't said another word until he was registering for them at the Broken Bone saloon-hotel. Slowly, carefully, he signed the big guestbook while Julie waited by the stairs. The bartender from the downstairs saloon, spun the book around, read what Micah'd written and smiled.

"Well, thanks, Mr. Benteen. You and your missus can have room number five. Top of the stairs on the right." He handed over a large brass key and assured Micah that the bath he requested could be provided for one dollar extra.

Micah slapped the money down on the counter, then turned to join Julie and walk her upstairs.

She felt the bartender's eyes on them, so she waited until they were safely in their room to demand, "Why did you tell him we are married? We could have had two different rooms, you know. I have given you my word not to run away."

Micah dropped the saddlebags on the bed, grabbed her hand, and dropped the key into her palm. "I already told you about why we're pretendin' to be married. Your granny's men should be about catchin' up to us, if they're ever gonna. No sense helpin' 'em out any." He walked to the door and yanked it open. "Besides, you may have more money than God, but I sure as hell don't. I can't afford to pay for two rooms when one will do."

"But I offered . . ."

"Yeah, I know. *Thanks!*"

Julie blinked at his sarcastic tone, and as he walked through the door, she tried not to sound frightened when she called out, "Where are you going?"

He glanced back at her. "Got to see to the animals. You lock this door till I get back, y'hear?"

But that was an hour ago. She sighed and pushed

away from the window. She'd watched for him, but hadn't seen him yet. Absently she scratched her head and felt at least an inch of trail dirt on her scalp.

She still hadn't gotten her bath, either!

Turning her back on the unchanging scene below, Julie walked to the wide, iron bed and plopped down onto the stained white quilt top. She glanced around the room and decided the only thing cheerful about the place was the fire blazing in the hearth. Thank heaven they'd gotten a corner room with its own fireplace.

Lord knew, there was nothing else in the room the least bit comforting. Two ladder-back chairs, a beige fabric dressing screen, a wash table with pitcher and bowl, and the most garish yellow, black, and rose wallpaper Julie'd ever seen.

She hugged herself tightly, fighting back the sting of tears. Why was Micah staying away so long? Was he going to come back? And why did she want him to? After all, if he left her alone, she could go back to Montana. Couldn't she?

He wasn't going to leave. He wouldn't do that. She'd already learned what his word meant to him. Strange how much better she felt, knowing that.

A pounding at the door brought her up short. She jumped off the bed and hurried across the floor. Before she turned the key in the lock, though, she called out expectantly, "Micah? Is it you?"

"Open up, lady."

A strange, deep voice. Fear shot through her. Could it be one of Doña Ana's men? God, why didn't she bring Micah's rifle with her to the room?

"C'mon, lady. I ain't got all day."

"Who are you?"

"Jesus! Did you order a bath or not?"

She exhaled in a rush, her shoulders slumped in relief. Of course. Her bath. She turned the key and pulled the door wide.

CHAPTER
···EIGHT···

A BIG MAN wearing a black, flat-brimmed hat, black jeans, and a black vest over a dirt-colored shirt stepped into the room and pulled the door shut behind him.

Julie backed up slowly, shaking her head, until the backs of her knees touched the iron bed. "Enrique?"

He smiled and jerked his head at the door behind him. "I met a boy in the hall, carrying your bathtub." He shrugged. "It seemed an easy way to get you to open the door."

"Enrique, I'm not alone here." Frantically Julie tried to think of something, anything, to stall him.

"*Sí.* I saw the redheaded man you rode in with. But he's not here, Julietta." He took one step toward her. "And we'll be gone before he returns. I've got the horses ready and waiting just outside of town. I even had the restaurant put some food together for us, so we won't have to stop."

Julie inched her way around the end of the bed and continued to back up toward the window. Keeping her eyes locked on Enrique, she tried to find some sign of compassion in his face. But there was nothing.

His dark eyes flat, his ax-sharp features hard, he

looked at her with complete disinterest. He was there to do his job. Nothing more.

And that was only one reason, she told herself, why Enrique and his partner, Carlos, were so important to Doña Ana. Neither of the men possessed any emotions that might get in the way of their carrying out *la Patrona*'s wishes.

"Get your things, Julietta," he commanded softly and held out one hand.

"No, Enrique. I won't go."

His hand dropped to his side, and he frowned at her. "Doña Ana is expecting you." He walked closer. "Your groom," he added with a smirk, "grows anxious."

"I won't marry Don Vicente." Panic rushed up to fill her lungs. She couldn't breathe. Her heartbeat staggered erratically.

Enrique's patience wearing thin, he said in rapid-fire Spanish, "Enough, Julietta. Carlos and I have wasted too much time already in the search for you. . . ."

In English, she asked fearfully, "Carlos is with you?"

He laughed and switched back to his excellent, unaccented English. "No. We split up, thinking to cover more territory. I don't know where he is, but it doesn't matter." Lunging forward, his hand shot out and grabbed her arm viciously. "I won't need help."

The door behind him crashed open, slamming into the opposite wall. Enrique let go of Julie, spun around, and dropped into a crouch.

"If I was you," Micah said calmly, "I'd call for all the help I could get."

Julie took two steps back, fighting down the swell of relief that had flooded her with Micah's appearance. It wasn't over yet. She and Micah weren't safe yet. She'd seen Enrique in a fight once and he was a remorseless, cruel opponent.

"Leave now, gringo," Enrique offered quietly, "this is not your business. Julietta knows what she must do. She is going with me."

Micah never took his eyes off the dangerous man just across from him, but he asked, "That right, Julie? You goin' somewheres with this ... *fella?*"

Somehow she forced out the words past a dry throat. "No. I am not going anywhere with him."

She watched Micah give the dark man a tight smile and heard him say, "Damn right, you ain't."

Enrique charged the other man from his crouched position, roaring like a wounded bear. Micah easily sidestepped his attacker, and as he moved into the clear, he laced his fingers together and brought his joined fists down on the back of Enrique's neck.

He dropped, stunned momentarily, but he was a strong man and was up and pivoting again in seconds. Micah moved around warily until he stood between Julie and the big vaquero. When Enrique swung his fist and it connected with a solid *whump* in Micah's mid-section, Micah felt the power of the blow right down to his socks. But because of the other man's strength, Micah couldn't afford even a moment's hesitation in retaliating.

He grasped the other man around the waist and rolled him over onto the floor, peppering the muscular body with short, hard jabs. In the back of his mind he knew that he couldn't hold back. He *had* to win this fight. Julie's safety depended on it.

As the two men crashed and rocketed around the room, Julie tried to keep out of their way as she watched, both terrified and somehow fascinated by their brute strength. Her gaze locked on Micah, she winced with every crash of Enrique's fists and clamped her lips together to keep from screaming out her own fears.

From a distance she heard a shout and someone running. And still she couldn't move. It was as if her feet were nailed to the floor, her knees locked . . . immovable. Then Enrique gave a mighty shove, throwing Micah off him and to one side.

As quickly as a streak of lightning shot across a night sky, Enrique was straddling Micah, holding a razor-sharp knife clenched in his fist. She saw Micah's grip on the other man's wrist failing. His arm trembled, and for an instant she thought she saw worry flash in Micah's eyes.

And suddenly she could move again. She had to *do* something. She had to help. Her gaze flew about the room until she spied what she needed. Forcing her legs into action, she raced, stumbling across the room and back again, holding the heavy, ceramic water pitcher. Standing directly over the still struggling men, she lifted the empty jug high overhead and brought it smashing down on the back of Enrique's skull.

He slumped over immediately, and Micah pushed him clear. Julie stood with her hands on her knees, trying to catch her breath, and Micah got wearily to his feet to stand beside her.

"What the hell's goin' on in here?"

Julie didn't even look up when the furious bartender rushed into the room hollering at the top of his lungs. Vaguely, absently, she heard Micah's winded voice giving the same explanation that he'd given the trapper a few days before.

This time though, he added the fact that Enrique had been sent by Julie's angry father, in an attempt to get her back and have their marriage annulled.

The burly bartender's practiced gaze moved over Micah's battered face to Julie, leaning heavily against him, before shifting to the unconscious troublemaker on the floor.

"Never could stand nobody stickin' their noses in where it ain't wanted," he mumbled. Without another word he walked to Enrique's side and effortlessly scooped the big man off the floor. Tossing the limp gunman over one shoulder, the bartender said gently, "Now, missy, don't you give this no-account one more thought. I'll see he's locked up for a week or so ... give him time to cool off and you two time to put some miles under ya."

"Thanks," Micah said softly through puffed lips. He ran one hand up and down Julie's back comfortingly, and she felt the warmth of his touch right through to her bones.

"Don't you worry about it. My pleasure." The bartender spoke again, and still Julie couldn't bring herself to step away from the tranquillity of Micah's embrace. "I'll have a boy set up the tub and bring you lots of hot water." He walked toward the door, adding, "My wife swears by havin' what she calls a good hot soak when she's troubled."

The door closed after him and they were alone. Slowly she raised her head and looked at the man who'd come to her rescue again. One eye was almost swollen shut, his bottom lip was split, bleeding, and puffy, and a bright red mark stained one cheek.

She'd never seen anyone more handsome.

"Thank you," she whispered and was sorry because it didn't seem like enough.

He smiled, then winced, and touched his tongue to his cut lip. "You're welcome. Thank you, too." He sucked in a gulp of air and moaned softly. "If you hadn't hit him with that jug when you did . . ."

"You would have beat him anyway."

Micah's gaze moved over her face slowly, lovingly. "Maybe," he acknowledged. "Let's just say I'm not a man to turn down a little help now and again."

She laid her head on his chest and listened gratefully to the reassuring, steady beat of his heart. When a knock sounded on the door, she jumped and squirmed closer, hating herself for a coward.

"Who is it?" Micah called.

"Got a bathtub out here for the lady."

"I'll let him in, Julie," he said and moved to disentangle himself from her arms.

But she grabbed one of his hands before he could get away. "Be very careful, Micah. It was a bathtub that started all of this."

He gave her a look that said plainly he thought she was still much too upset to be talking. Julie didn't bother to explain herself yet. Instead, she kept her eyes fixed on the door and didn't relax her pose until she saw a young boy, staggering under the weight of an empty hip bath enter the room.

Sighing her relief, she slumped onto the bed and let Micah take care of setting up the tub.

* * *

He could understand how she didn't want to be alone just yet. Shit, she must've been scared out of her mind when her granny's man walked into her room, big as you please. But still—Micah shifted position for the hundredth time in the last fifteen minutes—he wished he was anywhere but there.

Water splashed and his gaze flew to the worn, beige dressing screen. Behind that screen, directly in front of the roaring fire, Julie was taking a bath.

He let his head drop against the wall with a satisfying thump.

"What was that?" she asked, a hesitant note in her voice that he didn't much like.

"Just me, Julie. I ... uh ... hit my head is all."

She laughed, and the sound floated out to him on waves of the jasmine she'd added to her bathwater. "I would have thought your head had been hit enough for one night, Micah."

"Yeah, well ..." He closed his eyes and tried to ignore the sound of bathwater sloshing against the sides of the tin tub. But he couldn't. Instead, behind his lids, his brain conjured up the image of Julie, naked, rubbing soap all over her body.

In his mind's eye she cupped water in her hands and splashed her face. He watched tiny droplets race down the length of her neck, across her chest, and over her breasts. He imagined her erect, brown nipples peeking out of the water, as if eager for his touch. He envisioned her legs as she ran soap bubbles up and down her calves and thighs.

She began to hum tunelessly, and he heard her stand up to rinse herself off.

His breathing heavy, he swallowed and kept his eyes closed, determined to give her privacy. But at the same time, he gave his mind free rein.

The image his brain created was so clear, so beautiful, his heart pounded in response. Firelight danced on her ivory skin. Her black hair piled high on her head, she stepped clear of the tub and stood in front of the fire to dry herself. He let his gaze wander slowly from the tips of her toes, up her legs to the juncture of her thighs. She turned in his vision, giving him a heart-stopping view of her bottom.

When she reached up to undo the knot of hair, her breasts rose with the movement, and Micah had to curl his hands into fists to fight the desire to touch his imagination's too real vision.

"Thank you for staying with me," she said softly from behind the safety of her screen.

"It's all right."

His dream shattered, Micah shook his head and told himself he ought to be ashamed. But he wasn't. Hell, if you could shoot a man for his thoughts, Micah told himself, there'd be more dead than alive in this country. Besides, he'd wanted to see her, hold her, for so long now he didn't remember a time when he hadn't. And he knew, deep inside that *this* would be the only way he could ever realize that want.

He'd known it from the first. And it had been pointed up to him afresh only that afternoon. He opened his eyes again and stared at the water-marked ceiling.

She hadn't thought twice about offerin' to pay for a hotel room. Hell, she'd been raised with so much money, she didn't *have* to think about it before stayin' in a hotel. He snorted and glanced about the shabby room. And it was for *damn* sure she usually stayed in better places than *this*!

There were so many differences between the two of

them, he couldn't even name them all. And he didn't have to. It was enough that he knew it. You'd think, he told himself fiercely, that *knowing* it would be enough to stop all these damn-fool fancies about the two of them . . . together.

But it seemed, he silently acknowledged, that knowin' and wantin' was two separate things.

"Micah?"

Startled out of his imaginings, he turned to face her as she stepped out from behind the screen. Immediately he wished he hadn't.

On the trail she'd slept in her clothes. Like him. It just wasn't practical to be puttin' on nightshirts and the like out in the woods and then go huntin' your clothes in the pitch dark of early morning. But tonight she was wearing a nightgown she must've had tucked away in her saddlebags.

His throat closed, and his body tightened uncomfortably. Outlined against the firelight, her white cotton nightdress was practically see-through. Micah tried to avoid looking at the shadow lines of her body. He told himself that she'd had enough upsets for one night. She didn't need a stupid, fumbling mountain boy gawkin' at her to top it off.

But forcing his gaze up to meet hers was the hardest thing he'd ever done.

Her towel-wrapped hair sat atop on her head like a crown, and the high neck and long sleeves of the garment she wore made her seem even smaller, more . . . *breakable* than she had before.

"Huh?" he finally said. "What'd you say?"

"Nothing yet." She smiled, crossed her arms over her chest, and walked to the nearest chair. "I only wondered if you thought the town sheriff would keep Enrique in jail as the bartender said."

"Oh." Micah slid his legs off the bed and stood up, stifling a groan his quick movements brought. He had to get out of that room for a while. He had to get out in the cold night air. Take some deep breaths. Walk around a bit. Something. *Anything.*

An idea struck him and he snatched at her last statement like a drowning man at a floating log. "Tell ya what. I'll just head on down to the jailhouse and check to make sure."

"Oh, but . . ."

"It's all right, Julie. Won't be gone long." He grabbed up his hat, crossed to the door, and opened it. Glancing back at her, he ordered, "You come lock this door after me."

She jumped up and hurried to him. Her face pale, eyes worried. Micah felt terrible about leavin' her alone while she was still so upset. Then a whiff of jasmine drifted to him and he steeled himself. Better he leave now, while he still could, than cause her more grief.

His voice harsh, he said, "This time, don't you unlock that durn door for anybody but me. Y'hear?"

She bit her lip and nodded.

He was barely out the door when it slammed shut. Standing quietly in the hallway, Micah listened to the key turn in the lock. Satisfied that she was safe for now, he headed for the stairs.

His moccasined feet made little noise on the steps as he hurried outside. First, he'd go by the jail. Then the saloon. Maybe if he had a drink or two, it would slow down the wild imaginings his brain kept taunting him with.

On the boardwalk, when a cold wind slapped against him, he told himself that what he really needed was a lock on his own mind.

And to get her the hell to Texas as fast as he could!

* * *

Alone in her room at the Duffy rancho, Penelope leaned back against the carved walnut headboard. Her fingers moved gently over the creased paper in her hand, tracing the words she'd almost memorized.

Eustace's last letter. Penelope sighed and glanced down at her brother's spidery handwriting. Tears pooled in her brown eyes and spilled over, raining down her cheeks to fall on her neat, simple shirtwaist. Her eyes and nose bright red, her face puffy from too many tears, she sniffed loudly and pushed herself into a sitting position.

Spread out all around her on the wide mattress of her bed were pages and pages in Eustace's hand. She ran her fingers over the papers lovingly and curled her legs up, her feet tucked beneath the hem of her black skirt.

There was so little left of him. She didn't even possess a likeness of him. Penelope smiled softly and rubbed at her nose with a handkerchief she pulled from one sleeve. She smiled at her own foolishness. She didn't *need* a daguerreotype or a painting to bring her brother's image to mind. His face was as clearly marked in her memory as her own was in a mirror.

Much too skinny with thinning brown hair, a jutting nose, and curious, friendly eyes, Eustace was the only person who'd ever loved her. Loved *her*. Penelope. Just as she was, making no demands on her to be anything other than true to herself.

When he'd left London five years before, Penelope'd

thought the loneliness would kill her. But then the letters started arriving. She gathered up the loose sheets of paper and held them close to her breast. How he'd loved the West. And he'd shared that love with her. Made her see the wonders of such a strange country through *his* eyes.

Through all the cold nights in England, she'd warmed herself with his tales of cowboys and cactus and hot desert winds. She'd imagined it all so clearly from his loving descriptions that at first sight of the country stretching wide open for miles, she'd felt as if she'd come home at last.

Eustace had been so proud of his young but thriving law practice. He'd said that in America a man could become anything he wanted. Women, too, he told her, were free to discover their own way, and he'd begun saving his money so that she could join him in his new home.

She stared across the room at the glass-paned doors that opened onto the central patio, closed now against the night. Instead, it had taken almost two years for her to find enough money to make the trip alone.

All the hours spent hunched over poor light doing fine needlework rushed back into her mind. She remembered the time spent teaching untalented and uninterested children how to play the piano. In startling clarity she recalled the auction she'd held to sell her family home and furniture.

And when she'd finally earned enough money to see her to America and support herself until she could find a job of some sorts . . . the only thing waiting to welcome her was her brother's grave.

Penelope laid the collection of letters back down on

the bed, blew her nose, and vowed silently to stop feeling sorry for herself. It wouldn't do the slightest bit of good, anyway.

The thing to do now, she thought firmly, was to go through Eustace's letters again carefully. She must find everything she possibly could to help prove her case to Patrick Duffy.

Oh, he wanted to believe her, she knew that. His own hatred for Doña Ana was enough to gain her at least *that* much cooperation. And, to be fair, he *had* allowed her to stay at the rancho, which certainly helped her financial situation.

But she would need more, and she knew it.

Deliberately she tried to recall everything Eustace had said about these people.

He'd never written much about Duffy himself. Eustace *had* told her about Julietta, though, claiming she was a lovely child, despite her relations.

Gritting her teeth, she reminded herself grimly that he'd also written about Don Ricardo Santos and his wife, Ana. Though admiring of the old Don, Eustace hadn't trusted Doña Ana from the first. And when he'd written to her that the old man was seriously ill and had ordered a new will leaving his land to Julietta, Penelope'd felt a thrill of fear all the way in England.

Then she'd received that wire from the marshal in El Paso telling her about Eustace's death. On an impulse she'd sent her own telegram, inquiring after the health of Don Ricardo. She'd been informed that the Don was dead and that any further inquiries should be sent to Doña Ana Santos, who was now the sole owner of the Santos rancho.

Unthinkingly Penelope crushed the letter she held in

her hand as her eyes filled again with helpless, furious tears. It wasn't proof. She knew it. But deep in her heart, Penelope was convinced that the old woman was directly responsible for Eustace Butterworth's death. Surely there had to be a way to make Doña Ana pay.

She swallowed past the knot in her throat and hiccuped as her eyes began to fill again. Her jaw worked, and she blinked frantically in a futile battle to stem the tide of hurt threatening to choke her. It was no use, though. Then, realizing that she was at least alone, she gave in to the emotions rocking her. Lying down, she curled up into a tight ball of pain and let the memories flood her brain.

The back of her hand against her mouth to muffle her sobs, Penelope cried for all the things that would never be.

Patrick stopped dead in the hall. Just a couple of feet away, from behind his guest's partially opened door, came the unmistakable sounds of a woman crying.

He frowned thoughtfully. In the two days he'd known her, he somehow hadn't imagined Penelope Butterworth as the weeping kind.

A fragmented memory shot through his mind. He saw Elena crying gently, touching a lacy handkerchief to the corners of her eyes while at the same time watching him to judge his reaction. Calculated misery, conniving sorrow ... Elena'd known better than anyone that she was even more beautiful when she cried.

He could still see a solitary tear coursing its way down her smooth cheek to her trembling lips.

Patrick snorted and shook his head. It seemed that all women were pretty much alike, after all. He listened as the weeping from the room beyond grew stronger. Even Penelope Butterworth was not above using tears . . . the female weapon of choice.

Moving quietly he inched his way forward to sneak a peek at the woman. After all, if the tears were for his benefit he reasoned, the least he could do was *look*.

Through the crack of space between the door and its frame, Patrick saw the invincible Penelope Butterworth. Startled, he stared, amazed at the sight of his stiff and starchy houseguest, curled into a ball and sobbing as though her heart would break.

Abruptly he straightened and stepped away from the door. But the mental image wouldn't fade. He could still see her blotchy, plain face contorted with her effort to control the sounds of her mournful weeping.

For the first time in a long while, he admitted that a woman had surprised him. Penelope Butterworth wasn't crying to *win* something from him—but to *lose* her own grief.

He pushed one hand through his hair and stared down at the polished tile floor. For a moment he almost envied her the ability to cry.

She coughed and sniffed, obviously trying to control herself again. When sounds of movement came from inside the room, Patrick turned away and walked back down the hall. He knew he was intruding and didn't want to be caught at it.

CHAPTER
···NINE···

MICAH MOVED RESTLESSLY and cursed under his breath. One more time he tried to find a comfortable spot, and one more time he failed.

Staring at the ceiling, he shook his head and called himself all kinds of fool. Served him right. Next time maybe he'd think twice before offering to sleep on the damned floor.

The corn-husk mattress beside him rustled. He heard Julie sigh in her sleep and felt the now familiar tightening of his body. Dammit. How the hell was a man supposed to keep his mind off . . . Shit. Even when he tried *not* to think about . . . he was thinkin' about it.

He grabbed the flattened-out feather pillow, shoved it into a hard ball, and pushed it under his head. There was nothin' to be done about it. He was just gonna have to suffer, is all.

She sighed again.

Disgusted, he snorted and pushed himself to his feet. Looking down at the sleeping woman, Micah didn't feel the least bit better knowing she wasn't havin' any trouble at *all* gettin' some sleep.

What does she think I am? he fumed silently. Her *brother*? It's downright humiliatin' that a woman's not even a little worried about sleepin' in the same room with him. *Worried?* Hah!

He crossed the room, none too quietly, and plopped down onto a straight-backed chair. Watching the woman in the wide bed, he reminded himself that not only wasn't she worried—when he'd come back from cleanin' up at the bathhouse behind the barbershop, she'd flung herself at him. She was so durn glad to see him, she'd hung onto him so tight you'd have thought he was the last beefsteak at a church picnic.

He groaned softly and let his head fall back onto the chair back. It didn't take much effort to recall how good she felt pressed up tight against him, either. Why, through that nothin' of a nightgown, he'd been able to feel her every curve.

His hands ached to hold her again. To touch her.

Dammit!

He jumped up and walked to the window. Opening it a bit, he welcomed the blast of cold air that swirled around him. Breathing deeply, Micah felt a reluctant chuckle bubble up inside him, and he clamped his lips together to prevent its escape.

Hell, a few weeks ago, who would have believed that he could be feelin' like this about *Julietta Duffy?* From the time they first met in Montana right up until they started this blasted trip, she'd done nothing but rub him the wrong way. Now, her rubbin' up against him *any* old way was all he could think of.

Instead, he had to take her to a bunch of people who didn't want *or* deserve her.

He placed one palm on either side of the window and leaned forward. His gaze slipped to the jailhouse. Inside, he knew, Enrique sat on his cot, plannin' just what he'd do to Micah the minute he got free. Of course, the sheriff'd promised that wouldn't be for at least a week . . . but still, the man was a worry.

And he couldn't afford to forget there was another one out there somewhere, too. This . . . Carlos Julie'd told him about. Hard to believe a woman's own granny would send the likes of *them* after her. Shit. Judgin' by them two, the old lady wasn't exactly picky about the kind of men she dealt with.

Micah got cold chills just *thinkin'* about what Julie's groom must be like.

Groom.

He turned to look at her. Her thick black hair, fanned out on the pillow, her beautiful blue eyes, closed in sleep. Micah fought down an almost overpowering urge to lie beside her. To hold her. Protect her.

How in the hell could he hand her over to some other man? Especially when the man didn't give two hoots for her?

But how could he not?

His family was depending on him.

Her father was expecting him.

Micah sighed and closed the window. He walked back to his chair and eased himself down. His gaze locked on Julie, he gave up trying to sleep. There would be years for him to catch up on missed rest.

Years without her.

When he was alone.

* * *

Over coffee in the huge dining room, Patrick took a moment to study the woman seated opposite him.

Except for the red streaks in her eyes and a slight puffiness beneath them, no one would guess that she'd been crying the night before. Prim and starchy, Penelope picked at the food on her plate while her gaze kept slipping to a folded piece of paper lying on the cherry-wood table.

Patrick poured himself another cup of the strong, cinnamon-flavored coffee. He ignored the slight tremble in his hands and pushed aside his empty plate. Strange, he'd eaten more since Penelope'd arrived than he could remember eating in years.

Of course, he reminded himself with an inward smirk, he'd been *sober* since she'd arrived, too. That probably accounted for his appetite. Hell, even the *coffee* tasted better. And for two nights running, he'd actually slept under the blankets on his bed instead of being sprawled atop them. But more importantly, he admitted silently, he hadn't woken up in the middle of the night, out of breath. For too long, whiskey-inspired demons had haunted his dreams, making sleep damn near impossible.

Frankly it surprised him how little he missed his nightly ritual of drinking himself into oblivion. All he'd really needed, he supposed, was a *reason* to be sober.

And this tall, plain woman from halfway around the world had dropped that reason into his lap. If she was right, and he was praying she was, he finally had the opportunity to make Doña Ana pay for all the misery she'd heaped on him in the last twenty some years.

Lord knew, the old bitch was due her comeuppance long since. Why, if it wasn't for her, Elena never would have married him—there would be no Julietta—and he wouldn't have spent the last sixteen years searching out a target for his hatred the way most men sought love.

"If you're *quite* finished . . ."

"What?" He blinked and met Penelope's stern gaze.

"I *said*, if you're quite finished with your inspection of me, I'd like to show you something far more interesting."

"Sorry—"

She waved his apology aside. Picking up the paper and holding it tenderly, she said, "This is the last letter I received from my brother." Stretching out her hand, she gave it to him, adding, "In it, he mentions that Don Ricardo had commissioned a new will. One in which Julietta would inherit the rancho and Doña Ana would receive nothing."

Eagerly Patrick read the letter. He barely remembered Eustace Butterworth. Oh, he'd met him a few times, naturally. But on those occasions, Patrick had had far too much to drink to remember *anyting* very clearly. But, as he read the missive, the man's image became more distinct.

A fussy, tidy man, Eustace had also possessed a rare quality. Enthusiasm. Interested in everything and always ready to try a new experience, the thin young man had made a lot of friends in Texas.

"As you see"—Penelope's voice interrupted his thoughts, and he looked up impatiently—"Eustace goes on to say that he was sure Doña Ana would be furious at her husband's actions. He also says that his appointment with Don Ricardo was on the fifth of the month." She bit her lip before continuing. "I received a telegram the morning of the seventh telling me of my brother's death."

Patrick gave her a quick nod. He wanted to read the letter for himself. And he would. If she ever shut up.

"We know that Doña Ana inherited the rancho on her

husband's death a week later." She crossed her arms over her ample bosom. "So. What happened to the new will, I ask you?"

She was on fire and getting even more so. The soft brown eyes were lit from within, giving her unremarkable looks an almost seductive appeal. Her pale complexion flushed pink, her lips parted in anticipation, Penelope Butterworth, it seemed, was much more than she appeared.

Patrick shook the irrelevant thought from his head and held up one hand for silence. Forcing a smile, he said, "Give me a minute, Miss Butterworth. I'd like to read this myself. That *is* why you gave it to me, isn't it?"

"Yes. Of course." Pushing away from the table, she stood up, crossed the room, and walked out the double doors leading to the patio. "I'll wait for you out here."

"Fine, fine . . ."

She'd been dismissed. Penelope strolled across the stone floor of the patio and seated herself on a bench near the fountain. Cool, clear water danced and splashed, its soothing sounds reaching past the tumultuous feelings racing through her body.

It didn't bother her, she told herself, that Patrick Duffy hadn't the time to listen to her. It was enough that he was reading Eustace's letter.

Though it had been disappointing to discover that Patrick Duffy was a drunk, he was still her best hope for assistance in dealing with Doña Ana. But she'd done all she could. All Penelope could hope for now was that he was as convinced as she that his mother-in-law was responsible for Eustace's death.

Her brother's name brought a fleeting smile to her lips. She breathed deeply, inhaling the strange, exotic fragrances floating on the desert air. How odd it was to travel to a place so foreign to everything she'd ever known and yet feel completely at home.

Swallowing heavily, she straightened her spine deliberately. She was determined not to let self-pity rule her emotions again . . . but, it was so hard. Seeing all the things she'd planned on seeing with her brother.

"I read it."

Penelope looked up. Patrick stood in the open doorway. The morning sun peeked over the patio walls, bathing him in a soft, golden light, and she noticed for the first time what a handsome man he really was. It was a shame how'd he'd let himself turn to drink.

Though his blue eyes were clear and sharp, the shadows beneath them looked like bruises on his tanned flesh. She'd already noticed that occasionally his hands shook, and judging by his ready temper, he was not reacting well to an absence of liquor.

"What do you think, Patrick?"

"Pat."

"I beg your pardon?"

He squinted and frowned up at the sun as if it was directing its rays into his eyes purposely. Stepping into the cool shade of the patio, he repeated, "Pat. I said, call me Pat. Every time you say 'Patrick' in that tone of voice, I look for my mother."

Penelope's eyebrows lifted, but she nodded.

"As to what I think," he went on and plopped down on the bench beside her. "I think the old bitch had Eustace killed."

She released a breath she hadn't realized she'd been

holding. His apt description of Doña Ana, however true, sounded crude, bitter. But isn't that why she'd counted on his being willing to help? A giddy sense of relief swept over her. Patrick Duffy believed her. The release of her own anxieties was almost painful.

"But."

Her smile faded as she watched his stern features crease thoughtfully.

"Thinking it and *knowing* it are two different things." Patrick tilted his head to look at her. "Got any ideas about how we can prove this?"

"As a matter of fact, I do." She'd had two long years to think about this. To plan.

"Somehow, Miss Butterworth," he said, a sardonic smile on his well-shaped lips, "I'm not surprised."

One finely arched brow lifted, but she decided to ignore his sarcastic attitude. "I think the first thing we must realize is that Doña Ana cannot possibly have committed the murder herself."

He snorted.

"Therefore," she went on, a little louder than before, "we must concentrate on the people around her. Attack from her 'flank,' I believe is the proper term."

He shook his head slowly as if he couldn't quite believe his ears.

"We talk to her confederates, her servants, the town constable—"

"Marshal," he corrected.

"Fine. Marshal. Frankly I am most interested in speaking to him. Why he didn't investigate my brother's death more closely is something *I* would like explained."

"As I recall," Patrick tossed in, "Eustace was thrown from his horse and down a cliff face. . . ."

Penelope paled. She preferred not to think about her dear brother's body lying broken at the bottom of some forgotten desert gorge. Straining to maintain control, she managed to say, "Eustace was a proficient horseman."

"Yeah . . . Well, that kind of thing happens to a lot of people in this country, Miss Butterworth. Even the 'proficient' ones. It's not surprising the marshal called it accidental death."

"Perhaps. And I will most certainly find that out for myself when I speak to the man. To continue," she said softly, "I propose to speak to everyone I can find. To chip away at Doña Ana's secrets until they are finally revealed. Through bribery, persuasion, and whatever else is required, I feel sure we can bring this investigation to a satisfactory conclusion."

"And how much money do you have for these *bribes?*"

Penelope shifted uneasily and hoped to heaven she wasn't blushing. The embarrassing truth was she'd spent almost every cent she had just getting to Texas. She'd been hoping to sway Patrick Duffy into financing her quest for justice.

"I . . ."

"Yes?"

She forced herself to look at him. "I am a quite able teacher of art and music. No doubt I will be able to earn money quite quickly."

"Oh, no doubt," he agreed with a half smile. "I'm sure there's any number of cowboys and whores *eager* to learn to paint a pretty picture or pick out a tune on the piano. But until then, I'll wager you'll be wanting my support in this little game."

"This is not a game," she said hotly. But she couldn't afford to insult him, so she added, "Of course, if you feel my plan is worthwhile . . ."

"Before we start talking about your 'plan' . . ." Patrick handed her the letter, leaned back against the adobe wall, and stretched out his legs. After crossing his booted feet at the ankles and shoving his hands into his pockets, he asked, "How did you know to come to me with your information? Why not the marshal?"

She scooted mere inches away from him. Penelope'd never been that close to a man before. Except Eustace, of course. And she preferred to keep it that way. Of course, the men back home would never have presumed to sit so close beside a woman they hardly knew. And *no* man she'd ever met in England had had such a curious effect on her.

But then, Patrick seemed . . . *bigger* than most men. Not physically, of course. It was something else entirely. There was an air of danger, mystery, about him that suggested he was a man as imposing as the country in which he lived.

She blinked and realized he was staring at her. Mentally chastising herself for woolgathering, she spoke quickly. "As I told you, Eustace wrote to me faithfully. At least once a week. We were . . . very close. During his time here, he told me about the people he'd met . . . or heard about. The Don, his wife." She shot him a thoughtful look. "You, Elena, and Julietta."

He stiffened suddenly.

"And," she rushed on, "I thought that with the past

you and Doña Ana share, you would be the *one* person who would be willing to stand up to her."

"You thought right," he ground out and stood up.

Penelope leaned her head back to peer up at him. "I've noticed that Julietta isn't here, by the way. Will she be returning soon? I'd so enjoy meeting her after hearing so much about her. . . ." Her voice faded off as a change came over him.

His features tightened into a mask of anger. His brows lowered over narrowed eyes, and his lips pressed firmly together. It was a full thirty seconds at least before he spoke again.

"I don't want to discuss Julietta with you, Miss Butterworth. Or anyone else, for that matter."

"I don't see why not," she said, immediately on the defensive. "She *is* your daughter."

"Frankly I don't give a good goddamn if you 'see' or not," Patrick shot back. "I'm willing to help you go up against Doña Ana for my own reasons. For those same reasons, I'll thank you to not mention Julietta to me again."

Slowly Penelope stood up. Her height brought her to within a half inch of looking him directly in the eye. Pulling in a deep breath, she let her gaze move over him slowly, telling him with her eyes that his loud bluster and overbearing manner would not intimidate her.

She'd dealt with bullies most of her life. Usually, as soon as a man realized that a woman was on her own, with no man to defend her or speak up for her, his true nature revealed itself. Penelope'd ceased to be surprised at the number of petty tyrants there were in the world.

When she was sure she had his attention, she said

calmly, "I am not accustomed to being spoken to in such a manner, Mr. Duffy."

"I can't imagine why not, Miss Butterworth. With you stickin' that nose of yours into other people's business like you do."

Her toe began tapping viciously against the stone patio, but before she could say another word, he turned and walked back to the house. Before he went inside though, he glanced back at her. "You're welcome to stay here at the rancho. God knows there's plenty of room. But we will *not* discuss either my late wife *or* her daughter."

It wasn't until after he'd left in a huff that Penelope realized Patrick had referred to Julietta as Elena's daughter. Not his.

Curious.

*   *   *

Two hours on the trail and already Julietta was longing to stop. She hadn't lied when she'd told Micah that she'd been riding since she was a child. But she'd *never* spent day after day in the saddle without a reprieve.

And last night's stay in the hotel could hardly be counted as a reprieve, she told herself.

Thinking back on the scene with Enrique, before Micah came storming into the room, Julietta wanted to kick herself. Instead of fighting the man for her freedom, she'd backed away like a frightened child. There was no excuse for it.

She'd talked so much about having her own life. Making her own decisions. But, when the time came for her to stand up for herself . . . she hadn't had the courage. If not for Micah's timely return to the hotel room, she would be riding with Enrique right now.

"You all right?"

Julietta looked up to find that Micah had doubled back and was now riding beside her, concern in his eyes. The marks from his fight the night before stood out plainly in the morning sun, and Julietta winced just looking at them.

He'd been hurt because of her. He might have been killed.

All because she was a coward.

It was not a pleasant thing to learn about oneself.

"I am fine," she snapped and was immediately sorry for her tone.

He snorted and reared back, a look of surprise stamped on his features. "Pardon *me*, ma'am."

"Forgive me, Micah." She sighed and kept her gaze locked on the back of her horse's head as she said, "It is just that when I look at your face, I get so angry." Julie glanced at him.

His lips quirked, and one eyebrow lifted slightly. "Well now, guess *I* ought to be the one who's sorry. I know I ain't much to look at, but far's I know, you're the first to get mad just lookin' at me!"

"That is not what I mean," she countered quickly.

"Hope not, since there ain't much I can do about it." He grinned and pushed one hand through his hair. "And I'd hate like hell to have to tell Shad and Jericho they better start wearin' sacks over their heads."

Julie smiled halfheartedly. "You three do not look so alike, you know."

"Ain't many can tell us apart."

"Only those who don't truly *look*." She looked away

quickly and whispered, "You are by far the best-looking of the three."

Micah coughed, and she felt his gaze on her. But he didn't say anything. The horses kept moving in a slow walk. Julie watched the play of sunlight on the leaves of the trees. As they passed, birds lifted into flight, their raucous cries filling the air.

Wasn't it enough that she was a coward? she asked herself. Did she have to make a *fool* of herself as well?

After a long silence Micah asked, "So how come lookin' at me makes you mad?"

She inhaled sharply and forced herself to admit what was bothering her. "It is the marks on your face from the fight with Enrique."

He reached up instinctively and touched his bruised eye. "Hell, I've been worked over better than *this* by my own brothers!"

"That is not what I mean."

"Well, what the hell *do* you mean?"

She almost smiled. As used to Micah's bellowing as she was, it felt good to hear him shouting again. His gentle understanding and sympathy had only made her feel worse.

"I mean that it is because of me that you were hurt."

Julie risked a quick look at his thunderstruck face, then rushed on before he could interrupt. "You could have been *killed* because of me. And I was useless!"

Micah's jaw dropped. "What d'ya mean *useless*?"

"I mean I was a coward!" She spat, as if the very word was distasteful.

"Coward?"

"*Sí.* When Enrique walked in, I did nothing. *Nothing!*" She clenched the reins tightly. "It was as if my

140

body was frozen." Shaking her head, she stared straight ahead, seeing it all over again. "I could not move. It suddenly became so *real*."

"What?"

"My grandmother ... Enrique ... my father ...," she shuddered. "Don Vicente—everything. I was so *frightened*. Such a *cobarde*." Sneering, she added, "Even in my language, *coward* is an ugly word."

Micah stared at her. His reins dangled loose in his fingers, and he felt as though the breath had been kicked out of him. For a long moment there was silence, broken only by the sounds of their horses' hooves on the dirt.

A coward? Her? He caught a glimpse of her eyes before she looked down, and for the first time Micah saw the fear she'd been hiding. How long had she been plaguing herself with those kinds of foolish notions? he wondered.

Why, she was one of the bravest females he'd met. He couldn't imagine puttin' up with the family she'd been dealin' with for years. Yet she had, and still had managed to become a helluva woman.

Besides, he told himself— Shit! Don't just *think* it— say it.

"I don't know how in God's earth you could think yourself a coward." He waited for her to look at him. "You saved *my* bacon, didn't ya?"

"Yes, but that was not enough."

"Thank you very much!" He had shouted, and his horse lurched sideways, startled. "*I* think it was plenty. If you hadn't hit ol' Enrique like you done ... he might've killed me."

"But don't you see," she said, and Micah's breath

caught at the haunted shadows in her eyes, "I almost waited too long. Even for *you*, my ... *friend*, I could not move soon enough."

Friend. The word stabbed at him, though he told himself he should be grateful for *that* much. It wasn't her fault that he wanted more.

"Quit bein' so damn hard on yourself, Julie. From where I'm standin', ya done fine."

"No." She shook her head firmly. "You are being kind, Micah, but you shouldn't. There is still Carlos to be heard from, remember."

"Don't you worry about *him*."

"It doesn't matter anymore, anyway."

"Huh?"

She pulled in a deep breath. "Last night. Looking into Enrique's eyes, I saw a ... vision."

"In *his* eyes?" He narrowed his gaze and watched her warily, not sure of where she was going with this.

"*Sí.* I saw the ending of this ... journey. And despite our efforts here, I will still be married to Don Vicente. I know it. I *feel* it."

His jaw clenched, he struggled to hold on to his own self-control. He'd been having the same "vision," only he considered his a nightmare. And no matter what, he would see to it that it didn't come true. Now he had to convince her of that.

"It won't happen, Julie. I swear it."

A wistful smile curved her lips. "I know you will try, Micah. But my grandmother is too powerful. And my father does not care what becomes of me."

"Dammit!" He reached out and grabbed her arm, forcing her to bring her horse to a stop. "Look at me," he ordered. "I *swear* to you, Julie"—Micah's gaze met hers, and he tried desperately to make her believe—"I *won't* let your granny's men take you away."

She sighed and gave him a half smile.

"Julie." He leaned sideways, both hands gripping her upper arms, using the strength of his knees to keep his seat on the big horse. Inches from her nose, he said clearly, "I am *not* gonna let you marry that Don fella. You hear me? It ain't gonna happen."

Her bottom lip trembled, and he saw the quick rush of tears fill her eyes. Then, just as suddenly, she blinked the tears away, and her hesitant smile blossomed into a grin.

He'd *done* it! He'd convinced her! She believed in him!

"Micah," she said, her warm breath fanning his lips, "I *know* how you can stop my grandmother."

He gave her a quizzical look.

"I have had a wonderful idea."

"What?" he said and somehow knew he'd regret asking.

"Marry me."

"WHAT!"

CHAPTER
···TEN···

MICAH'S BALANCE DISSOLVED. He felt himself sliding sideways out of the saddle, and there wasn't a damn thing he could do to stop it. Satan leaped toward the right as his rider slammed to the ground on the left.

The horse danced nervously around, and Micah curled his arms and legs in. With one hand he slapped out at the animal's hind legs. "Damn your hide, Satan! Get the hell off me!"

When the big black skittishly moved away, Micah still sat where he'd landed and stared up at Julie. He kept his gaze locked on her even while she dismounted, stepped around her horse, and joined him on the ground.

"Would you mind sayin' that again?"

"Of course," she said, her smile bigger than ever. "Marry me."

There it was again. Calm as you please. His heart pounded, his blood raced through his veins. At a complete loss for words, Micah's mouth opened and closed repeatedly. Holy hell, how did she come up with *that*?

"You're talkin' crazy," he finally mumbled and was astonished to find his voice still worked.

"Why is this crazy?"

"Us? Married?"

"*Sí.* If we are married, Don Vicente won't be able to force me into a marriage with him! It is the perfect answer!"

"No, it ain't."

"But, Micah—"

"No, ma'am. It's crazy, I tell ya. I can't marry *you*!"

She sat up straight, hands at her hips, her legs crossed Indian style. "Am I so terrible a person?"

"No. . . ."

"Do you find me so ugly to look at?"

Hardly, he thought, but said only, "No."

"Then why won't you marry me?"

"Quit sayin' that, will ya?" He pushed himself to his feet, then stretched out one hand to help her up. Micah tried to step back from her, but she moved in close.

"But, Micah," she went on, and he could see that she was warmin' up to her own idea, "as a married woman, *none* of them could force me to do *anything* I did not want to do."

He backed up. "This is crazy, Hoo-lee-edda!" Holding his hands high and shaking his head, he said, "Just stop talkin' foolish! I can't marry you."

"Why not?"

"Because . . ." Frantically he tried to come up with a good enough reason for her. Jesus! Didn't she know what she was doin' to him. Just the *thought* of havin' her as wife was makin' his body sit up and take notice.

Good Lord. Micah Benteen? Married to Julietta Duffy? With all her fine education and fancy talk and pretty clothes and such? Hell, no.

"Just because!"

She cocked her head and looked at him through

wounded eyes. "You will not do this for me as my friend?"

Friend? Hah! Friends help you home when you're drunk. They bring you supper when you're laid up sick. They help you celebrate the good times and talk you through the bad. They sure as hell don't marry you!

"No."

Julie lifted her chin, sniffed, and said stiffly, "Fine. Then will you marry me if I *pay* you to?"

He couldn't believe what he was hearing. He shook his head as if to clear his ears and stared at her, dumbfounded.

"Pay me!" He jumped back, glaring at her. Viciously he kicked a stone across the trail and into the bushes opposite. Then he shouted, "What the hell kind of man do you take me for, woman?"

"I am not sure anymore."

"What's that supposed to mean?" He took a half step toward her, then stopped dead. "Goddammit! Have I ever *once* took money from you? For *anything*?"

"No," she acknowledged softly.

"You're damn right, I ain't. You can't *buy* me, Julie! I ain't a new hat or a pretty horse or even a night's sleep in a hotel!"

"But if you won't do this as a friend, I thought perhaps you could use money. For your ranch. Your family."

Even through the red haze of his anger, he noticed her face, how she managed to look both proud and pleading at the same time. He knew what it had cost her to make such a request, but that did nothing to take the sting out of her words.

"My family and me can take care of ourselves. Been

doin' it for years. We *don't* need some rich woman tossin' us a handout like we was standin' on the road beggin' a meal!"

"That is not what I meant."

"You'd better damn sure start doin' and sayin' what you mean then, woman! 'Cause I just ain't got the time nor the patience to deal with anything else!"

His chest worked like a blacksmith's bellows, dragging air into his lungs, then shoving it out again. Micah's head hurt he was so mad.

"Can't you think of marrying me as a job?"

"A job?"

"Sí." She took a step toward him, then stopped nervously. Her fingers twisted together, and she wasn't quite meeting his eyes. "We would be married only as long as it took to convince my father and grandmother that I was safely out of their reach."

He couldn't believe it. She was still tryin' to convince him. Jesus! This had to be the most stubborn female alive.

"Then," she went on, "we would leave Texas together."

"And go where?" He couldn't help himself. He had to find out just how far her idea went.

"Anywhere." She shrugged and spread her hands wide. "You would want to go back home, I know. Perhaps you would let me ride with you as far as your ranch. Then I could go on to Montana."

"Back to your friend?"

"Sí."

"Then what?"

"Then we would get a divorce."

"Just like that."

"*Sí.* We would both be free again to marry whom we choose."

He stared at her.

"Surely," she said carefully, as if leery of his temper, "there would be a use for extra money at your ranch house?"

He clenched his jaw tight. It angered him that she felt his home not good enough as it was. What did she think they needed her money for? Expensive paintin's and a couple of servants to carry their coffee for 'em? His home was just fine like it was. Maybe it wasn't some fancy rancho like she was used to . . . but at least none of them had wanted to run from it like a wanted man!

Of course, a voice in the back of his mind whispered, there *were* things they could use. Like payin' off that bank mortgage they'd had to take out a couple of years ago. And maybe two or three good mares to bring some new blood into their breeding stock.

No. It didn't matter. No matter what the Benteen's needed, they'd find a way to get it. They always had. And they'd done it without marryin' somebody just to get their hands on some quick cash.

It was on the tip of his tongue to say so, but then he noticed her eyes. That fear he'd glimpsed so briefly was back again. Her teeth worried her bottom lip and for the first time, he saw that her hands were now balled into fists so tight her knuckles stood out white against the pale brown of her flesh.

Hell, how could he blame her for tryin' to think of a way to stay safe? Especially after meetin' Enrique. If her granny's *other* man was half as tough, Micah knew he'd have a time of it keepin' her protected.

But if he did what she wanted, what would that make him? A kept man? Some kind of fortune hunter, marryin' some poor girl for her money? No. It'd be more like a favor.

Hah! He flicked her a quick glance. No matter what she thought, money wouldn't be what he'd do it for. Hell, what was he thinkin'? Was he actually startin' to consider it?

Micah rubbed one hand over his beard and tried to think. It wasn't easy with her starin' at him through them big, blue eyes.

Hell, there must be *worse* things than bein' married. And like she said, it'd only be for a while. He shook his head furiously. He was gettin' as crazy as her! Besides, he knew himself too well. If he *did* marry her— it'd be pure hell lettin' her go.

Julie's mare suddenly shied, tossed her head back wildly, and whinnied. She pranced agitatedly in one place and looked like she was about to run. Instinctively he reached for the animal's bridle and caught her before she could pull out of reach. He glanced at his own mount and noticed his stallion's alert posture. Satan's ears were cocked, and his long, elegant legs looked poised to take off at a dead gallop.

Quickly Micah yanked the rifle from Julie's saddle scabbard and began to carefully look around the surrounding trees and bushes. Something was out there. Something affecting both horses.

Dammit. He'd been too busy arguin' to pay attention to what was goin' on around him.

"What is it?"

"Hush!" He shook his head, reached out, and grabbed Julie, then pulled her behind him. "I don't know," he whispered. "But something's wrong. Them animals don't act like that for no reason. Stay quiet."

Mouth dry, breath coming in ragged staggers, Micah squinted into the shadows alongside the trail. His sharp gaze moved over every clump of bushes and every tree trunk, searching for the hidden enemy. It *had* to be an enemy, he knew. Anything friendly would've shown itself by now.

Then he heard it. He froze in place and cocked his head slightly, straining to identify the noise. From a distance a low, grumbling snuffling broke the silence. Micah's heart stopped. If he was right, they were in big trouble.

"Jesus," he whispered more to himself than Julie.

"What?" Her voice came from behind his ear.

He heard her strangled breathing and wanted to kick himself for getting her into this. If he hadn't been so caught up in bein' insulted by her proposal, he would've heard the danger signs when there was still time to run. As it was, they'd just have to take their chances.

Spinning around, he grabbed her, dragged her to the nearest pine, and told her to climb.

"What?"

"You heard me, dammit. Move." He handed her the rifle, held her around the waist, and lifted her to the first branch. "There's a bear out there. Close by." His whispered urgency finally reached her, and she began to pull herself higher into the tree.

As she climbed, she whispered, "If there is a bear, *you* should keep the rifle."

"I'm gonna be right behind you. Get as high as you can and hang on for all you're worth. With any luck, that bear will leave us be." He tossed a nervous glance over his shoulder. He'd give *anything* to be able to get his shotgun out of his saddle holster right now. If he had his way, they'd *both* be armed. But he'd have to settle for making sure Julie could defend herself.

"The horses?"

Micah frowned but shook his head. "They got to take their chances same as us. Now climb."

"Micah! Look!"

Even knowing what he would see didn't prepare him for the lightning bolt of pure fear that shot through him. Not fifty yards away, a huge, lumbering grizzly pushed through the bushes onto the trail.

Vaguely Micah heard Satan's and the mare's snorts of distress and then the sound of their hooves as they ran off the trail in opposite directions. But he didn't move. He couldn't seem to take his eyes off the bear.

The grizzly's massive head turned slowly first one way, then the other. It lifted its nose into the air, and Micah knew the animal had caught their scent. Slowly the bear stood on its hind legs, tossing its head back and forth and roaring a challenge. Its huge forepaws raked at the air, as if showing the man what those long claws would do to him.

The hair on the back of Micah's neck stood straight up in response to the almost deafening roar.

"Micah!" Julie's whispered shout reached him, though, and he spared her only a quick look. "Micah, come on!"

He ignored her pleas and desperately tried to think of *something* that would help.

At that same instant the grizzly dropped to all fours and charged.

Micah knew he wouldn't be able to climb high enough, fast enough to escape the animal. The only thing he could do now was try to draw it away from Julie. Deliberately he stepped away from the pine and into the middle of the trail. His eyes on the closing bear, he reached down into the cuff of his moccasin and drew out the knife he kept there. Not much of a weapon to use against an animal that had to weigh at least eight hundred pounds . . . but it was all he had.

The bear kept coming, its shoulder muscles rippling with every lumbering step. Micah'd known bears to make a false charge . . . running to within a few feet of their target, then stopping abruptly, as if to show their strength. But not this bear.

Even its labored breathing sounded like a warning. Danger. Danger.

Closer. Its dark eyes seemed to hold him captive. The animal's snuffling snorts were obscenely loud in the otherwise still air.

"Micah!"

He didn't turn to look at her. He couldn't. His grip on the worn, bone-handled knife tightened. His knees bent, preparing for the impact of the grizzly's body.

Closer still.

Micah could almost feel the animal's hot, steamy breath. He found his own breathing matching the rhythm of the bear's.

Seconds crawled by. He noticed everything around him while still concentrating on the approaching animal. The sun on his neck, the soft breeze rustling the pine needles, and most especially, the faint scent of jasmine drifting to him from Julie's body.

With regret he realized that he wanted to marry her.

For however long she needed him. If he could protect her from her enemies ... that would be enough. Or it would have been. Now it was too late.

Too late for anything.

And then the bear crashed into him, and he knew nothing but pain. The jarring blow staggered him and threw him to the ground as if he were no more than a rag doll. For a moment all he could see was teeth. The animal's powerful jaws hung open as it roared into his face. Micah frantically stabbed with his knife even as he tried to roll out from under the huge animal. The bear swung one paw at him and by a weird twist of fate, knocked his useless knife from his hand, sending it flying into the brush.

A woman's scream joined the bear's bellow, and he only had a moment to pray that Julie would have the sense to stay put. To save herself.

Hot breath blew onto his face and neck, and he spun over onto his belly instinctively to protect himself as best he could. He managed to curl his left arm up and over his neck, hoping to keep the grizzly's strong teeth from clamping down on his head. Then he tensed, waiting for the pain to begin.

As if from a distance, Micah thought he heard a gunshot, then another. But the bear didn't flinch. If Julie was shooting at him, the grizzly was either unhurt or too enraged to notice. Besides, he knew it would take a perfectly aimed shot to kill the rampaging animal.

When the razor-sharp claw sliced across Micah's back and shoulder, he heard himself scream. Another gunshot echoed, and the bear roared and stood up in response. Almost at the same instant, two more shots were fired. Micah hazarded a look over his shoulder and saw the grizzly's head snap back and the massive body turn completely around before dropping to the ground.

He couldn't move. Dazed, shaken, his shoulder throbbing, Micah could only lie on the trail and stare into the lifeless eyes of the bear lying not five feet away. And still, he didn't trust the animal. Behind him, Micah heard Julie as she scrambled out of the pine tree. He wanted to shout a warning. Tell her not to believe that bear was dead just because it wasn't moving.

But he couldn't. It was all he could do to breathe.

Her footsteps came hurriedly across the ground. He heard her pause beside him before circling around to stand behind the bear. His eyes opened to slits, Micah saw the chalk white pallor of her face. He saw her clenched jaw and the determined gleam in her eyes. He watched silently as she calmly and carefully fired three more rounds into the back of the animal's head.

Satisfied at last, she came to his side. And only then did Micah allow himself to pass out.

* * *

She whispered the same prayer for the hundredth time in the last hour and hoped desperately that God was listening. Reaching for the nearby pile of wood, Julie picked up a thick branch and laid it across the already blazing fire.

She sighed, drew her knees up to her chest, and wrapped her arms around them, shivering. Julie told herself she'd done the best she could. Lord knew their shelter wasn't much, but she hadn't had any choice. Micah was too big for her to drag very far and he'd been unconscious since the bear attack.

She shivered, bit down on her bottom lip, and

watched the steady rise and fall of his bare back with his deep, regular breathing.

"Thank you," she murmured and tried to close her mind to what had almost happened. But it was impossible. Julie knew that for as long as she lived, she would remember the charging animal crashing down on Micah.

Once more she felt the strangling fear that had clamped around her heart as she watched Micah's much smaller body disappear under the overwhelming size of the enraged bear. Squeezing her eyes shut and clapping her hands over her ears did nothing to soften the memory. She could still hear the furious roar. She heard Micah scream as the bear's claws ripped through his flesh.

She should have been quicker.

Rubbing her hands over her eyes, she brushed back useless tears and told herself that she'd almost waited too long again. First, Enrique. Then, the grizzly.

But this time she'd had no choice, she thought desperately. She'd *had* to wait for a clear shot. Wounding the animal would only have made it more dangerous.

Stop it! she thought silently. Rethinking the attack would do no good at all. It was over. Finished. Micah was alive.

That was all that mattered.

From somewhere not too far off, a wolf howled. Julie's head snapped up, and she stared through the surrounding bushes. Darkness crept closer, and she knew the wolves would come soon. The smell of blood drew them to the bear's carcass, but there was nothing to be done about that. She'd had to leave the huge animal where it had fallen, just off the trail.

For one fleeting moment she wished she'd been able

to take Micah farther away ... somewhere safer. But the best she could do, instead, was to keep the fire built up and stand watch over him until morning. Maybe, she thought hopefully, the wolves would be too busy with the bear to bother with them.

Another howl split the silence, and Julie gripped the rifle tightly.

Letting her glance slide over the canopy of tree limbs and brush she'd thrown together, she told herself it was better than nothing. At least, her crude shelter would keep most of the cold night wind off them and with any luck hide them from anyone passing by on the trail.

She only wished it was strong enough to withstand wolves.

Micah moved slightly, groaned, and before he could open his eyes, Julie was beside him. Laying her hands gently on his back, she urged him to be still.

"Julie?"

"Micah, do not move. Please. You will start the bleeding again."

"Bleeding?" He raised his head, then let it drop to the ground again. Sighing, he opened his eyes and mumbled, "Bear?"

"*Sí.*"

"How bad is it?" he asked and slid his arms under his chest as if to push himself up.

"Be still," she ordered and tried to hold him back.

"Dammit, Julie. How bad did the bastard get me?"

"There are long, deep scratches across your right shoulder."

"Shit."

"It is not as bad as I feared it would be," she said

156

hurriedly. "I think perhaps because you kept rolling, the bear was not able to do more damage."

He winced when he moved his right arm. "Feels like the damn thing did plenty." Raising his head slightly, he looked at his shoulder from the corner of his eye. "Where'd you get the bandage?"

"My extra shirt," she said and added, "I found some whiskey in your saddlebags. So I poured it on the wound."

"*All* of it?"

She smiled for the first time in what seemed hours. He sounded so disgusted to hear that what little liquor he'd had was gone. "No. There is a little bit left."

"I guess since you found the whiskey, that means Satan came back."

"*Sí.*" Julie shifted around on the dirt until she could look at him directly. "It was a miracle. I thought surely he would run and run until he was lost. But no. He simply walked up to me out of the woods. An hour later the mare returned as well."

He grinned. "That's one of the tricks I told ya about. Trained him to always come back to me." Micah groaned and shifted his weight uncomfortably. "That damn mare thinks she's Satan's mama. Always has. She'd follow the ol' boy straight to hell."

A chorus of howls echoed around them, and in response, Satan and the mare pranced nervously, pulling at the ropes tying them to a tree trunk.

"Damn," Micah muttered and tried to sit up. "Gonna be hip deep in wolves any time now. Help me sit up."

"Don't be foolish," she snapped. "I will stand watch. The horses are tied securely. And the wolves are not interested in us. Only the bear."

"Julie—"

"No. I will not help you up, and if you start bleeding again, I will not bandage you! *Then* you can worry about wolves."

His eyes challenged her, but Julie knew he was in no shape to argue with her. Whether he liked it or not . . . it was *her* turn to look after *him*.

CHAPTER
···ELEVEN···

"WHO IS THIS gringo?" Doña Ana stared down at the wire in her hands. She read it one more time, unwilling to believe that she'd been interfered with again. But there was no mistake. Enrique was in jail, and Julietta was once more on the road for home. Accompanied, it seemed, by a gringo who'd proven to be a surprise to Enrique.

"Fool!" she whispered and crumpled the wire. Her fingers tightened around the paper, squeezing until her own fingernails dug into her palm. Enrique should have been prepared. Did he think so much of himself that he gave no thought at all to an enemy?

She stared blankly at the pale ivory wall across from her, letting her mind create images of what Enrique'd described. "*¡Maldición!*" she mumbled and thought again, damn him, for ruining what should have been an easy task.

And where, she asked herself silently, was Carlos while Enrique was being bested by a gringo? Did she have to do *everything* herself? Disgusted, she tossed the crumpled piece of paper into the empty hearth.

The old woman took one last sip of tea from the cup

on her desk and shuddered delicately at the cold, bitter taste.

Doña Ana hurled the fine English bone china teacup to the floor. Fragile, hand-painted fragments shattered over the red tile and were crushed under the soles of her shoes as she marched out of the study toward the main staircase.

One of the servants scuttled out of her way as *la Patrona* hurriedly climbed the soft pink, marble steps. In the glow of oil lamps lit against the coming dark, the hand-turned walnut banister gleamed from recent polishing. Doña Ana lay her fingertips on its cool, smooth surface and found the touch . . . reassuring.

The sharp click of her own heels on the stairs irritated her. As she got closer to the top, she gripped the banister tightly, convulsively.

Julietta and her gringo were in Colorado. If they continued traveling quickly and, she thought furiously, *unimpeded*, they would be at the Duffy rancho within the next week or so.

Her head began to pound in time with the tapping of her heels. She could not allow that to happen! Breathing rapidly through gritted teeth, Doña Ana told herself that there was still time. The girl had still to evade Carlos. Hopefully he would prove to be more competent than Enrique.

At the head of the stairs she stopped and swayed slightly. One hand on the banister, she laid the other, fingers splayed, on her bosom. Her sharp, black eyes narrowed in confusion, she winced as a small tingle of discomfort snaked across her chest.

Only a small twinge at first, it slowly built until a strange heaviness settled over her. Tilting her head back, Doña Ana deliberately drew slow, regular breaths, telling herself that it was nothing. It would go away.

Seconds stretched into minutes, and the empty hallway seemed to mock her. There was no one to call for help, even if she'd been so inclined. And despite the discomfort, Doña Ana smiled. It was as it should be. She'd spent years training the servants to disappear when she entered a room.

She hated looking into their stupid, vacant faces. And after a time, even the fear in their eyes was not enough to compensate for having to talk to them.

The pain began to subside and with it went the tenuous thread of fear brought on by the unexpectedness of the attack.

Straightening again, Doña Ana took a few more deep breaths, relieved to be herself again. A rest. That was all she needed. The cool, dark silence of her own room beckoned her. Slowly, cautiously, she made her way down the length of the hall to the open door of her bedroom.

She stepped through the wide, arched doorway and came to a sudden stop. Across the room, on the far side of the four-poster oak bed, a young maid held a match to the wick of a lamp. For heaven's sake! Hadn't she just congratulated herself on the training of her staff? That lamp should have been lit an hour ago. Her bed should have been turned down and the room empty, waiting for her. The realization that the maid was young and most certainly new to her job, did nothing to relieve the flash of temper shooting through Doña Ana's body.

Hadn't she *enough* to put up with? Wasn't it *enough*

161

that one of her most thorough, efficient men had been bested by a girl and a gringo?

As the flame caught on the wick, Doña Ana snapped, *"¡Estúpida!"*

Startled, the young, plump girl jumped and dropped the lamp chimney.

When the glass splintered on the shining oak floor, the sound pushed Doña Ana into motion. Striding across the room, her black skirt flapping wildly about her legs, the older woman felt a brief satisfaction as she watched the girl back up, terrified.

Though no more than fifteen, the maid had a full bosom that heaved and strained against the plain white, off-the-shoulder blouse she wore. The girl's hands clutched at the fabric of her bright red cotton skirt, and her sandaled feet made a shuffling noise as she retreated until her back was up against the bedroom wall.

Her soft brown eyes wide, mouth open, she appeared to Doña Ana as the embodiment of the stupidity she was forced to deal with daily. As the older woman got closer, she saw the flame of the lamp reflected in the girl's eyes and then her own image covered the flame.

In fluid, elegant Spanish, Doña Ana cursed the girl, her parents, and whatever children she might deliver in the future. Her voice whipped through the silence, slashing at the maid until the girl was quivering and tears pooled in her cowlike eyes.

Bringing her right hand up, Doña Ana slapped the girl's face so hard she felt a slight sprain in her own wrist. With satisfaction, the older woman watched the bright red imprint of her hand blossom on the maid's plump cheek.

Tears began to rain down the vapid face, and Doña

Ana shouted, "Leave me! Find someone in this house to bring a broom up here and clean the mess you've made. But not you. You stay out of my sight."

The girl nodded and inched carefully around *la Patrona*.

"Find me someone with intelligence!"

She bobbed her head again, rounded the edge of the bed, and ran for the door—and escape.

"Intelligence!" Doña Ana mumbled, glaring down at the slivers of glass littering her floor. She doubted very much that there *was* such a person in her employ!

Suddenly the tight stranglehold on her chest clutched at her again. The now oddly familiar feeling staggered through her, building to a degree of discomfort quicker than it had before. But this time she knew what to do.

Slowly, deliberately, she pulled air into her body and forced a calm she didn't quite feel. Doña Ana turned the force of her legendary will onto her own body. Leaning only slightly on the bed beside her, she concentrated until the mysterious pain faded away once more.

* * *

Micah opened his eyes, rolled over, and bit off a groan that accompanied his too quick movement. What the hell? he wondered as pain lashed at his shoulder. Then in an instant he remembered everything. Julie's proposal, his own stupidity. The goddamned bear.

Slower now, he levered himself up until he was leaning on his left arm. Right beside him, her back against an ancient pine, Julie sat straight up, sound asleep. His rifle lay across her limp hands in her lap, her chin on her chest.

Morning sun filtered through the pine branches,

throwing a dappled light on the crude shelter she'd been able to put together when he was unconscious. A half smile on his lips, he conceded silently that she'd done a good job.

Satan whickered from nearby, and a glance told him she'd tied the horses close enough to camp that she could keep an eye on them, too.

He looked back at the sleeping woman. She had to be *real* tired to be able to sleep in that position. And why shouldn't she be, he asked himself silently. Look what all she'd done just to take care of *him*. Lord, no wonder she was wore out.

Slowly, carefully, he sat up. The pain in his back and shoulder was bad, but livable. Heaven knew, he'd had worse in his life and probably would again.

With his good hand, Micah reached out, lifted the rifle from her, and set it aside. Then he managed to get his left arm around her shoulders and began to lower her to the ground. At the very least, he could see to it that she got *some* sleep before they had to start riding again.

As soon as he laid her down, though, Julie's eyes opened and she stared up at him.

He had to bite his tongue to keep from telling her how pretty she looked.

" 'Mornin'," he said, smiling.

"Good morning."

"I was tryin' to lay ya out so's you could sleep some."

"Sleep?" She pushed herself up to a sitting position. A faint flush stained her cheeks as she realized, "I fell asleep, didn't I?"

"Yeah." Reluctantly he sat back.

"But I was supposed to be watching."

"Don't matter."

She looked at him, and Micah felt his heartbeat stagger slightly. Her blue eyes looked soft, dreamy. Her open-throated white shirt had come unbuttoned somehow, and he could just see the top edge of some lacy thing stretched over her breasts. He forced himself to look away. Desperate, he searched for something to say and finally blurted out, "That was some damn fine shootin' you done yesterday. How'd you learn to do that?"

"When I was a child. On the rancho." Julie pushed her hair back from her face and smoothed her skirt and blouse. Micah's eyes locked on her fingers as she buttoned up and covered his glimpse of lace. "My father's foreman, Roberto, taught me well. In case, he said, I should ever need to take care of myself."

"Yeah, well, reckon I owe that Roberto fella a thank-you, too."

She pointed to his bandaged shoulder. "I am sorry I was not faster."

"What this?" He shrugged, then winced. "It's all right. Could have been a sight worse."

"*Sí.*" She frowned briefly at the thought, then added, "I could not get a clean shot at the bear's head because I was afraid of hitting you, instead."

"I appreciate you takin' the extra time to be sure." He smiled at her. "How'd ya manage to get a good shot at him? I hate to admit it, but what I most remember about the whole damn thing is teeth. I swear that bear had more teeth than any *three* bears need!" He shook his head slowly. "And that's as close as I *ever* want to come to seein' the inside of a bear's mouth again!"

"*Sí*, Micah. I, too, have no wish to see another bear." She reached out, grabbed his hand, and squeezed it. "I was very frightened."

He looked down at the small, soft hand covering his much larger one and felt his throat close. The warmth of her flesh on his brought on an overwhelming rush of desire. Her slightest touch was enough to get his blood boiling and his body hard. If she knew what he was thinking, he told himself, she'd probably be more scared now than when faced with that bear!

But she didn't—and *wouldn't* know. Micah breathed deeply, swallowed back the urge to hold her, then slowly raised his gaze to hers. "I don't even mind admittin' it. I was pretty damn scared, too, Hoo-lee-edda."

She smiled at him, and Micah's heart stopped for a long moment before thudding into life again. Good God. One smile from her and all he could think about was easing the ache in his groin. A too vivid image blossomed suddenly in his brain, and he closed his eyes against the vision of his body sliding into hers. Of her arms around his neck, her mouth locked on his. Of the damp heat of her surrounding him.

Micah's eyes flew open guiltily. His thumb moved over her palm, and he covered his action by asking, "So, how'd you manage to get that damn critter anyhow?"

Julie sighed and moved her hand against his thumb. He nearly died when she licked her lips. She shifted position uneasily and cleared her throat before speaking in a hushed, distracted tone.

"I, uh . . . first had to shoot him in the, uh . . . backside. To make him rear up. Then I took my shot."

Micah laughed and groaned immediately as pain shot through his wounds. He squeezed her hand tightly and smiled to feel her fingers curl over his.

"What is so funny?" Her index finger drew patterns on the inside of his wrist.

"Nothin', I guess," he said, smiling at the delightful sensation of her fingers moving over his skin. "It's only that for some reason my shoulder hurts a helluva lot less, knowing that bear got shot in the behind before he died!"

Julie leaned toward him, a distracted smile on her face. Micah's breath caught. Even after a night spent sittin' up, leanin' against a tree, she was far too beautiful for her own good. He stared into her clear, blue eyes, tightened his grip on her hand, and let the smile on his lips fade away.

"I, uh . . . just want to say thanks, Julie."

"But, Micah—"

"No. Hush up a minute. Let me get this said." With his left hand, he reached out and cupped her cheek tenderly. "You really did save me this time, Julie. If not for you, that bear woulda had me for supper."

"I only—"

Urging her closer, Micah cut her off again. "You *only* shot that damn, flea-bitten, fur-covered piece of meat before he could do me in. And I thank you."

Her face only inches from his, Julie whispered, "You are welcome. Micah," and her breath fanned his cheeks temptingly.

Even though he knew he shouldn't, Micah pulled her closer. He couldn't seem to stop himself. She came to him without hesitation, her eyelids drifting shut just a heartbeat before their lips met.

At the first touch of her mouth against his, Micah groaned silently at the softness of her lips. She pressed closer, and Micah slid his hand from her cheek to the back of her head. Threading his fingers through her thick hair, he held her mouth to his with a gentle, but firm pressure.

A flood of emotion raced through him. Desire, gratitude at being alive and able to feel her warmth, and finally, reluctantly, guilt.

When her tongue touched his lips, he knew it was time for him to call a halt or he never would. From the depths of his soul, he summoned up every once of self-control he possessed and broke the kiss.

Surprised, Julie opened her eyes and met his gaze. Micah almost crumbled under the soft shine of hurt in her eyes. He felt her tremble and knew she was caught by the same driving need that gripped him. But she was a virgin, for God's sake. His responsibility. A trust.

He couldn't betray that trust. Could he?

No.

Before he could talk himself out of his own better judgment, Micah scooted back from her a bit and tried to ignore the throbbing ache between his legs. In an unsteady voice, he said, "Uh, Julie, maybe you could make us some coffee before we get goin'?"

"Coffee?" She blinked and he looked away. "But, Micah, I—"

"I'd really appreciate it, Julie."

He risked a glance at her from the corner of his eye and saw disappointment fill her eyes. Jesus, God. If she only knew what it had cost him to set her aside!

He didn't say anything, though. Not even when she pushed herself to her feet and walked to the horses. He watched her take out the coffeepot and the canteen, then turned his head away. It wasn't safe for him to watch the sway of her hips. It wasn't safe for him to look into her eyes.

Hell, he finally admitted silently. The only way they'd be safe was if she was at home in Texas and he was in Wyoming.

Where he belonged.

* * *

The morning sun was already hot as it streamed down on the two women standing in the open courtyard.

"Please, Señora," Juana said, wringing her hands. "It would be best if you waited for Señor Duffy to return."

"Nonsense, Juana." Penelope smiled at the shorter woman and pulled on her left glove. Smoothing the soft, gray material over her palms, she almost smiled at the neatly darned fingertips. Unless you looked closely, the signs of repair were almost invisible. "Please don't concern yourself. I shall manage quite nicely on my own, I'm sure."

"But, Señora . . ."

"Now, now, you mustn't fuss so." Pulling a lacy handkerchief from the sleeve of her black wool riding habit, Penelope dabbed at the beads of perspiration on her upper lip. For one brief moment she wished she had *something* else to wear, but there was nothing to be done about it. Her old black wool had served her well in England, as it would here.

If only, she thought, the sun weren't *quite* so hot. She adjusted the knot in her white cravat, then checked that her no-longer-fashionable black felt hat was at the proper tilt. Penelope allowed herself a moment of vanity and assured herself that the new net veil and jet beadwork she'd affixed to the little hat was just enough to give it a saucy air.

She knew that she looked as good as was humanly possible for a thirty-year-old spinster to look. She'd never been a beauty, heaven knew. And now was certainly not the time to be wishing for fine feathers! But she'd always prided herself, at the very least, on a genteel appearance.

Tucking the handkerchief back into her sleeve, Penelope slipped the strings of her bag over her wrist, tugged at the hem of her short jacket, and straightened her shoulders. "Now then." She threw a wide smile at the boy standing to one side, holding the reins of an enormous horse. "Come along, Alejandro," she called, wagging one finger at him. "Bring the animal over here."

"Señora Penelope," Juana said once more, stepping closer. "Señor Duffy will not be happy about this, I am afraid."

"Pish-tush!"

"Señora?"

"I said, pish-tush, Juana." The housekeeper's round, placid face was drawn into lines of confusion. Worry. Penelope hated to upset the woman, but she'd come too far to be stopped now. "It means . . . oh, never mind. The point is, I haven't the time to wait for Patrick Duffy to return from his morning ride."

"He is not on a ride, Señora. He is checking on the north range, and I know he would want—"

"Ah!" Penelope smiled and patted Juana on the shoulder. "You see what I mean, then! Patrick is off doing what he has to do . . . as must I."

"*Sí*, but—"

"But me no buts, Juana." Penelope frowned when she noticed Alejandro hadn't moved a muscle. Tapping her foot, she signaled to him again and didn't take her eyes off the boy until he'd begun to walk the horse toward her. Then she glanced back at Juana again. "I am only going into town to speak to the marshal, Juana. I will no doubt return long *before* Patrick does."

Warily she turned her eyes to the horse in front of her. The brown-and-black animal seemed much larger than the few horses she'd had occasion to rent for an hour's ride back home. And, she told herself, she didn't much care for the look in the beast's eyes, either.

However. Penelope lifted her chin and stood up straight. It was important to let the brute know just *who* was in charge.

Determinedly she pulled back the hem of her skirt, stuck her left foot in the stirrup, and pulled herself up into the western-style saddle. She'd forgotten that this was *not* a sidesaddle. Not to be deterred, though, she wavered uncertainly for a moment, balanced on one foot. Then, because she couldn't think what else to do, she hooked her right leg over the saddle horn and plopped down onto the saddle. She wobbled dangerously for a long minute.

A precarious seat, indeed! One would think, she told herself, that a rancho of this size would be properly equipped with ladies' riding accouterments! The horse beneath her seemed to sense her unease and pranced skittishly.

"Stop that at once!" she ordered and tightened her grip on the reins.

Alejandro grabbed the bridle and began to stroke the animal's nose until it quieted.

Penelope used that extra moment to settle herself more firmly. Though uncomfortable, she had no doubt that she would be able to control the horse during her short trip. Besides, it was unthinkable that she show the slightest hesitation.

"Señora?" Juana asked carefully and took a half step back. "Perhaps you would wait long enough for a carriage to be brought around and cleaned up?"

Penelope threw the thoughtful woman a bright smile. So kind. "Nonsense, Juana. This beast will do nicely, I'm sure. Besides," she added with a solemn wink, "it is as I've always said, Make do—or do without!" Gesturing to the boy, she said, "Stand clear, dear boy. Wouldn't want you to be injured." She held the reins in a firm grip and said clearly, "Very well, horse. When you're quite ready."

The big animal began to walk, but as he neared the gate, he broke into a trot.

Juana watched as Penelope Butterworth bounced and leaned dangerously from side to side in a desperate effort to keep her seat. The housekeeper frowned at Alejandro's giggle, then slowly crossed herself.

* * *

Micah picked up the shirt Julie'd dug out of his saddlebags for him. As he drew the faded blue material carefully up over his injured arm, he told himself he'd have to get Hallie to make him a new buckskin shirt once he got home. A too familiar thought flashed through his brain in response. It was only due to Providence and Julie's aim that he'd be gettin' home at all.

As his left hand clumsily did up the buttons on his shirt, he watched her as she crouched beside the fire.

He shook his head and reminded himself that it was *twice* now, she'd saved his worthless hide for him. And the second time, she'd pulled him out of a tight spot just after he'd turned down her proposal.

Proposal! Hell, she'd practically *begged* him to marry her. To keep her safe. And he'd refused her. Then what does she do? He groaned softly.

She saved your ass, that's what.

His brain was a jumble of thoughts, each one crowding in on the one before. And through them all, he saw her face as she asked him to marry her. Shit. That *she* should be beggin' *him*! It just wasn't right. Not right at all.

And anyway. Who the hell was *he* to turn her down? Didn't Trib himself say to keep Julietta Duffy safe? No matter what? Why the hell *shouldn't* he marry her? It was what she wanted. . . . Huh! He snorted at his own thinking.

All she wanted was to be safe. To escape her pa and her granny and go back to her friend's place in Montana.

She's not exactly pinin' away for love of a dumb mountain boy, so don't go tryin' to fool yourself any, he silently warned himself. But did that matter? Did anything matter except what he *owed* her?

Dammit, how could he *not* marry her? If not for her, he'd be dead now for sure. Either Enrique or that damned bear would have cleaned his clock for him.

A soft, lilting melody spun out into the quiet, and Micah paused, listening. Whatever tune it was that Julie was humming, he liked it. With her left side facing him, he could see the half smile on her face and the muted sunlight shining on the braid that hung over one shoulder.

Even after days of rough travel and more troubles than one body had a right to, she could still smile. Even when the one person who could help her had turned away from her, she could still smile.

His heart turned over in his chest, and a sharp spasm of near pain shot through him. Cautiously Micah pushed himself to his feet and stood quietly for a moment, just watching her.

If she *really* needed him—he would do whatever he could for as long as he could.

CHAPTER
···TWELVE···

HUMMING SOFTLY, JULIE set the coffeepot close to the flames, brushed her palms together, and stood up. It was good to have something to do. Something to think about besides . . . She reached up and ran her fingertips across her lips, remembering the feel of Micah's mouth. The strength of his hand as he held her close. The warmth of his breath.

It began and ended so quickly, though, Julie couldn't help but think she'd been too bold. But she was only doing as he'd shown her before. She chewed at her lip thoughtfully. He'd broken away the moment she'd touched her tongue to his lips. Perhaps that was wrong. Perhaps it was not what a lady should do.

Frowning, she stared down into the campfire. Her gaze locked on the swaying flames, Julie saw Micah's face again as he set her away from him. He hadn't *seemed* angry. But if he was not, why did he stop kissing her? Was she not very good at it?

A stir of movement told Julie that Micah had come up right behind her. The strength of his gaze pulled at her. She felt his eyes move over her body as surely as if he had touched her. With that thought came unbidden images of Micah's hands moving over her flesh. The rough calluses on his palms rubbing over her breasts. Julie's nipples hardened in response to the too real vision, and she had to forcefully push her wayward thoughts aside.

Slowly she turned around to face him. Hot color flooded her face, and she only hoped he would think it was merely from the heat of the fire.

Her wild imagination was embarrassing enough without him being aware of it. When his hand cupped her elbow, she reluctantly looked up at him. For the hundredth time, she found herself wishing that he had no beard. Perhaps then she might be able to read his features. As it was, his feelings were always hidden from her.

Julie swallowed nervously and forced a calm she didn't feel into her voice. "The coffee will be ready in just a few minutes."

He nodded but didn't speak. She watched his gaze move over her face, and when he finally met her eyes again, there was a new, unreadable emotion shining at her.

"Does your shoulder pain you?"

Micah sucked in a gulp of air before answering. "Hurts some—it'll be fine."

"Good." Nervously she added, "I will check your bandage."

"Later."

"It will only take a moment, Micah."

"Dammit, Julie—"

"There is no need to curse at me." *Madre de Dios.* Could he really change from soft and loving to irritable so quickly? "I only wish to help."

"If you'll just shut up a minute—"

176

"Shut up?" She stared at him. "You tell me to shut up? Very well. If that is how you feel, you may change your own bandage."

"Julie—"

"No." A knot formed in her throat, and she swallowed past it. There were too many raging emotions battling in her body. Too many things to think about. To ignore. To wish for. To forget about. "I shot a bear for you—cleaned and bandaged your wounds—even sat up during the night to protect you from the wolves—"

"And fell asleep."

"I was not asleep. Merely resting."

"That's not what I want to talk about, dammit. I want—"

"I am not interested in what you want." She held up both hands and shook her head fiercely. Foolish tears filled her eyes, and she blinked furiously to keep them at bay. She was only interested in what he was most obviously *not*. Taking one step back from him, she went on, "Your temper is a foul one. I may excuse it because of your pain—but that does not mean I want to listen to it!"

His left hand shot out to grab her upper arm, and he pulled her close to him.

"Let me go, Micah. It is best, I think, if we do not talk any further this morning."

"Julie, will you listen to me?"

"No. I will get us both some coffee, and then we can be on our way again."

"I don't want any damned coffee!"

"Fine. *Señor Testarudo!*"

"What?"

"Hardhead," she translated. "What is it you want?"

He released her, rubbed his chin thoughtfully, then smoothed back his unruly hair.

Julie waited. She wished only that he would hurry and say whatever it was he wanted to say. Then perhaps she could keep her distance from him long enough to banish her ridiculous longings.

"I want you to marry me."

"What?" She'd heard him. She was sure of it. But she wanted him to say it again. Just in case. "What did you say?"

"I said, I want you to marry me."

There. It was true. Her knees suddenly weak, Julie slipped to the ground. She looked up at him and found his eyes linked with hers. She opened her mouth, but nothing came out. She kept her gaze locked on him as he slowly lowered himself to sit beside her.

"Julie?" he whispered. "You all right?"

"You mean this?"

"Yeah. Yeah, I do."

"But I do not understand." Julie rubbed her temples with her fingertips. This was not what she had expected. And after the way he'd pushed her away from him earlier, she could hardly believe it was something he wanted.

There seemed to be only one explanation. Though she wasn't sure she wanted to hear the answer, she knew she had to ask the question. Lowering her gaze to her own clenched fingers, she said softly, "Have you decided then that you could use the money I offered you?"

He snorted a muffled curse, and she looked up at him.

"I don't want your damned money."

"Then I do not understand, Micah."

"Don't have to. Ain't it enough that I want to marry ya?"

"I do not know."

He reached for her hands and held them in a firm grip. Meeting her gaze squarely, he said, "Just let it be enough, Julie. We'll get hitched, and I'll take you to your pa's. We'll show him and your granny that you already got a husband, and that should get 'em to leave you alone."

"And then?"

"Then," he released her, "then, I'll take you back to Montana. To your friend."

"And we would divorce?"

He jerked his head. "Yeah."

"Would that be easy?"

His fingers plucked at a new blade of grass, and he stared at it with the concentration of a blind man suddenly made to see.

"Prob'ly. You could even get one of those. . . . I forget what you call 'em. Y'know, that thing that says you was never married in the first place?"

"Annulment."

"Yeah, that's it. You could get one of them." His brow furrowed, he raised his gaze to hers. "Who knows? You might find somebody, someday, you really want to marry up with."

Divorce? Annulment? Strange things indeed to be discussing with the man who had just agreed to marry you. But, Julie reminded herself, it was *she* who'd first suggested all this.

But that was *before*, she cried silently. Before she'd come so close to losing him. Before that horrifying moment when the bear came so near to killing Micah. Perhaps it was *then* that she began to realize that she loved him.

She blinked. Looking into the depths of his gentle green eyes, Julie admitted to herself that, yes, she *did* love him. Excitement, surprise, and worry warred in her soul for supremacy. Watching him silently, Julie knew that if he realized her feelings, he would so something foolish like take back his offer. She'd already heard the truth in so many things that he'd said over the last few weeks.

He didn't believe himself good enough for her.

She wanted to laugh. Micah was the best man she'd ever known. Kind, despite his impatience . . . loyal, despite the cost to his own feelings . . . and gentle. Despite his strength.

She loved him. And Micah, she knew, wanted her. She'd seen the way he looked at her. She'd felt it in his kiss. Perhaps, she told herself silently, if they were together long enough, perhaps he could come to love her.

It was as though a boulder had been lifted from her chest. With the realization that she loved him had also come the decision to stay with him. All she had to do now, was to convince him how much he needed her.

A slow smile crept onto her face, and she watched his eyes take on a wary shine.

"What're you thinkin', Hoo-lee-edda?"

"It is nothing," she said softly, "only that . . ." Julie tilted her head and looked at him slyly. "Did you know that the only way one can receive an annulment is if the marriage is not consummated?"

She wasn't sure because of the too concealing beard,

but Julie thought she saw a stab of discomfort across his face.

"Uh, yeah." He nodded and inhaled sharply. "But that's no problem, though."

"No?"

"No. 'Cause we won't be, uh ... well ... we won't, is all."

She hid a smile and threw herself at him. Locking her arms around his neck, Julie squeezed him tight and deliberately pressed her breasts against his chest. "Thank you, Micah. For marrying me."

He groaned aloud and dipped his right shoulder in an effort to protect his wound. Immediately she released him. She hadn't meant to cause him pain.

"I am so sorry, Micah."

"It's all right, Julie."

"I only wanted to hug you. In thanks," she added with an innocent smile.

"Yeah." He cleared his throat and stood up. "Now, Julie, I got to tell you right off."

"Yes, Micah?" She stood up and moved in close.

He backed up. "If this marriage plan is gonna work without makin' me crazy"—he wagged one finger at her—"there's got to be no more huggin' and kissin' and such. Understand?"

"But we will be married."

"Not for real, we won't." Shaking his head, Micah took another step away. "It's only ..."

"Temporary?"

"Yeah."

"When?"

"When what?"

"When will we be married?"

"Oh. As soon as we hit New Mexico, I guess. I want to put some miles between us and ol' Enrique first."

"*Bueno.* Then I will pour us both some coffee and then pack our things so we can be off." She took two quick steps and stopped when less than an inch of space separated them. "But first," she added and rose up on her toes to plant a quick kiss on his parted lips. Before he could say anything, she said, "A kiss to seal our bargain, Micah." She grinned up at him and turned to get their coffee.

When she glanced back at him, Julie smiled. He was still standing where she'd left him, watching her through skeptical eyes.

* * *

Don Vicente Alvarez smiled down at the small oval portrait in his left hand. It had been too long. Sixteen years since Elena died. Sixteen years since he'd felt that rush of desire that only *she* could create.

His thumb stroked the surface of the tiny oil painting as his tongue darted out to lick suddenly dry lips. Merely *thinking* about the one week he'd had alone with her was enough to make him hard.

Don Vicente groaned and leaned back in his oversized leather chair. His right hand dropped to his lap, and slowly, lovingly, he began to rub his throbbing erection. A soft sigh escaped him, and his fingers moved to unbutton his trousers.

When his swollen member was free, he grasped himself tightly and began to caress his flesh.

Elena's dark eyes looked up at him from the painting, and he saw them again as he once had. Full of pain. Fear. He arched into his hand, but fought back the climactic release. It would be better, he knew, the longer he waited. Stifling a groan of pleasure, he worked his fingers expertly. If only he could have her now, he told himself breathlessly. . . .

Immediately, colorful visions of just how he would use her filled his brain. He closed his eyes to better enjoy the delicious images. As he mentally teased himself, Don Vicente felt his release building. Almost, almost—

A timid knock at his study door shattered his concentration. Opening his small, dark eyes, he glared at the door across the room and snapped, "What is it?"

"Con permiso, Don Vicente." A young woman, no more than sixteen, opened the door.

"Yes, yes," he said, his fingers still caressing his erection beneath the cover of his oak desk.

"I must clean out the hearth, Señor."

He watched her silently. Two long, black braids fell across her small breasts. When she moved her head warily, he could just see the shadows of her dark nipples pressed against the white of her shirt. A peasant, she stood uneasily in the doorway, shifting her sandaled feet as if she wanted to run.

He smiled.

Surprised, the girl gave him a hesitant smile in return.

"Go on then," Don Vicente said, waving his left hand toward the fireplace. "Just be quiet about it."

"Sí, Señor. I will hurry."

He nodded and watched her walk across the wide room to the cold hearth on the wall opposite him. Her wide hips swung from side to side, and he heard the soft hush of flesh on flesh as her thighs moved together.

His right hand paused its movement. He squinted at

the girl and told himself that in the right light, with the right clothes, she would almost look like Julietta.

A slow grin curved his thin lips. Soon, he promised himself. Soon, he would have Julietta. And though she was a little older than he usually preferred, the fact that she was Elena and Patrick Duffy's daughter more than compensated.

It wouldn't be the same, he knew. Taking Julietta. Using her. It would never be the same. She wasn't Elena. But she would have to do.

And until she arrived . . . Don Vicente's gaze locked on the girl across the room. On her knees, her right arm stretched out, sweeping at the ashes, the girl's firm, rounded behind wiggled with her every movement. He swallowed heavily and felt the throb of new need course through his groin.

He glanced at the door. Closed.

And no one would enter without his permission.

"You!" he called. "Girl! Come here at once!"

She pushed herself to her feet and cautiously walked toward him.

Yes. If he didn't look carefully, she could pass for Julietta. He smiled.

"Come around here, girl. Now."

Ah, good. He saw the fear flash into her eyes. Her breasts rose and fell rapidly with her anxiety. Don Vicente could hardly breathe.

She stepped around the edge of his desk and stopped short. Eyes wide, she stared down at the sight of Don Vicente grasping his own engorged flesh. As she watched, he stroked himself and almost purred with satisfaction.

"What is your name, girl?"

She swallowed. "Rosa."

"Rosa, you need not finish with the hearth. I have another 'duty' for you, instead."

Terrified, the girl could not look away.

"Stand close to my desk, Rosa, and bend over it."

"*¿Que?*"

"Do it. Now." He stood up and pulled her closer. "Lie across the desk, Rosa. Curl your fingers over the far edge."

He heard her sharp intake of breath. He felt the tremors begin to quake through her body. But she did as she was told. They all did.

Breathing deeply, Don Vicente stepped up behind the girl and slowly lifted the hem of her skirt. Her long, bare, cinnamon-colored legs enticed him. He ran his damp palms over the outsides of her thighs and up the curve of her behind.

"You are beautiful, Rosa. Too beautiful to clean a hearth," he murmured and tossed the hem of her skirt up until it covered her back and head. He heard her muffled whimper and smiled. "You will tell the housekeeper that you will be moving into the room next to my own bedroom for a time. No more cleaning for you, Rosa." His pale, veined hands cupped her buttocks and squeezed. "Until I bring my wife to this house, you will . . . keep me company. *¿Sí?*"

His fingers pinched at her flesh until she whispered, "*Sí, Don Vicente. Sí.*"

"Good." He rubbed the tip of his swollen flesh over her behind and released a groan of need. He'd waited long enough. He wanted to feel again. Feel the rush of ecstasy as he spilled himself into her.

Grasping her rounded cheeks, he pulled them apart

slightly, positioned himself and plunged deep inside her. Rosa's scream echoed through the room, drowning the Don's satisfied sighs.

* * *

Patrick Duffy wiped his sleeve across his sweaty forehead. Even in spring the damn sun was enough to cook a man alive. Shoving his hat back down on his head. Patrick pulled on the reins and started his horse for home.

Home. Hell, he hardly knew the place anymore. He didn't get a moment's peace. What with Juana running around like a chicken without a head. That woman had cleaned more in the last few days than she had in the last ten years.

And he knew why, too.

Penelope Butterworth.

His horse walked lazily along, and the easy, rocking motion gave Patrick plenty of time to think.

It wasn't as though Penelope had taken over. She never *ordered* any of his servants to do a damn thing. In fact, he hadn't once heard her be less than kind or considerate to anyone on the rancho. Except him, of course.

No, it was Juana herself, and all the others, too, who'd decided to please this interloper. They just couldn't seem to do enough for her. And whenever they thought he couldn't hear them, it was, "Señora Butterworth said this. Señora Butterworth did that."

For God's sake, who would have thought a plain-faced spinster from England could turn his well-ordered world into chaos! Now that's hardly true, his brain argued. Nothing in that rancho had been well-ordered for years.

That wasn't the point, though, he argued silently. Everything had been the way he liked it. Until *she* came. Now *nothing* was the same.

A movement on his left caught the corner of his eye. He turned his head to get a good look and muttered, "Goddammit!"

No more than a hundred yards away, Penelope Butterworth was strolling down the road, leading one of Patrick's best horses. What in the hell?

As she came steadily closer, he watched her, fascinated. He noticed her limping and didn't even want to guess at the reason for that. Shaking his head, he let his gaze survey the country surrounding the stubborn woman.

For miles, on either side of the narrow road, there was nothing but sage, mesquite, sand, and snakes. Early afternoon sun beat down on the woman in black, and he told himself it was a wonder she hadn't fainted dead away already.

What the hell kind of women *is* she? he asked himself. And why the hell did she have to come to *him*?

Only fifty yards away now and he could see that her black riding habit was covered in dust and dirt. The useless hat she wore was tilted over her right eye, and the reason for her limp was clear. She'd broken a heel on one of her shoes.

Patrick folded his hands on the saddle horn and leaned forward. In spite of himself, he was impressed. No matter that she looked like she'd been dragged for miles behind an ornery horse. She held her shoulders straight and walked with her chin up.

Nope. She wasn't like any other woman he'd ever

met. Even in these unlikely circumstances, Penelope Butterworth was every inch a lady.

Lady.

He snorted. The word didn't mean a damn thing. A frown creased his face as he reminded himself that Elena was *supposed* to be a lady. And look what she'd done.

His hot Irish temper flared just thinking about his late wife. She'd used him. Lied to him. *Cheated* him out of everything! Then she died, leaving him to stew in his own futile rage for years!

When Penelope finally came alongside him, Patrick's anger exploded.

"What the *hell* are you doing out here?"

CHAPTER
···**THIRTEEN**···

PENELOPE SMILED GRATEFULLY. "Thank heaven you found me, Patrick."

"*Found* you? I wasn't looking for *you*. I was just heading back to the rancho."

She sniffed. "That will do just as well." She handed him the reins of her horse. "Perhaps you would return this beast to his stable and send a carriage back for me? I shall wait right here."

Patrick's long fingers curled around the reins. "Oh, I'll take the horse back. But there won't be any carriage coming for you, so you might as well climb back on that animal."

The horse behind her snorted, and she shot it a savage glance. Turning back to the man, she shook her head decidedly. "Thank you, Patrick. I've had more than enough of riding this particular animal." She shifted her weight to her other foot and dropped one and a half inches.

"How'd you lose the heel on that shoe?"

Frowning, Penelope raised up onto the ball of her foot to compensate for the missing heel. "I stepped into a hole."

His lips quirked, and she bit her tongue to keep from

lashing out at him. How dare he laugh at her? After the day *she'd* had?

"All right." He sighed and kicked his left foot out of the stirrup. "Stick your foot in here and hop up. You can ride with me."

Hop up? Penelope's eyebrows lifted. Surely he couldn't be serious. "I prefer to wait for a carriage."

"Maybe. But like I said, there won't be one." He let his gaze wander over the sky before looking back at her. "It's already late afternoon. By the time I get back to the rancho, get a carriage hitched up and sent back for you, it'll be black as pitch out here."

"Surely no later than twilight."

"Lady, there *is* no twilight in the desert. The sun goes down like a rock in a river. And it gets almighty cold out here, too."

Penelope ran one finger under the collar of her now gritty shirt and shrugged under the cloying heat of the black wool riding costume. "I would be *grateful* for the cold, Patrick."

"Hell, woman!" He pushed his hat to the back of his head. "Why don't you take off that damnfool jacket you're wearing?"

"That would hardly be proper."

Patrick shook his head and laughed. His deep voice boomed out around her, and Penelope couldn't help noticing what a fine-looking man he was when he smiled. Of course, his smiles came so infrequently it was hardly surprising she hadn't noticed it before.

"You don't look very proper right now, Penelope!" He waved one hand at her disheveled appearance.

Ruefully she let her own gaze sweep over the clothing that had looked quite presentable only that morning.

Black wool covered in pale, fine dust. A rip in the hem of her skirt, dirt edging the cuffs of her white shirt, and she knew from the angle of the veil over her eyes that her hat was completely askew.

Perhaps he had a point, she told herself.

Grudgingly she smiled and pulled off the constricting, short jacket. Immediately she felt relief as the desert breeze flitted gently over her. She sighed and ran her hand across the back of her neck.

Suddenly awkward, Patrick looked away. With that damn jacket off, Penelope's voluptuous figure was entirely too noticeable. Her long-sleeved shirt was just a bit small, emphasizing all too clearly her firm, generous breasts.

He pulled in a deep breath and told himself to remember who this woman was. Why she was there. He snorted at his own primal reaction to her figure. This was not the type of woman he would be interested in . . . *if* he were looking for a woman, which he was not.

And yet she stirred something inside him that had lain in ashes for longer than he cared to think about.

To conceal his reaction to her, Patrick snapped, "Come on, Penelope. Climb up here."

She eyed the horse warily and he noticed the look she gave *him* was scarcely any better.

"If you don't mind, Patrick," she said, "I believe I'll walk."

He reached down abruptly and grabbed her arm. "I *do* mind, Penelope. If I leave you alone out here, you'd most likely get lost. Then I'd only have to come back out and look for you—in the dark. Frankly, I'm too damned tired for that. So stick your blasted foot in the damn stirrup and swing aboard."

Lips twisted in a mutinous frown, Penelope stepped into the stirrup, grabbed hold of the saddle horn, and pulled.

Patrick guided her up and scooted back in the saddle to make room for her. As she plopped down in front of him, his arms closed around her, holding her securely. With that first touch, though, *something* happened. Lightning seemed to crackle between them. Alive. Dangerous.

She turned to say something and stopped.

Eye to eye, nose to nose, they stared at each other.

Looking into those soft, brown eyes of hers, Patrick suddenly had difficulty breathing. He heard Penelope's short, rapid breaths and knew he wasn't the only one affected.

This had never happened before. He'd never known his heart to beat so wildly. He'd never experienced such a *jolt* of awareness. His gaze moved over her face and for the first time Patrick saw that Penelope wasn't really *plain*. She simply possessed a different sort of beauty.

One that took more than a passing glance to recognize.

She licked her lips, and Patrick's gaze locked on her tongue. Her left hip lay cradled against the juncture of his thighs, and when she shifted slightly, it was all he could do to hold still.

"Patrick . . ."

"Yes?" His eyes continued to rake over her features. He couldn't seem to help himself.

"I . . ."—she paused breathlessly—"perhaps I *should* walk."

"No." He shook his head and forced a deep breath of

air into his lungs. Whatever it was that had gotten into him would surely pass. "No, you'll ride with me. Just . . . turn around and sit still, all right?"

She did as he asked, and Patrick tried to ignore the warmth of her back leaning into his front. It was a short ride to the rancho. He could do this.

"Patrick?"

Shit. Why couldn't she just be quiet? Why had he noticed *now* what a husky, promise-filled voice she had? "Call me Pat. . . . Remember?"

"I prefer Patrick."

"Oh, for—what is it?"

"I only wanted to say that if you would allow me the use of Julietta's sidesaddle while I am visiting—"

"Don't have one." Surprising how simply the mention of Julietta's name obliterated all the crazy wild notions he'd been forming. "She never used one. Liked to ride astride. Besides, it's safer in this kind of country."

"You're hurting me."

"What?"

"Your arms, Patrick." She pushed at the hold he had around her waist. "You're holding me too tightly."

Dammit. Immediately he loosened his hold. "Sorry. Just . . . be quiet—will you!"

Suddenly, all he could think about was the whiskey waiting for him at the rancho. At least when he was drunk, no one spoke to him . . . or if they did, he didn't remember or care.

"Someone in town mentioned that Julietta is engaged to be married."

Maybe if he stayed quiet, he told himself, she'd let it go. He should've known better.

193

"They say that Doña Ana arranged a marriage with Don Vicente Alvarez. . . ."

"Won't happen." There. He'd answered her. Now be quiet, Penelope, he silently ordered. Let it rest.

"Why not?"

Hell. "That's none of your business."

"Does she *want* to marry this Don?"

"No. But it doesn't matter anyway." Why wouldn't she shut up?

"Why not?"

"You are the *nosiest* female I have ever met!" But it was for damn sure she wasn't about to let the subject drop. Best to just get this over with. He took a deep breath and said, "Because whether Julietta wants it or not—if Doña Ana wants it, I'll stop it. *You* should understand that, Miss Butterworth."

"I *do* understand your animosity for Doña Ana. It is your indifference to your daughter that has me perplexed."

She shifted clumsily in the saddle to face him. "Julietta must be pleased by your support in this situation."

He refused to look at her. Instead, Patrick kept his gaze locked on the rancho in the distance. In his mind he'd already poured a full glass of *aguardiente*.

"Patrick!"

Unwillingly he looked down at her and found her eyes boring into his.

"Don't you *care* in the slightest about your own child's happiness?"

Through gritted teeth, he shot back, "I already told you. I will not discuss Julietta with you."

"But why not? She's your daughter!"

His lips twisted into a mocking smile. "Is she?"

* * *

Four days of hard, almost constant riding had brought them deep into New Mexico. Skirting the mountains, the two riders had instead passed through open plains, miles of desert, and even some fine-looking valleys.

More than once Micah'd been tempted to stop and look the land over more closely. But he couldn't. Not now, anyway. Maybe someday, he told himself, he'd come back. Explore a bit.

For now, though, he pulled back on the reins, drawing Satan to a stop. Standing in the stirrups, he looked back over his shoulder for Julie. He smiled to see she was right where she'd been the last four days. About fifty feet behind him and comin' up quick.

He'd pushed her hard these last few days. They'd had almost no rest—sleepin' in snatches when they stopped long enough to give the horses a much needed break. She hadn't complained any—not even about doin' without hot food. Hell, Micah was pretty sure *he* missed his hot coffee more than she did.

Julie'd made do with strips of jerky and some canned peaches they'd picked up at a store in a one-horse town they'd slipped through night before last. She'd kept up with him, no matter what pace he set her, and she hadn't once questioned his decision to travel fast. Of course, *she* didn't want to meet up with Enrique or his pal, either.

A sudden gust of wind blew his hair across his eyes, and he shoved it aside. He stared west, at the jumbled collection of adobe and wood buildings that huddled together just a couple of miles off. In the still, empty desert, sound carried quite a stretch, and Micah heard the muted clang of a blacksmith's hammer stirred up with the unmistakable sounds of some kind of party.

He smiled. Looks like they'd picked a good night to stop. If there was a hoo-rah goin' on in town, folks would be less likely to notice a couple of strangers.

Micah tilted his head back to check the late afternoon sky. High and wide, it seemed to go on forever and then some. Tall, banked clouds backed up against the distant mountains, and the dying rays of the setting sun reached out and colored them a soft orange-gold. Though there wasn't much sign of it, he could smell rain on the wind.

Storm comin'. Sometime soon.

He glanced back at Julie as she got closer. She was really something, he thought. Made him kind of sorry now that he'd thought her just a spoiled, pampered rich girl. She'd done better on this trail than a lot of men he knew would have.

Micah curled his fingers over the saddle horn and leaned forward. Yeah. She was all woman. *And*, he told himself wryly, she'd been remindin' him of that every chance she got, too.

She'd started in lettin' her hand slide over his when she gave him the canteen. And she had a way of stretchin' her muscles here lately that damn near stopped his heart. Every time she raised her arms over her head and twisted from side to side, he had to look away. But lookin' away didn't close his ears to her soft, contented sighs as she worked the kinks out.

He tilted his head and watched her ride up. If he

didn't know better, he'd believe Julie was tryin' to *seduce* him!

And doin' a damn fine job of it, too!

"Why have we stopped?" Julie asked as she drew the mare up alongside Micah.

"Look there," he pointed. "There she is. Good-sized town. Not too big, but big enough to have a hotel, and maybe a judge or sheriff to marry us."

Julie raised up in her stirrups and looked at the little town set down in the middle of the desert. The soft, pale pink of the adobe buildings almost glowed where they were touched by the sun. And at the far end of the village—a church bell tower, crowned by a simple wooden cross. She sat back down in her saddle and hid a smile.

"Micah."

"Yeah?"

"Can you see that bell tower?"

"Yeah, why?"

She shrugged. "It is a church."

"So?"

"Are you Catholic?"

Micah shook his head.

"Well, *I* am." She lowered her gaze, then looked at him through her lashes. "Would you mind if the town priest married us?"

"A priest?"

"*Sí.*"

"Wouldn't it be easier if we just rustled up the sheriff? The justice of the peace?"

She lifted her gaze to his. Looking him squarely in the eye, she said, "If we are married by a priest, the marriage will seem more real . . . to my family, I mean."

"Oh." Slowly he nodded, and she released the breath she'd been holding. "Sure, Julie. Don't matter much to me, I reckon."

"Thank you."

"That's all right." He glanced down at his trail-worn clothes and smacked himself in the chest. A cloud of dust swirled up, and he waved one hand at it. Smiling, he offered, "Before we go see this here priest, though, how about we first stop at a store for some decent clothes?"

"That would be wonderful," she said and plucked daintily at the front of her own shirt. She felt as though she'd been born in the clothes she was wearing. "Do you think we might also find a bath?"

He grinned. "Y'know, that sounds almighty good to me, too. Let's do it."

Before he could urge his horse into a trot, Julie asked quickly, "Micah . . . do you—would you—"

"What is it?"

She sucked in a gulp of air and blew it out in a rush. Julie'd been thinking about this for the last few days and there would never be a better time to ask.

"I was wondering if you would consider shaving off your beard."

"My *beard*?"

"*Sí.* I would very much like to know what my future husband looks like beneath all that hair."

He rubbed one hand along his jaw, lovingly smoothing the rust-brown beard. "I pretty much figured on keeping it—at least till I got back home."

She tilted her head and watched him.

"I usually grow the damn thing over the winter 'cause it's too blasted cold to shave."

"It is not that cold now. . . ."

"No . . . but it will be when my chin's naked."

"If you would rather not . . ."

"Ah, hell." He shrugged and smiled. "Don't make that much difference if I shave it now or later. And I reckon you got a right to say what you want your husband to look like at the weddin'."

"*Gracias*, Micah."

"It's all right. Hell, we don't want that priest of yours thinkin' this weddin' ain't just right, do we?"

Julie picked up her reins again and began to follow Micah as he led the way to the nearby town. Soon she would be a married woman. And she *had* to be married by the priest.

She would see to it.

*　　*　　*

Penelope swallowed her doubts and pulled open the top desk drawer. She frowned at the messy contents. Crumpled receipts, a water stained ledger. Her eyes opened wide when she spied a Derringer pistol tucked into the corner of the drawer.

Carefully, as if the gun might go off by itself, she slid the drawer shut. Shaking her head, she reached for the knob on the next drawer. If only she could rid herself of the guilt nagging at her for going through Patrick's desk.

But she needed writing paper, and she couldn't very well ask him for it. He'd hardly spoken to her since that afternoon four days ago when he'd found her walking back from town. And even then she thought, pursing her lips, he hadn't *spoken* to her. *Shouted* was the correct term.

She leaned her palms on the desktop for a moment. Since that ride they'd shared, he'd avoided spending any time with her at all. It was as if he was a phantom in his own house. She never saw him, never heard him. He left the rancho each morning before anyone was up and didn't return until long after supper each evening.

And as for his hinting that Julietta was not his child— well, she didn't believe that for a moment. No matter *how* much he hated Doña Ana, *no* man would go to the trouble he had to protect Julietta unless he loved her.

After some spirited questioning, Juana had at last told Penelope about the man Patrick had hired to escort his daughter home. Surely, if Julietta meant as little to him as he claimed, he wouldn't have bothered trying to ensure her safety.

She straightened up and brushed her palms together. Patrick Duffy, it seemed, was no different from any other man she'd encountered over the years. Excepting Eustace, of course. Logic had little to do with their actions.

Quickly she opened and shut three more drawers in Patrick's massive desk. She tried not to look at anything that might be private and told herself that with everything in such a jumble, it was unlikely that Patrick kept his personal papers there, anyway.

Her fingers slipped through stacks of documents, searching for blank paper. She wanted to write a few letters. No, she thought firmly, she *needed* to write the letters. One to the marshal of El Paso, one to the mayor, and one to Doña Ana Santos.

With or without Patrick Duffy's help, she *would* get to the bottom of Eustace's death.

Disgusted and about to give up, Penelope yanked open the bottom and final desk drawer. It was empty but for a framed daguerreotype.

Penelope bent down and picked it up. Turning the portrait toward the window, she stared at the image of a pretty, young woman. Black hair framed her oval face, pale, haunted eyes looked directly into the camera, and a soft, sad smile curved her lips.

Julietta. It had to be.

Penelope stepped closer to the window and tilted the framed image a bit, allowing the last of the sunlight to fall directly onto it. She shook her head as she studied the young woman's features.

Though not an exact replica, the girl certainly carried the stamp of her father on her. The resemblance was in their eyes, mostly, and the shape of their mouths. How could he look into that face and harbor any doubts at all?

"Patrick Michael Duffy, you're a fool."

"Thank you very much," a voice answered, and Penelope jumped, startled. She looked at the open doorway and met Patrick's infuriated gaze.

"Who the hell do you think you are, rooting through my desk?"

"I had no intention of *rooting* through anything," she countered and felt the blush of shame creep up her cheeks.

"Intention or not, that's precisely what you've done!" He crossed the room in a few angry strides. "Just what are you up to now, Miss Butterworth?"

She swallowed back her nervousness and lifted the portrait until he looked at it. "I *believe*," she said, "that I am finally meeting Julietta. Your daughter."

CHAPTER
···FOURTEEN···

THE ENTIRE VILLAGE of Vacio had turned out for a fiesta.

Micah gave the blacksmith a dollar and left the livery stable to join Julie. She stood in a slice of candlelight thrown from a hanging lantern, her eyes fixed on the party in the small plaza.

He stepped up behind her and followed her gaze. It seemed theirs wouldn't be the only wedding that day. A young couple, obviously bride and groom, danced together in the middle of a cheering crowd. The bride's white lace dress flew out around her ankles as her new husband spun her in circles to the delight of their audience.

Micah glanced down at the woman beside him. A soft smile tugged at her lips, and he noticed her right foot tapping in time with the musicians. That's what she ought to have, he told himself solemnly.

A real weddin', with her friends and such around her. Not some make-believe ceremony in a nowhere town all alone. Maybe seein' all this, he thought, would make her change her mind. Make her see this idea of hers for the craziness it really was.

He gripped his shotgun a bit tighter. Even crazier, he

told himself, was how the thought of *not* marryin' her left him with such a lonely, miserable feeling.

Foolishness. If she changed her mind, he couldn't hardly blame her.

"Are you ready, Micah?" she asked, turning to look up at him.

"Yeah, Julie. I am." He shifted the saddlebags a little higher on his shoulder and steeled himself to give her a chance to back out. "How 'bout you? You still want to do this? You know, don't ya, that I'll see ya safe home even if we ain't married?"

"I know." She laid one hand on his arm. "But I will feel much safer knowing that I am your wife." She looked away and mumbled, "If only for a short time."

"All right then." He straightened up, more relieved than he'd admit. "Let's us get over to the store first, then find a hotel."

A half hour later, Micah stood in a tavern called El Gato Desierto. Julie'd told him it meant the Desert Cat, but he didn't much care. As long as the place had a room with a bed and a bath for Julie, that's all he'd ask.

The little man behind the desk smiled up at him and spoke in rapid-fire Spanish. Micah could only shrug and point at the sign-in book.

"*¡Sí, sí!*" The man grinned and turned the book toward his guest.

Staring down at the page filled with names, Micah hesitated only a moment before slowly writing *Mr. and Mrs. Benteen*. He hid a smile as he admired his handiwork. Imagine that. *Him*. Married.

Well, he would be soon, anyhow.

"*¿Su esposa?*"

Micah looked at him through squinted eyes. *Esposa.*

What? "Sorry, mister. I just don't understand Spanish much."

The little man looked frustrated for an instant, then smiled, pointed to his ring finger and repeated, *"¿Su esposa?"*

Esposa. Spouse. Wife.

"Oh! She's over to the store." Hell, the man didn't understand English any better than Micah did Spanish. Pointing at the general store across the street, Micah said firmly, *"Esposa."*

"Ah, sí."

"Can you fix up a bath for her, mister?"

"¿Que?"

Hell. Micah rubbed his chin thoughtfully. This language thing was gonna be a problem. He should've waited for Julie. But the way she was wanderin' around that store, fingerin' everything the owner had, he'd known she was gonna be there for some time.

Still went against the grain some, how Julie'd insisted on payin' for her own clothes. But at least, he'd held his ground about payin' for the hotel room. Havin' a wife with money was no easy thing.

But it was too late to worry about that now. Now all he wanted to do was get Julie all set here and then find a barbershop. Most times barbers had a bathhouse, too. He could get cleaned up there. By thunder, he wasn't about to sit in a hotel room listening to her takin' another bath.

There wasn't a chance in hell he could survive *that* again.

Bath. How was he supposed to make this man understand what he needed? The fella seemed helpful enough, but his face was all screwed up like Micah was something that had just dropped out of the sky.

Another burst of Spanish shot out of the man, and Micah stared at him helplessly. "Bath?" he repeated a little louder this time. Then he caught himself. The man wasn't deaf!

Realizing he'd have to show the man, Micah sighed, set his gun, saddlebags, and packages down on the desktop and began to take a pretend bath.

When his host nodded and began to mutter, Micah told himself there was an answer to every problem. All you had to do was find it.

Julie stood in front of the warped, wavy mirror and grinned. It truly was amazing how much better a hot bath and fresh clothes could make a person feel. She tilted her head and smoothed her palms down over her hips.

It was not exactly the wedding dress she'd dreamed of as a child . . . but somehow this was better. The sunshine yellow, off-the-shoulder cotton blouse skimmed across the tops of her breasts, displaying to perfection her honey-colored flesh. Red-and-blue embroidered flowers stitched along the neckline matched the handwork along the hem of the full, black skirt that fell to the middle of her shins.

Making a half turn, she glanced over her shoulder to check the hang of her skirt. When she caught her own reflected gaze, she stopped and smiled. A leap of excitement burst through her as she realized that she would be married in just an hour or so.

Married. How she'd dreaded that word. But now,

knowing it was Micah—not Don Vicente—who would be her husband, it filled her with an eager anticipation.

At the knock on the door, Julie spun around, slipped her feet into a brand-new pair of brown leather sandals, and snatched a white lace mantilla off the end of the bed.

She yanked the door open and stared, openmouthed at the man on the threshold.

He looked wonderful. His unruly hair had been trimmed and neatly combed. The beard he'd hidden behind so long was gone, revealing a stong jaw and just the hint of a cleft in his chin. He wore a dark green, long-sleeved cotton shirt tucked into the waistband of his freshly brushed buckskins, and for the first time since she'd known him, he wasn't carrying his shotgun in the crock of his arm.

"Micah!"

He smiled self-consciously and rubbed one hand along his clean jaw. "Can't say I didn't warn ya."

She stepped into the hall and slipped her hand through the bend of his elbow. Looking up at him, she said softly, "I was only surprised because I had no idea my husband would be such a handsome man."

A rush of pent-up breath left him, and Julie realized that he was *nervous*.

"You all set, Hoo-lee-edda?"

"I am all set, Mr. Benteen."

At the small, adobe church of San Paulo, Micah stood to one side while Julie spoke to the priest. Father Garcia's dusty black cassock pooled around his sandal-clad feet and in one beefy hand he held a clay mug filled to the brim with foamy *cerveza*.

"Padre," she said in Spanish, shouting to be heard above the villagers attending the fiesta, "we wish to be married tonight."

"Tonight?"

The short man's round, red face screwed up in confusion. His bristle of gray hair stood out around his head like a tarnished halo, and Julie could smell the beer on his breath. He swayed unsteadily until Julie's restraining hand caught his arm. Obviously the little priest had been celebrating with his congregation.

"Sí, Padre. Tonight." She flicked a quick glance at Micah, then looked back at the priest.

Candles inside the multicolored lanterns hanging in the square tossed a rainbow of light over his gentle features. The cleric paused, then turned to look at the tall gringo curiously before asking, "Why tonight, my child? This is not proper. The banns must be read."

Thinking fast, Julie looked directly into the man's kind, gray eyes and lied. "Forgive me, Padre," she said, "but I am pregnant." Another quick glance at Micah to see if by some wild chance he recognized the word *encita.* She sighed in relief. He appeared to be as confused as ever.

The priest, though, turned disappointed eyes on her and shot Micah a malevolent look.

"What? What is it?" Micah asked.

Julie ignored him. "My father," she explained, silently pleading forgiveness, "does not approve of my sweetheart."

"Perhaps your papa is right, my daughter," he answered, never moving his disgusted gaze from a bewildered Micah. "I am sure, if you go to your papa with your ... *problem*, all will be forgiven." He hiccuped and covered his mouth guiltily.

This was not going well, Julie told herself. She had expected the priest to be more willing.

"Is he at least a Catholic?" the priest asked hopefully.

"No, Padre."

He shook his head, wobbled a bit, then straightened again carefully. "This is not good. A gringo, not a Catholic, *and* he has gotten you with child."

"He did not do that alone, Padre."

A quick intake of breath was his only reply, save for the narrowing of his bushy gray eyebrows.

"Julie, what's goin' on?"

She waved one hand at him and kept her attention fastened on the priest. Desperate, she said quickly, "Padre, if you will not marry us tonight, I will live in sin with this man, and it will be *you* who must answer to God."

"What're you tellin' him?" Micah demanded, "and why's he lookin' at me like he wants my scalp?"

"One moment, Micah. Please." Staring at the befuddled priest, she asked, "Well, Padre? Will you marry us?"

The man was clearly unhappy with the whole situation. After what seemed like centuries, though, he nodded. "I will. In your ... condition, I suppose even a *pagan* is better than no husband at all."

Julie almost crumpled in relief. *"Sí, Padre. Gracias."* She hurried to Micah's side and together they followed the priest into the church.

The inside of the small, adobe building was cool and dark. Whitewashed walls sparkled with the shadows of dozens of candles. High in the bell tower, a single, stained-glass window, its colors quiet in the dark, waited for sunrise and the chance to shine again.

At the altar Micah stood tall, with Julie's hand tucked firmly in the crook of his arm. Behind the little priest hung a hand-carved crucifix and even more candles clustered at its base. Sounds of the fiesta were muted by the thick adobe walls, and the tiny church seemed alone, set apart from the rest of the world.

Micah shifted from foot to foot nervously while the cleric's fingers riffled through the pages of a prayer book.

Julie squeezed his arm, and he covered her hand with his own. Studying her from the corner of his eye, Micah told himself again what a lucky man he was. Her dark head bent, white lace fell down over her shoulders and settled on her lightly bronzed flesh. The scent of jasmine clung to her and Micah knew that however long they were together, he'd always be grateful.

When the priest began to talk, Micah listened carefully, even though he didn't understand a word of the ceremony. Julie gave the padre their names and told Micah when to say, "I do." Before Micah knew it, the whole thing was over, and he was a married man.

Father Garcia slapped his book shut, looked at Micah, and rattled off a stream of Spanish in a none too friendly voice.

"What'd he say?"

Julie looked up at him and smiled. "He says congratulations. You may kiss the bride."

Micah glanced at the old boy again, and he was willing to bet that congratulations didn't have a blessed thing to do with that speech.

"Micah?"

He looked back at his new wife. Her eyes shining, she asked, "Will you not kiss me to seal our marriage?"

You better not, his brain warned. Best if you just keep your distance.

Julie ran one hand up his arm and cupped his face gently. The feel of her hand on his jaw was like a match set to dry brush. Telling his brain to shut up, Micah bent down and slanted his mouth across hers.

She leaned into him, and his arms went around her instinctively. His wounded shoulder well on the mend, he ignored the small twinge of pain. He would endure much worse to be able to hold her.

When she opened her mouth to him, Micah's tongue swept inside her warmth and all conscious thought stopped. His body reacted immediately. Pressing her tightly along the length of him. Micah held her hips firmly against his until he heard her moan softly.

He felt her fingers lace through his hair and tasted her hunger with her every touch. A groan escaped him, and he broke away desperately, breathlessly.

"¡Basta! ¡Violador!"

Micah looked up through passion-glazed eyes at the priest. The little man was hopping up and down rattling off Spanish at a frightening speed.

Quickly they signed the church register the little priest thrust at them. Julie began to tug at Micah's arm until she had him moving quickly down the short center aisle. Even outside, over the noise of the fiesta, Micah could still hear the priest ranting and raving. Coming to a sudden stop, Micah demanded, "What the hell is he yellin'?"

She looked at him, licked her lips, then tossed a

glance back at the closed door of the church. Quickly she said, "He was inviting us to the fiesta. He wishes us Godspeed."

Micah laughed inwardly. Judgin' by her sweet, innocent look he thought, a body'd never guess she was such a liar. He knew damn well that priest wasn't callin' down a blessin' on them. More'n likely, a curse.

But, if Julie didn't care ... why the hell should he? Laying his arm around her shoulders, he pulled her close. "Well then, as long as we're invited, why don't we go join the party?"

Everywhere they walked they were met by smiles and laughter. It seemed folks from miles around had gathered to celebrate, and they'd pulled out all the stops. When the music started up again and the square filled with the soft sounds of guitars, Julie drew him to the outskirts of the crowd.

"Dance with me, husband."

He looked around at the other couples and hesitated. "I don't know, Julie. You give me a square dance, and I do all right, but I ain't sure about this slow movin'."

"Please?"

She held her arms out to him, and Micah knew he would brave anything to be able to hold her close again. As she fit her body tightly to his, Micah's right hand moved over her back to settle on the curve of her hip. She laid her head on his chest, and the scent of jasmine clinging to her filled him until nothing in the world existed except Julie.

Her left hand encircled the back of his neck, and her fingers began to slowly tease his flesh. A tremor shook him, and he deliberately took long, steady breaths, trying for control. Then she tilted her head and kissed the base of his throat, lingering on his pounding pulse.

Micah groaned and slid his right hand down over her behind. Cupping her gently, he pulled her against him and held her until he knew she was aware of his need. But she didn't pull away. Instead, she ground her hips slightly, as if trying to get even closer to him, and Micah was lost.

Lowering his head, he took her mouth in a firm, yet gentle pressure that grew stronger with their growing hunger. She threaded her fingers through his hair and held his head down on hers, demanding more from him. Her tongue met his in a clash of passion, and her soft groan of pleasure stabbed at Micah like a hot knife.

The sounds of the fiesta faded away. The other dancers ceased to exist. As if they were alone, they clung together desperately, and when Micah's hand moved to cup her breast, Julie broke away from his mouth and gasped for air. Throwing her head back, eyes closed, she covered his hand with hers, telling him without words what he needed to know.

"Julie . . ." He bent and ran his lips and tongue down the length of her neck. His thumb and forefinger circled her nipple through the thin fabric of her blouse, and he felt her tremble. "Julie, if I don't stop now . . ." He straightened up and waited for her to open her eyes to look at him. Raw hunger and passion glazed the clear blue of her eyes, and it was all he could do not to take her right there. But he had to give her one last chance to change her mind. "If I don't stop now . . . I won't stop at all."

She licked her lips slowly and then lifted his hand from her breast. Bringing it to her lips, Julie kissed each of his fingers, letting her tongue move over his callused flesh.

His jaw clenched, he waited, struggling for breath.

When she'd kissed his palm, she moved his hand back to cover her breast and deliberately held it there. Then she said softly, "Don't stop, Micah. Please don't stop."

He groaned, bent, and swept her up into his arms. Cuddling her close, Micah moved through the crowd like a madman. Stepping around the revelers, he hurried to the hotel.

Micah set her on her feet, then tossed the worn, flowered quilt to the foot of the bed. With the hush of the surrounding thick, adobe walls and the feeble light of a single oil lamp, the little room seemed a cozy haven.

Nervous, Julie looked up at him and felt her heart skip as his eyes moved over her hungrily. Slowly he bent and took her lips in a gentle kiss, playing with her mouth, teasing her flesh until she could think of nothing but him.

His arms slipped around her, and she was grateful for his strength. Micah's hard body pressed close to hers, she felt their hearts pound in tandem. Her eyes closed, she leaned into him.

With every caress of his mouth, Julie's breath quickened. His tongue traced warm patterns on her lips until she opened her mouth and welcomed him inside. Her hands clutched at his shoulders, and she boldly matched his tongue, stroke for stroke, with her own. She heard her blood rushing through her body, her heartbeat pounding in her ears. She heard him groan gently as he broke away from her mouth and moved his lips to her neck.

Inch by glorious inch, his lips and tongue slid down her flesh, and she tilted her head to give him access. The warmth of him, the incredible heat of his mouth on her body, melted the strength in her legs, and she wobbled uncertainly.

Tenderly he backed her up until her knees met the edge of the mattress. Then he eased her down to sit on the bed. His hands moved up to her shoulders, his callused fingers dancing gently across her skin.

She opened her eyes and found his gaze locked on her. His features strained, breath rapid, he seemed to be waiting for a sign from her before continuing his magic. Deliberately Julie raised her palms to his face and cupped his cheeks. Drawing him close, she dropped soft kisses on his mouth, his cheeks, his jaw. She felt his hands tighten on her shoulders and then the unmistakable feel of her blouse as it slipped down.

Straightening her shoulders, she sat perfectly still and watched as Micah slowly lowered the edge of her bright yellow shirt. As each new inch of flesh was exposed, Micah leaned forward and claimed it with a kiss.

Julie shuddered and swallowed heavily. When cool night air moved across her naked breasts, she inhaled sharply and watched. Micah's fingers moved over her breast, each in turn, with care. The thumb and forefinger of each hand encircled her erect nipples and stroked them gently. Julie gasped and arched her back.

An incredible bolt of pure pleasure shot through her, and she wanted to tell him to do it again. But she couldn't find her voice. When his fingers continued to toy with her flesh, she smiled and let her head fall back on her neck.

She heard him groan and in the next instant felt his mouth close over her nipple. Julie's head snapped back up, and her eyes locked on his mouth as he suckled at her.

"Dios mio," she whispered and cupped the back of his head tenderly. Her eyes closed to slits, she shifted position, moving her hips against the mattress in response to a sudden, warm tingle between her thighs.

On his knees in front of her, Micah moved in closer to the bed, spreading her legs apart and kneeling between them. With a last, slow lick of his tongue he moved to her other breast, and the sensations coursing through her came again, stronger this time.

Forcing herself to open her eyes, Julie watched Micah's mouth close on her right breast. With her left hand she cupped the nipple he'd abandoned and shivered at her own touch on the sensitive flesh.

Her hips twisted again seemingly of their own volition, and Julie licked her lips before saying softly, "Micah?"

"Yes," he murmured and drew his tongue across her hard brown nipple.

"Ah, Dios," she sighed and arched into him. "Micah, why is it I feel your touch in . . . other places?"

She felt his smile against her breast, and then he slid his right hand up under the hem of her skirt and along the line of her leg to her thigh. Julie jumped slightly.

He pulled his head back to look at her. When he noticed her hand at her breast, Julie immediately lowered it, embarrassed. Quickly Micah lifted her hand and placed the palm back where it had been.

She looked down, unwilling to let him read the brazenness in her eyes. But Micah dipped his head until he could see her face, then kissed her gently.

"Don't look away, Julie. Not from me." His breath fanned her cheek. "Not ever." Then, beneath her skirt, he moved his hand to cup her center, the core of the tingling that threatened to drive her mad.

"Micah." Even through the thin fabric of her underdrawers, she felt the heat of his touch. "What . . . ?"

"It's all right, Julie," he whispered, lowering his head to taste her nipple again. "Everything is all right. Lay back, now, darlin'."

She nodded and did as he asked. In truth, with this hand stroking fire across her throbbing body, she could not have argued had she wanted to. Staring up at the whitewashed ceiling, Julie felt him untie the strings around her waist and slide the petal-soft fabric of her drawers down over her legs.

His hands smoothed back up her limbs, and his touch on her bare body stoked the fire in her blood to a raging blaze. When he tugged her skirt free, then joined her on the mattress to pull her blouse off, Julie lay, for the first time in her life, naked against cool sheets with the night air caressing her body.

She watched him as he undressed, and her throat tightened at first sight of his broad, muscled chest with just a sprinkling of fine, blond hair. He held her gaze as he removed the rest of his clothing, and when he stood naked beside the bed, looking down at her, Julie felt only a moment's hesitation at the sight of his hard body.

And then he was beside her on the mattress, his hands moving over her flesh. He kissed her gently, then moved his lips to explore the body his hands knew so well. As his mouth caressed her breasts, his hand slipped down past the small patch of dark curls just below her abdomen.

Julie instinctively opened her thighs for him, arching into his hand. And when his fingers slipped inside her, she groaned aloud. His thumb rubbed slowly across a tender bit of flesh while his fingers moved in and out of her body, coaxing the tingling she'd felt before into something that threatened to consume her.

Propping himself up on one arm, Micah looked down into her eyes, silently demanding that she not look away. Julie licked her lips, pulled her knees up and began to twist her hips furiously in a maddening quest for something she couldn't even name.

He lowered his mouth to hers, and after kissing her, pulled back only a breath and whispered against her mouth, "Feel it, darlin', let it take over now. Don't fight it. Don't think."

She nodded, swallowed, and gave herself up to the fire between her thighs. With every stroke of his thumb, shots of fire raced through her. Every time his fingers left her body, she wanted to cry out, only to sigh as he plunged back into her warmth again.

Her hips lifted from the bed. Her head tossed from side to side, and still her body climbed toward some distant peak.

"Micah . . ." Something was happening. She felt as though she was about to burst apart. Desperately she reached for him, holding his naked shoulders with a fierce grip. She arched once more into his hand, looked into the deep green of his eyes, and cried out as something deep inside her splintered, sending her beyond anything she'd ever known before.

And before her body had quit its trembling, Micah moved to kneel between her legs. She opened her thighs wide for him, eager to give him what he'd given her. He lifted her hips slightly and inched his body into hers.

Slowly, agonizingly slowly, he entered her. As their bodies became one, Julie reached down and ran her fingers across his thighs. His features tightened, but he didn't hurry his movements. A heartbeat at a time, Micah's body became a part of her. And when he stopped, she wanted to shout at him to go on . . . to go deeper.

"This might hurt some, Julie," he whispered through clenched teeth. "But only a bit and only the first time, I swear it."

She reached her arms out to him and wiggled her hips. "Fill me with you, Micah. I want to feel all of you."

He raised up, leaned over her, and as he plunged himself home, he caught her lips with his. A brief stab of pain and then there was only Micah. Moving in and out of her body, rubbing against her still throbbing skin, bringing her to even higher peaks than she'd reached before.

Her legs locked around his middle, she moved with him, instinctively urging him on. Julie's hands coursed up and down his broad back, reveling in the feel of him. And as the now familiar tingling began to explode in her, Micah whispered her name and convulsed as his body shattered in hers.

CHAPTER
···FIFTEEN···

HE COULDN'T BELIEVE it! He wouldn't have thought Penelope Butterworth the kind of woman to go snooping through a man's desk!

Everything he'd heard in El Paso faded from his mind. Racing his horse at breakneck speed for the rancho disappeared from his memory. In fact, everything he'd planned on saying to Penelope was forgotten in an instant.

Never had he expected to find her rummaging through his papers! And then to face him down without the slightest bit of shame in her eyes, waving Julietta's portrait like a broadsword at an enemy!

Jesus! Who in heaven had he offended to such a degree that they considered Penelope Butterworth just punishment? Why the hell hadn't she stayed in England, where she belonged? And as long as she was here, why didn't she have the decency to stop pouring salt on old, infected wounds?

Patrick snatched the picture from her hands. "You had no right." He spoke through clenched teeth, hoping to salvage at least *some* of his normal control.

"She's lovely."

Two words. Two simple words and they took the breath from him as easily as a punch to the stomach.

Unwillingly his eyes strayed to the portrait. In the half light of early evening he couldn't see it well. But that didn't matter, God knew. Even blind, Patrick would know every shadow, every line, of that portrait. It was ingrained in his soul.

It had been months since he'd last had the nerve to look at it. And then, he remembered, he was reeling drunk and took his courage from the bottom of a bottle of *aguardiente*.

Dead sober now, he stared at the image behind the glass. Julietta's eyes seemed to bore into his. Accusing, reproachful. But that was in his mind, he knew. In life, Julietta had never commented on his treatment of her. Maybe it would have been better if she had.

He shook his head. Too late for any of that now. And yet, it seemed important that he answer Penelope's statement. "Yes, she is lovely."

"Well done, Patrick!"

"What?" He looked at the aggravating woman and wasn't the least bit surprised to see a self-satisfied smile on her face.

"I said, well done!" She took a half step toward him. "You actually *spoke* about your daughter."

His lips twisted. God, what he'd come to.

"She has your look about her, you know."

Patrick flicked a quick glance at the portrait. Did she? he wondered. Was it there for anyone to see? Or did Penelope see what she expected to see? Lord knew, there was a time when he'd stared into Julietta's face, trying to convince himself that there was something of him in her. But then, each time he found a resemblance, he'd put it down to wishful thinking. Until finally he'd stopped trying, unwilling to torture himself *or* the girl any further.

And now, he told himself, this woman had stirred it all up again. Anger flared up deep within him. And though he *knew* it was unreasonable to blame Penelope for the pain of old wounds, he did. It was much safer for everyone concerned if he remained shuttered behind the now familiar wall of bitterness.

And he wouldn't let himself dwell on what might have been anymore, either. It was too late for him *and* for Julietta. Whatever chance they'd had at a normal father-daughter connection had long since slipped away. What's past was past and best left there.

He pulled in a deep, ragged breath. "She looks like her mother."

"Her coloring, perhaps. Except for the eyes, of course."

Penelope stood beside him, almost touching him. He inhaled the soft, clean scent of her and felt something inside him quake unsteadily. She looked down at the image in the frame.

"But her features, Patrick, are yours."

He pushed the renegade feelings aside. There was no place for them in his life. Besides, he thought with a silent laugh. He could just imagine Penelope's reaction if she ever guessed the effect her nearness had on him.

Instead, he concentrated on the image in the frame. What does Penelope see? he asked himself silently. How can she be so certain? And why can't *I* feel that certainty, too? His fingers tightened on the ornate frame until his knuckles stood out stark white against the honey gold tan of his hands.

221

"Patrick?" she whispered, and he felt the warmth of her hand as she touched his forearm. "Patrick, what is it?"

He stared at her hand for a long moment. Long enough to notice how deceptively fragile it appeared. Fragile. Hah! Penelope Butterworth might be many things, but *fragile* wasn't one of them.

Too close. She was too close. He swallowed heavily. Deliberately he backed off a pace. He tried to ignore how suddenly lonely he felt when he moved away from her touch. Patrick kept his eyes averted from her, not daring to look at her. If he risked it and saw sympathy ... compassion in her eyes ... No.

He breathed deeply and walked to his desk. Fanciful notions and a wild, unreasonable hunger for the woman faded with each step. Distance. He needed distance between them.

Gently he slipped Julietta's portrait back into the drawer and firmly closed it. Leaning his palms flat on the big desk, Patrick looked up at the woman across the room from him.

She stood as straight as a well-made arrow. Her hair done up in a no-nonsense upsweep, her hands clasped together at her waist, the very image of composure. Patrick told himself that to look at her, no one would believe the fiery determination behind that placid, plain face. No one would believe the amount of trouble she was capable of stirring up.

Trouble. A mild word indeed for what she'd begun with her clumsy questioning of the people in El Paso. He shook his head again and drew another long breath.

"I have to talk to you."

"Good," she said quickly and began to walk toward him.

"No." He shook his head and stood up straight. "Not about Julietta. About you. And what you've done."

"I?"

"Yes, Penelope. *You.*"

Her hand at her breast, she tilted her head and stared at him curiously. "For heaven's sake, Patrick. What on earth have *I* done?"

Patrick's booted foot kicked out at his overstuffed leather chair, and he watched her jump as it crashed into the opposite wall. Running one hand over his jaw, he mentally counted to twenty. This was *not* the time to lose his temper.

Besides, he wasn't sure any longer if he was angry about what she'd done or about his own body's traitorous response to the woman's presence. And it was hardly fair to blame *her* for the latter.

Telling himself to go slowly, carefully, Patrick said, "When you went to town a few days ago . . . what exactly did you do?"

"Do?" Penelope lifted her chin defiantly. "I did precisely what I came here to do. I started asking questions."

"Who'd you talk to?"

"The deputy, for one."

"Uh-huh." He nodded abruptly. "Go on."

She sniffed delicately. "Do you want a complete list of everyone I spoke with?"

"Yes." Patrick stepped out from behind his desk. The calm he'd hoped for hadn't come, and as he looked into her eyes and saw not the slightest *hint* of regret, he realized that *calm* was not an emotion associated with Penelope.

"Then," she said, with more than a note of annoyance, "I suggest that instead of *kicking* the furnishings"—she pointed at the leather chair, now five feet away from the desk—"you sit down. This may take quite a while. I spoke to many people, you know." She seated herself in a straight-backed chair alongside the desk and folded her hands neatly in her lap. "One doesn't travel several thousand miles to shilly-shally!"

His eyebrows shot straight up. "Shilly-shally?" Patrick gave her a brief nod. "If *that's* the way you asked your questions in El Paso, it's no *wonder* at least three different people stopped to tell me that 'Señora Butterworth is in danger.' "

"What?"

* * *

Micah stared at the ceiling and tried to catch his breath. Julie snuggled in close and he wrapped his left arm around her, pulling her tight against him. He'd never felt so complete—and yet so empty—in his life.

Lord, he thought with a silent groan, how in the hell had he let that happen? He was supposed to protect her—not take advantage of her. For God's sake, he'd acted like some rutting, out-of-control boy.

Julie ran her fingers lightly across his chest, and his body shook. Just the touch of her hand was enough to wipe away his last best intentions. Holy Hell, what a mess they were in now! Her fingers danced across his flat nipple, and he grabbed her hand, stilling the action.

"Micah . . ."

"Yeah?"

"Do not feel badly. We are married. We did nothing wrong."

He looked down and found her watching him through wide, blue eyes. Jesus, she even knew what he was *thinking*.

"Not wrong, maybe," he said and couldn't quite stop himself from sliding his hand up and down her naked back, "but it surely wasn't smart."

She kissed his side and pushed herself up until she was half lying atop him, her chin resting on the forearm stretched across his chest. Her foot moved over his leg slowly, and Micah sucked in a great gulp of air.

"I wanted this, too, Micah. Do not be so worried about me."

Looking into her eyes, Micah wanted to believe that it would be all right. But how could it be? They would still be getting a divorce. And now she'd never be able to get that durned annulment she'd talked about.

She pulled her fingers from his grasp and began to stroke his chest idly, thoughtfully. He tried to close his mind to the incredible sensations her touch aroused, but it was impossible. And when she ran her tongue over his nipple, Micah damn near came off the bed.

"Julie," he ground out and lifted her chin until she was looking at him, "you best, uh . . . get some sleep now. We got to get back on the trail early."

She turned her head and kissed his palm. "How early?"

"Real early," he answered, his jaw tight.

Julie levered herself up higher, pulling her body along the length of him until she was able to touch his mouth with her own. Her teeth nibbled at his bottom lip, and her tongue flicked quickly against his mouth, demanding a response from him.

A man could only stand so much, he told himself before threading his fingers through her hair and slanting his lips across hers in a kiss that left them both breathless. Finally, reluctantly though, he broke away and said softly, "We got to stop this, Julie. It's no good."

"You didn't enjoy it?"

A half grin tilted his mouth. "Hell yes, I enjoyed it. And you know good and well that ain't what I meant."

She smiled, propped her elbows on his chest, and let her long, loose hair fall on either side of his face like a thick, black curtain. "I am glad to hear it because *I* think it is *very* good."

"You cut it out now, y'hear? You ain't makin' this any easier on me." He tried to sound stern, but the curve of her lips defeated him. "Hell, Julie. I'd like nothin' better than to spend the rest of the night lovin' you."

"Good."

"But"—he raised up and planted a quick, light kiss on her mouth—"we can't. We're too close to the end of this now."

"What do you mean?"

"I mean, if we push on hard, we should be to your pa's place inside the week."

She stiffened, and the playful expression on her face slipped away. Hell, he hadn't *wanted* to remind her of all the things waitin' on them. But there was no way to get around any of them, either.

She laid her head down on his chest, and instinctively his arms closed around her. Was she still scared? Didn't she believe him when he said he'd protect her from her pa and granny? Didn't she know that he wouldn't leave her with her family? He'd promised to take her back to Montana before going his own way . . . and that's just what he was gonna do.

"Julie?"

She heard the regret in his voice. It matched the ache deep inside her. Julie didn't want to answer him. She didn't want to talk about the end of their journey. She didn't want to think about him leaving her.

"Julie?" he went on softly, "don't you worry about your folks, now. Everything's gonna be fine."

His hands moved over her back, and she concentrated on the rough, gentle slide of his flesh on hers. Didn't he understand? She wasn't concerned about her family. She trusted Micah completely and knew that he would keep her safe from Doña Ana and Don Vicente.

What he'd said only a moment ago kept rattling over and over in her brain. Inside the week. Their journey would be finished inside the week.

She slid one hand up along his arm and around his neck. Julie listened to the steady beat of his heart beneath her cheek and knew that she had to try harder.

She didn't have much time left to convince him that they should not be separated. Somehow, in the next week, she had to show Micah that he would not be happy without her.

"Micah," she whispered and blew gently at the few golden hairs on his chest, "thank you for allowing the priest to marry us."

He gave her a quick squeeze. "That's all right. Didn't

bother me any"—a deep chuckle escaped him—"but it sure didn't seem to set too well with the padre."

Julie grinned, remembering all of the colorful words the little priest had hurled at an unsuspecting Micah's head. She would never have guessed that a *priest* would know such language!

"Here, now, I can *feel* that smile of yours. . . ."

"I am *not* smiling," she shot back and muffled a giggle against his chest.

"I can see that. Well, s'pose you answer me a question then, Miss Solemn Face. What was that little fella yellin' at me there in church right after the weddin'?"

"After?" she asked and bit down on her lip.

"Yeah, *after*." Micah tilted her chin up with the tip of a finger. When their eyes met, he lifted one eyebrow and said, "When I was kissin' you, that little priest commenced hoppin' up and down and yellin' like a Comanche!" His eyes screwed up and he added, "I remember him sayin' somethin' about a violin. . . ."

Laughter burst from her throat before she could hold it back. Micah's confused expression tickled her even more, and she had to fight to catch her breath.

"What's so damn funny?"

"Oh, Micah . . ." Julie touched his cheek, then traced her fingers up to his forehead, where she smoothed his hair back. "He did not say 'violin.' He said, *'¡Basta! ¡Violador!'* "

"Yeah. That's it." A half smile curved his lips. "So what's it mean?"

Julie grinned and looked directly into his eyes. " 'Stop! Rapist!' "

"RAPIST!" Clearly outraged, Micah's eyebrows shot

straight up and his face flushed a deep red. "I don't see what's so goddamned funny about *that*!"

"Ah, Micah," she whispered and slid her body to lie full length atop his, "it is funny because there is so much the good father did not understand...."

"Like what?" he mumbled and let his hands trail down her back to the curve of her hips.

"Like ..." Julie moved to straddle him. Sitting up straight on his flat abdomen, she reached behind her to cup his already eager response. Micah groaned when her fingers closed around his erection. "He did not know that it was *I* violating *you*."

Surprise was etched on his features. "You violated me, did ya?"

"*Sí.*" She threw her head back when his hands moved up her rib cage to capture her breasts.

"You plannin' on doin' it again?"

"*Sí.*" Julie ground her hips against him and arched into his hands. His fingers plucked at her erect nipples, and she felt the pull of his touch fire her blood. "I am."

Slowly, deliberately, she raised up onto her knees.

"Jesus, Julie."

With her fingers, she guided Micah's body inside hers. Luxuriating in the tight, hard feel of his flesh becoming one with hers, Julie sighed as he filled her. She rotated her hips slightly and felt him go even deeper than he had before.

"Micah," she whispered, "I believe I would enjoy violating you again."

He pushed himself up on one arm until he could taste her breasts. Then, encircling her hips with his free arm, Micah teased her nipples until she was half mad with the need coursing through her.

"Micah . . . I . . ."

He pulled back slightly. "Julie darlin'. How do you say, 'Stop talkin',' in Spanish?" He moved his hand from her hip and began to stroke the hard bud of her sex.

Julie groaned and trembled. *"Silencio,"* she finally answered.

"Right."

* * *

Esteban hunched his shoulders and cocked his ear at the partially opened door. Warily he cast one quick glance behind him at the hall leading to the kitchen and sighed his relief at finding the corridor empty.

It was only by chance that he'd seen the man from El Paso ride up to the rancho. But as soon as he had, Esteban knew there would be trouble.

He moved a half step deeper into the shadows and waited impatiently for the two people in the study to speak. When Doña Ana's voice sliced through the stillness, Esteban held his breath.

"This gringa asked about *me*? In particular?"

"Sí, Patrona."

Esteban's nose wrinkled. The deputy from El Paso whined like a dog for favors.

"Her name?"

"Butterworth," the deputy said slyly. "She says she is sister to the old Don, your husband's, lawyer."

A long, breathless pause, then finally Doña Ana muttered, "What did she want?"

"The marshal. But he is in Houston." An incredulous snort of laughter shot into the quiet, then he added, "This crazy gringa thinks that her brother was murdered!"

Esteban shook his gray head. He heard the disbelief in the younger man's voice and wished for a moment that *he* was as ignorant as Doña Ana's visitor.

"Murder?'" a too silky voice asked. "As I recall, the man fell off his horse."

"Sí, Señora. And then down a cliff."

"Foolish man," Doña Ana muttered, then asked briskly, "This woman is his sister, you say? Where is she now?"

"Ah, this is the surprising part, Patrona. It is why I have come. Señora Butterworth is at the home of your son-in-law."

Even from the hall, Esteban heard Doña Ana's sharp intake of breath. Cautiously he straightened up and slipped down the hall toward the kitchen and the back door. He'd heard enough.

He didn't notice the cook offer him a cup of coffee as he crossed the too hot room. He didn't hear her call after him as he stepped outside and closed the door behind him. Esteban kept walking, the quiet, cool night a welcome reprieve from the doings of the rancho.

From the long, adobe bunkhouse came the sounds of men arguing, the bark of a dog, and the occasional pluck of a guitar string. Horses in the corral moved about lazily, and he heard the muted voice of the cook, shouting at someone to bring more firewood.

Everything so normal.

And yet . . . Esteban turned his steps toward the barn, eager to avoid having to speak to anyone. He had to think.

He was too old for this business and no match for Doña Ana. But he could not stand by and let another "accident" happen.

If only the young fool had not reported his findings to the Patrona. Esteban muttered under his breath, calling himself an old woman. *Of course*, the deputy would come to Doña Ana. He would wish to make himself look important in the eyes of a very powerful woman. It was well-known that a word from Doña Ana could help or destroy a man's career.

He sighed heavily and told himself he should have done more. He should have tried long ago. But instead, he had let his own safety and comfort and his fear of Doña Ana come before what he knew to be right.

But at least, he reminded himself, he *had* sent that telegram to Julietta at her friend's house, to warn her of *la Patrona*'s plans. But that fact brought no peace. As soon as the thought entered his brain, he shoved it aside. It was not enough.

But what more could he do?

The tired old man stopped, let his head drop back on his neck, and stared up at the night sky. The longer he stared, the brighter the stars seemed to shine. It was as if *Someone* in the heavens wished to give him comfort. Strength.

A sense of purpose slowly filled him. A fragile thread of the courage he'd taken for granted as a young man wound its way through his body until Esteban felt its power renew him.

A hesitant smile touched his lips. He straightened up suddenly and continued on toward the barn. There was nothing else to be done here. But there was *much* to be done elsewhere. His conscience had troubled him for too long. Too many nights had he lain awake, drowning in his own helpless fear.

It was finished.

No more. He was old. Soon he would be called to give an accounting of his life before the Almighty. And a man could not stand in shame before his God.

He *must* find a way to warn Señor Butterworth's sister.

CHAPTER
···SIXTEEN···

Two more days.

Only two more days until they reached the Duffy ranch.

Julie rolled her head around on her neck, wincing at the stiffness in her muscles. Every inch of her body screamed out with aches and pains. She felt as though she hadn't slept a wink since leaving Vacio, and she didn't think she'd ever be warm again.

A sharp desert wind swept through the campsite, and she huddled deeper into the blanket thrown across her shoulders. Not for the first time, she wished they'd been able to have a fire.

But, she thought as she stared out at the black night, Micah was right on that point. They couldn't chance a fire. In the wide, open darkness of the desert, even the tiniest of flames could be seen for miles. And now they had not only Enrique and Carlos to worry about—they were also deep into Apache territory.

So far they'd been lucky.

Reflexively Julie's fingers tightened around the stock of Micah's rifle. In the distance a lone coyote howled and the hairs at the back of her neck stood straight up. For a moment, her too active imagination conjured up the image of Indians stealthily closing in. A quick glance at the horses told her that there was nothing out there in the darkness. If there had been, the animals would have their heads up, listening.

She yawned and told herself she could wake Micah. But it wasn't time yet. They'd agreed to keep watch in two-hour shifts, hoping that several short periods of sleep would serve well enough to keep them alert. Julie glanced at the sleeping man opposite her and knew that she couldn't wake him yet. Just a half hour more, she promised herself.

Deliberately she forced her eyes wide open and breathed in the cold night air. The picketed horses stamped their hooves, and Julie jumped nervously. Almost immediately the animals settled down again, and she didn't even notice when her eyes began to drift closed.

She remembered how good it felt to cuddle in close to Micah and sleep with the sound of his heart beating beneath her cheek. She recalled the feel of his arms wrapped tightly around her and the warmth of his body pressed to hers. It was all she could do to stop herself from stretching out beside him, just for a moment. She wanted to feel that closeness again. Before it was too late.

Since their wedding night in Vacio, they'd been little more than traveling companions. And with the rancho only two days' ride away, it didn't appear likely that the situation would change. In fact, her new husband had neatly avoided all of her affectionate efforts. Her slightest touch was enough to make him take a step back.

It seemed as though Micah had focused every

thought and every ounce of his will on getting her to her father's ranch. Even when she was able to distract him from his duty long enough to *talk* to him, Julie felt a strange distance in him that hadn't been there before. It was as if he'd already said good-bye to her.

But it wasn't over. Not yet. She would just have to use the next two days wisely. Somehow she *would* reach him.

Her head fell forward onto her chest, and she told herself that she'd only rest her eyes for a moment. Just a moment.

His hand covered her mouth and wrenched her backward before she could think what to do. Instinctively she lifted the rifle, but the man's free hand snaked around her body and yanked the weapon away from her easily.

Julie twisted and kicked in his grip. Frantically her gaze flew to her husband. But her captor'd been too quiet. Exhaustion had claimed Micah. He didn't stir as the unknown man dragged her from the camp.

Pulling at the fingers covering her mouth, Julie sucked in a gulp of air and would have screamed but for the harsh, Spanish whisper in her ear.

"Scream, Julietta, and I will kill your gringo so quickly he will be dead before the echo of your scream fades away."

Carlos.

She jerked him a nod and breathed furiously through her nose. He pulled her up against his barrel chest, and Julie's features screwed up in protest. He smelled of stale sweat, horse, and tequila.

The momentary hope that perhaps he'd had too much to drink died almost before it was born. His step was steady and the strength of his grip told her he had no intention of letting her get away.

Julie stumbled, and he yanked her back up viciously. Determined to be as much a trial to him as possible, she went limp in his grasp, forcing him to half carry her. A muttered curse was his only comment as he continued to drag her farther from Micah.

He didn't even slow down. Julie's fingers pulled at the dirty hand clamped across her mouth, but it was useless. A big man, Carlos' strength was well known in their corner of Texas. It was said that Doña Ana relied on Carlos' muscles and Enrique's brain to carry out her wishes.

Tentaclelike branches of ocotillo grabbed at her as she passed. Carlos dragged her through a patch of mesquite, and she felt the thorns snag, release, then snag again on her split riding skirt. The lumbering man moved on single-mindedly, oblivious to Julie's muffled groans of pain as her body slammed into the ground again and again.

From somewhere nearby she heard a horse snort gently.

It was over then. After all she'd been through. After all she and Micah had done and endured to come this far, the fight was finished. And Doña Ana had won.

Frustration boiled up inside her, and Julie knew that once she rode away from this place with Carlos, there would be nothing else she could do. Nowhere else she could run.

In a blinding flash of hope, she realized that they were far enough from the camp now that Carlos' threat against Micah was futile. Frantically, instead of pulling at the hand covering her mouth, she pushed it into her mouth and bit down hard.

Carlos inhaled sharply, snatched his hand back, and shoved her away from him all at once. His push sent her sprawling onto the ground, and once more she felt thorns scratch her arms.

"*¡Bruja!*" he whispered, and Julie scooted back farther, ignoring the sting of rocks and sand on her palms.

His round face set in grim lines, he took a half step toward her. "If not for your grandmother, I would kill you now, you stupid bitch."

She couldn't take her eyes off him. Not even for the instant she would need to leap up and run. One mistake and he would have her. And this time she knew there would be no escaping him.

"But it is better that I don't kill you." A slow, taunting smile curved his lips, twisting the small scar on his left cheek. "Instead, Don Vicente will make you wish you were dead."

She swallowed heavily and tried to think.

"Enough, Julietta," he said in Spanish, his voice low, threatening. "Have you forgotten my promise? I swear to you I will kill your gringo."

"How?" She forced the word past the knot in her throat. "You cannot shoot him, Carlos. Even *you* would not be so foolish. One gunshot would bring the Apaches down on all our heads."

"You think I need a gun to kill that scrawny man?" He held up his two huge hands and took another step closer. "With these, I could snap him in half."

From the corner of her eye, Julie caught a shadow of movement. Something, or someone, was inching up behind Carlos. A blast of wind rushed past, and she realized that whoever it was, was standing upwind of Carlos' horse. It was the only reason the animal hadn't reacted.

Her gaze shifted to the unknown stalker, and Carlos used that brief moment to leap for her.

At the last instant Julie rolled to one side, and the big man landed on an oversized clump of mesquite instead. Before he could do more than groan from the pain of the tenacious thorns tearing into him, Micah rushed at him from out of the shadows.

Heart in her throat, Julie watched terrified as her husband struggled with the much bigger man. The solid smack of a fist connecting with flesh sounded uncommonly loud in the stillness. Carlos shrugged his shoulders, tossing Micah a good five feet from him.

Micah landed flat on his back, but before the big man came at him, he was back on his feet, moving in a wary circle around his opponent.

As the two men began to edge around each other, Julie moved too, always keeping Micah in sight. She began to work her way toward Carlos' horse. Surely there was a rifle in the scabbard. Lord knew she didn't have the time to search for the rifle Carlos had taken from her. And, though she couldn't shoot it for fear of attracting Apaches, she could at least threaten their enemy with it. If worse came to worst, she would use the cold steel barrel as a club.

"Stay clear, Julie," Micah warned her without taking his eyes off Carlos.

"*Sí, Julietta,*" Carlos agreed in halting English. "When I finish with this *bastardo*, we will be on our way."

Micah snorted and kept moving. "Now my Spanish

ain't all that good, but I reckon even *I* know what you just called me, mister."

Carlos laughed, took a step, and pulled a knife from the leather scabbard at his waist. "Let us end this, gringo."

Nodding, Micah half bent, wrapped his fingers around his bone-handled knife, and slipped it out of the sheath stitched into his moccasin.

Julie moved closer to the horse, now straining his neck against the picket pin.

When Carlos raised his knife arm and stepped forward, Micah bent double and raced to meet him. Ducking under the big man's weapon, Micah hit the man hard around the knees. Carlos' balance dissolved, and he fell backward with a crash. In a heartbeat Micah straddled the other man and with his free hand delivered a solid punch to his opponent's jaw.

Carlos grunted and swung his knife. It sliced across Micah's shoulder, ripping into his already battered shirt. Quickly Micah grabbed the big man's wrist in one powerful hand. With the other, he held his own knife to the tender flesh of Carlos' thick neck.

Immediately all noise ceased. Julie snatched the rifle from Carlos' saddle and raced back to the two combatants.

"Drop it, mister," Micah said quietly.

Carlos' eyes bored into the smaller man's, but his grip on the knife didn't loosen.

Micah touched the tip of his blade to the man's flesh and pressed gently.

Julie watched as Carlos' eyes widened in fear. Slowly a single drop of blood formed on the man's neck and slid across Micah's blade. She looked into her husband's face and couldn't understand why Carlos refused to do as he was told. She'd never seen such a fierce expression on Micah's features before. At that moment he looked as though he would have no trouble at all slicing his enemy's throat.

"Mister," Micah whispered, his grip on the man's wrist tightening, "you got about a second here before I lose my temper." His breathing ragged and labored, he leaned down closer and stared directly into the flat, black eyes beneath him. "I'm a easygoin' man, but I been pushed too hard and too long by that old bat you're workin' for. I'm about at the end of my tether, and it don't much matter to me if you live or not. So you decide. Now."

For a long, heart-stopping minute, Carlos seemed to weigh Micah's words. Julie gripped the rifle tightly and held her breath. Finally, though, she saw defeat shine in Carlos' eyes and knew the battle of wills was over.

"Julie," Micah said, his gaze still locked on Carlos, "pick up the man's knife, will ya? I'll get his hip gun." He slid the other man's gun from its holster and pointed it at him. Slowly he backed off. Motioning with the pistol, Micah ordered, "All right, mister. You get up and climb on that horse of yours." When Carlos didn't move, Micah cocked the pistol. "Now."

Carlos clumsily pushed himself to his feet then faced the man who'd beaten him.

Micah backed up a pace. "Julie. You come on over here. Behind me." He smiled. "Wouldn't want you shot by accident if my friend here does somethin' stupid."

Julie stood behind her husband and watched Carlos fight a losing battle to hide his rage.

"Now, son," Micah said in a deceptively soft tone, "I want you on that horse of yours ridin' for Vacio."

"Vacio!"

"That's right. It's that little town a couple days back down the trail? See, me and Julie are headin' for Texas and her pa's ranch, and I don't want to have to spend my time worryin' about the likes of *you* sneakin' up on me."

"Do not worry about *me*, gringo," Carlos snapped. "It is *la Patrona* you should think about."

"La Patrona?"

"My grandmother," Julie explained.

Micah shook his head. "Ah. The old bat. Well, mister, I can't say I'm too scared of whoever'd hire the likes of you."

Carlos' meaty hands curled into fists at his sides, and Julie saw what it cost him to stand still for Micah's insults. The big man looked as if he'd like nothing better than the chance to kill Micah Benteen.

"Julie darlin, . . ."

"¿Sí, Micah?"

"I want you to stay out of the line of fire, but go on over to this fella's horse and let loose the saddle."

"The saddle?"

"That's right."

She moved off without another word and felt Carlos' eyes follow her. As she pulled at the cinch strap, she heard the big man say, "What are you doing, gringo?"

"Just fixin' it so's you'll have your hands full stayin' put on that horse of yours." Micah answered. She didn't have to see him to know he was smiling again. "If you ain't got a saddle, you're gonna be so busy holdin' on to the horsehair, you won't give us another thought."

"You would send me bareback across the desert?"

"Mister, you're lucky I'm lettin' you go at all." The teasing tone was gone from his voice. "The way you was draggin' my wife hither and yon, I'd just as soon shoot ya right here. And that's the damned truth."

"Your *wife*?"

"That's right."

Clearly outraged, Carlos shrugged, "You are *married*?"

"Can't have a wife without doin' that, mister."

"Julietta!"

With one last tug, the strap was loosened, and the worn, leather saddle dropped to the ground. Julie squared her shoulders and turned to face Carlos. Even in the darkness she saw the deep, mottled splotches of red and purple marking his hard features.

In Spanish he shouted. "This is true? You have married this . . . *trash*?"

"Shut your ugly mouth," she shot back. "*You* who is paid to hunt down a woman is not a man to call others trash."

"Talk English!" Micah tossed in, looking from one to the other of them.

"You stupid slut!" Spittle ran down Carlos' chin in his rush to speak. He wiped his forearm across his mouth, pointed to Micah, and went on, "To bed this worthless gringo you have risked much!"

"Now I understand what *puta* means, mister, and I ain't about to let you go callin' my wife a whore!"

"Shut up, gringo," Carlos snarled at him and turned his venom back on Julie. "When Don Vicente finds out that you are no longer virgin, what do you think he will do to you, eh?"

"I am not worried about Don Vicente."

"Then you are more stupid than even *I* thought you to be!" He laughed, waved one hand at Micah, and added, "You think your gringo will be able to save you from Don Vicente? You have much to learn, Julietta."

"That's it." Micah cocked the pistol.

"Go ahead and shoot, gringo," Carlos said in English. "You no more than I wish to see the Apache this night."

"Get on the horse, mister, and head out."

"My rifle?"

"Nope."

"You will leave me in the desert two days from a town with no weapon?"

"If it wasn't for your horse needin' water, mister, I'd send ya without a canteen." Micah's eyes narrowed. "But I'll see no animal suffer. Not even *your* horse."

Carlos stared at the other man for a long moment before finally shrugging his massive shoulders negligently. "Very well, gringo. You have won this time. I will go." With slow, careful steps, he moved through the brush to his horse's side. He heaved himself onto the animal's broad, bare back, wrapped the reins of the bridle around one hand and threaded the fingers of the other through the horse's mane. When he was ready, he threw the couple one last glance.

Julie stood beside her husband, Micah's arm draped protectively across her shoulders.

Carlos' lips twisted into a smile that held more pain than pleasure. His gaze moved up and down Julie's body with brazen contempt. In a quick rush of Spanish, he said, "I hope he made you scream your delight, bitch. Because Don Vicente's pleasures bring screams

244

of pain. It is too bad your mother is dead. She could have told you all about how to *please* the Don."

"My mother?" Julie whispered.

"*Sí*. Your mother." In English, he added for Micah's benefit, "Watch your wife, gringo. Like mother, like daughter. And Don Vicente is a man who will not be refused."

Micah glanced at Julie's face momentarily and saw the shock in her eyes. Glaring up at the fat bastard in front of him, he said quietly, "Get goin', mister, or so help me God, I'll fire this gun. I'm willin' to bet the Apaches would rather go after *one* rider than two." He smiled and added, "Me and Julie can travel a helluvalot faster than you can. And you wouldn't stand a gambler's chance in church without a weapon."

Their eyes locked, and for the second time Micah watched a flash of fear shoot through the other man's gaze. In an instant Carlos turned away, kicked at his horse's belly, and took off at a dead run in the direction of Vacio.

Micah waited until the pounding of hooves faded away into the stillness before tucking the pistol into his waistband and enfolding Julie in his arms.

"What was all that about a mother?"

"You understood?"

"Only the word *madre*, honey. What'd he say?"

She tilted her head back and looked up at him. In a soft, halting voice, Julie told him everything. Including the pain Carlos promised she would feel at Don Vicente's hands and the fact that her mother had already learned that lesson.

"What did he mean?" she whispered. "What did my mother have to do with Don Vicente?"

"I don't know, darlin'." Leaning down, he kissed her forehead before saying, " 'Sides, who says ol' Carlos was tellin' the truth? He don't strike me as a real honest sort."

"*Sí,* perhaps."

She wanted to believe that Carlos was lying. It was etched into her furrowed brow and confused gaze. The problem was, both of them knew Carlos had no reason to lie. So what did it all mean?

Micah smoothed her hair back and pressed her face into his chest. He felt her trembling and couldn't rightly blame her. Between Carlos and Enrique she'd already had plenty to deal with. And now that damn fool Carlos had given her *more* to wonder about. And worry over.

Shit. He should've shot the bastard before he ever got a chance to open his damned mouth. Apaches or no Apaches—it would have been worth it to spare her.

There was a lot more goin' on here, he told himself, than even *Julie* realized. And for some reason, all the trouble boiled back down to her granny and Don Vicente. Micah's instincts told him that there would be no easy answer to any of this, either. Julie wouldn't be safe until everybody's secrets were out in the open.

And if that meant Micah had to reach down the old bat's throat and drag the truth out of her . . . then so be it.

After all he'd been through already, hell, he could hardly *wait* to come face to face and toe to toe with Doña Ana. Somehow, someway, he was going to get to the heart of this business. Either that, or die tryin'.

Julie's arms reached around his middle and squeezed him tight. He rested his chin on top of her head and tried to think of something to say. But, hell, what *was* there to say? He didn't know any of these folks yet. He didn't know spit about her mother . . . and what he *did* know about her pa convinced him he didn't want to know much more.

Besides. All that mattered this minute, he thought, was Julie.

He breathed deeply and smoothed his palms over her back until he felt her begin to calm. Lord knew, his own insides could do with a little calmin' down.

For a while there he'd been afraid that he wouldn't be able to get her away from the fat man at all.

A flash of memory shot through his brain, and he recalled with perfect clarity the moment when Carlos snatched her from camp. He hadn't been able to do a thing while the man had the drop on him and his hand around Julie's throat.

Micah'd had to wait his chance. That surely wasn't easy. He'd never been a patient man anyway. That was Shadrack's way. Not his. And havin' to learn patience this night had damn near killed him.

Now, after listenin' to everything she'd had to say about this Don Vicente, Micah wanted to run all the way to Texas and shoot the bastard before he had a chance to hurt her. But he couldn't. Again, he'd have to wait. He'd have to go slow. Careful. Wait his chance.

"Micah?" she whispered, shattering his thoughts. "Yeah?"

"Can we go now? I would like to get far away from this place."

"Sure thing, darlin'." He pulled back, looked into her tear-filled eyes, and forced a smile he didn't feel. "I don't reckon I'll be gettin' much more sleep tonight anyway."

A soft, reluctant smile curved her lips, and before he could think better of it, Micah bent down and kissed her gently. His soul came alive again with her first touch, and he realized how lonely he'd been since that night in Vacio.

For that one, perfect night he'd let himself believe that they belonged together. That there would be no separation. But with the following dawn came the realization that he'd built up a fool's dream.

He'd tried to keep a distance between them since their wedding night. Even seeing the hurt in her eyes when he avoided her touch, he'd remained strong. Determined.

And it hadn't done a damn sight of good, he thought resignedly. It didn't matter if he touched her or not.

His blood still raced.

His body still ached.

The wanting never quit. Prob'ly never would.

Micah firmly pushed all thoughts from his brain and gave himself up to the pleasure of holding her, tasting her sweetness. He wouldn't deny her or himself again. For as long as he was able, Micah knew he would accept each kiss, each touch, for the gift it was.

She responded to his kiss eagerly, hungrily. Throwing her arms around his neck, she pulled him down onto her mouth and kissed him as if the last breath of air on earth was inside him.

Micah held her tightly, trying to tell her silently that all would be well. That he wouldn't leave her. Not yet.

Not until she was safe.

And still, one niggling thought crept through his mind. He would give plenty to know where Enrique was right now.

CHAPTER
···SEVENTEEN···

PENELOPE SIGHED AND set the book down in her lap. It was simply no use. Despite Mr. Charles Dickens' clever way with words and an intriguing story, she could not concentrate on *A Tale of Two Cities*.

Of course, she thought wryly, that should hardly surprise her. For two days she hadn't been able to think about anything save her last conversation with Patrick.

In her mind's eye she again watched his furious pacing and listened to him carry on about what she'd "done."

"Everybody in El Paso is talking about you, dammit!"

"Really, Patrick. There is no need to resort to vulgar profanity."

"Dammit, Penelope. I am trying to tell you that you've really put your foot in it *this* time."

A serene expression on her face, she asked, "What in heaven are you raving about?"

He crossed the small study floor and stood not three inches from her. Hands on hips, he faced her down and she saw the unmistakable flash of aggravation in his blue eyes.

"According to the town gossips, you all but accused Doña Ana of murder!"

"Certainly not! At least, not in so many words." She drew herself up to her full height and stared at him calmly. "I never *once* made an accusation. My brother, after all, *was* a lawyer. And slander is such an ugly word." She nodded slightly, then continued. "I simply let it be known that Eustace was a fine horseman—that some paperwork he'd done for Don Ricardo had disappeared with Eustace's death—and that I wished Doña Ana had been a *bit* more forthcoming regarding the circumstances of Eustace's death."

"Is that *all*?"

"Sarcasm, Patrick, is as ugly as slander."

"Forgive me." One hand pushed through his thick hair, leaving it in untamed tufts on the crown of his head.

Penelope swallowed back the urge to smooth it down. "Of course, Patrick."

He stared at her and shook his head. "You don't get it, do you?"

"What?"

"This is *not* London, for God's sake! There aren't constables on every street corner. There are no gentle manners for civilized living. Dammit, Penelope!" His hands had fallen to her shoulders and gripped her tightly. "Don't you understand? If Doña Ana *did* have Eustace killed . . . what would stop her from doing the same to you?"

Penelope shook her head sharply, ridding herself of that entire conversation. A futile gesture, she knew. After all, she'd been over and over it countless times in the last two days and was no closer to answering Patrick's question now than she was then.

Hmmph! He was making far too much of the whole thing. It was absolutely ludicrous how one small, elderly woman could reduce everyone around her to frightened children. Well, that would not happen to Penelope Butterworth! she vowed.

She folded her hands on top of the book and lifted her feet to the small footstool in front of the overstuffed chair she sat in. Penelope let her gaze wander over the huge, well-appointed main room of the rancho.

Bright, vivid landscapes hung on creamy, whitewashed walls. A splash of sunshine fell across the wide, gilt mirror above the hearth, reflecting the light into the room.

Cozy chairs and settees were clustered near the empty grate, encouraging conversations that never took place because Patrick avoided her company so studiously. She sniffed and glanced across the room at the magnificent piano in the far corner.

Though no one ever played it, Penelope knew it to be in tune, having tried it for herself only the day before. Her gaze strayed to the portrait standing on a lace runner stretched across the top of the piano. Thoughtfully she stared at it.

At some point in the last two days, Patrick had taken Julietta's portrait from his desk and placed it in this prominent position. Although she was glad to see it, Penelope couldn't help wondering what had caused his change of heart. And it was highly unlikely that he would actually *tell* her. In fact, he still hadn't mentioned why he was so convinced that Julietta was not his child.

"¿Con permiso, Señora?"

She looked up to see Juana hovering in the doorway, balancing a laden tea tray. The china teapot, she knew, held cinnamon-flavored coffee instead of her preferred beverage. But Juana's abilities with pastry more than made up for her ineptitude with tea.

"Thank you, Juana," Penelope said with a smile. "If you'll set the tray here . . ." She waved her hand at the long, low, intricately carved table before her.

The older Mexican woman hurried into the room, set her burden down, then gave a flick of her apron to some imagined speak of dust on the shining wood surface.

"Anything else, Señora?"

"No, thank you."

Juana was almost out of the room again before Penelope asked, "Has Mr. Duffy returned yet?"

"Lo siento, Señora. I am sorry. No." The woman's lined face wrinkled in concern.

"It's quite all right, Juana, I'm sure."

Alone again, Penelope sat up and reached for the china pot. As she poured the steaming brew into a fragile cup, she found herself wishing she was as confident as she sounded.

What on earth was Patrick up to? Since warning her to stay near the house, he'd absented himself daily. The confinement was becoming weary. She was unused to being so sedentary.

All her life Penelope'd faced her problems head on, chin up. And truth to tell, she had little desire to behave differently now.

She took a small sip of the too hot coffee, then replaced the cup in its saucer. As she set it down on the table again, Juana's voice shattered the quiet.

"*¿Con permiso, Señora?*"

"Yes, Juana."

The older woman turned slightly, looked down the hallway, and waved one hand. "*¡Venga! Venga aquí!*" Exasperated, she looked to Penelope. "I am sorry, Señora. I tell him to come here, but he is ..." She rolled her eyes, obviously trying to think of the right word. Finally she came up with, "*Inquieto.* I mean, not easy."

"Uneasy?" She rose to her feet slowly and crossed the floor toward the doorway. "But why? And who is 'he'?"

"*¡Caramba!*" Juana muttered and tapped her forehead with the palm of her hand. "*Lo siento.* I did not say." She shot one more look down the hallway before turning back to Penelope with a sigh. "It is Esteban. He works for Doña Ana Santos, Señora. It is because of *her* he is uneasy."

A thrill of excitement coursed through Penelope before she squashed it. First things first, she reminded herself firmly. She stepped into the hallway and looked where Juana pointed.

Not ten feet away, an old man, his shoulders stooped as though he carried the troubles of the world, stood watching her through the saddest brown eyes she'd even seen.

She smiled and whispered, "Does he speak English?" to Juana.

"*Sí, Señora.* Not so good as me, but *sí.*"

Instinctively Penelope smiled, hurried toward him, and gently took his arm. "Good afternoon, Esteban."

He twisted the brim of an ancient, battered straw hat and hesitantly returned her smile. *"Buenas tardes, Señora."*

Patting his arm softly, Penelope began to guide him down the hall to the main room. "It was so good of you to come to see me, Esteban." She turned her head for a moment and said, "Juana, would you please bring an extra cup for my guest?"

The housekeeper's eyes widened in surprise as the oddly matched couple walked past her into the sun-splashed room. Then she moved off quickly to fetch the cup.

Over his mumbled protests, Penelope seated Esteban in a chair beside her own. He sat stiffly, ill at ease in the fine surroundings, and she used his momentary distress to study him.

His features were marked heavily with the passage of years, but there remained a . . . *kindness* that gentled the harsh lines and leathery flesh. Penelope saw his hands shake slightly. That he was frightened was obvious.

Well, she told herself, she was going to find out why!

After Juana brought the fresh cup, Penelope poured the man some coffee and offered it to him.

"Gracias, Señora," he whispered, taking it from her. He then set the dainty cup gingerly on the table without even tasting the cinnamon brew.

Laying her hand on his arm, Penelope tilted her head and looked at him gently. "Now, Esteban. You've come to see me about something important?"

"Sí, Señora."

"What is it?"

A deep, shuddering breath racked his too thin frame,

and as he exhaled, he murmured, "I have come to warn you."

"About what, precisely?"

"Doña Ana, Señora."

"Ah. Here we are, then." Perhaps this would finally be the proof she'd longed for. Perhaps Esteban would be able to tell her what she so needed to know. Carefully she tamped down any trace of excitement and waited.

"Your brother, Señor Eustace?"

"Yes?"

"He was a kind man, Señora." Esteban nodded thoughtfully and stared into space as if seeing the man he spoke of. "The last time he left the rancho, I myself saw him go. A few moments later I also heard Doña Ana send two men after him. They were to bring to her some papers Señor Butterworth carried."

The will. She felt the blood drain from her face. Suspecting something and having it confirmed as fact were two different things, it seemed. A flash of raw, new pain swept her body, and Penelope had to force herself to listen as he continued.

"Though *la Patrona*'s men returned with the papers that afternoon, it was not until days later that I learned Señor Eustace was dead. It was then I knew. Enrique and Carlos. They killed him."

A soft moan escaped her, and Esteban turned at the sound. Looking her directly in the eye, he spoke in a hurried hush.

"Now I have come to save you, Señora. I am an old man, Doña Ana is a powerful woman, but if I die?" He shrugged. "What would it matter? I will not see her harm another *inocente*."

She squeezed his hand, blinked back tears, and smiled bravely at him. "You are a brave man, Esteban. I thank you."

"Por nada."

Disjointed thoughts shot crazily through her brain, but finally one fact became clear. She still needed proof. Hastily she asked, "Do you know? Does Doña Ana still possess the will?" He frowned slightly. "The papers Eustace was carrying?"

"Ah." The old man shrugged again, throwing his threadbare shirt back on his narrow shoulders. "I do not know, Señora. But I would not think so."

"Nor I, I'm afraid," she muttered, then looked up as he pushed himself to his feet. "Are you returning to Doña Ana?"

Esteban chuckled mirthlessly. "No. I am old, but I am not ready to die yet." His narrow shoulders straightened perceptibly. "I will go . . . somewhere."

"Nonsense!" Penelope stood up and took both his gnarled, work-worn hands in hers. Smiling gently, she said, "You will stay right here."

"¿Aqui?" His busy brows gathered in confusion. "But Señor Duffy—"

"Will agree," she interrupted firmly. "There is always a place for a brave man."

He stared at her in stunned silence, and Penelope had to turn from his grateful gaze. "Juana!" she called.

The woman appeared quickly in the doorway, and Penelope was certain she'd been in the hall the entire time, listening. Of course, Penelope thought helplessly she could hardly blame her! It was something she might have done herself if the situation had warranted it.

"¿Sí, Señora?"

"Juana, I'd like you to give Esteban a room of his own in the servants' wing, please."

The older woman's eyes again widened in surprise, but her quick smile indicated her pleasure. "*Sí, Senora.*"

"I shall see you both later, then." Penelope nodded at the two people and hurried from the room, already making plans.

In Spanish, Juana said easily, "Come with me, Esteban. We will find your room, and then I will feed you the best *chili colorado* you have ever tasted."

He breathed a sigh of relief and smiled at the woman so close to his own age. "That would be welcome, *gracias*. The Señora Butterworth is very kind."

"*Sí.*" Juana grinned and winked. "But not *too* kind. She is a strong woman, Esteban. Doña Ana, I think, has finally met the woman who will best her."

Esteban crossed himself nervously, but Juana only smiled and drew him to the kitchen.

*　　*　　*

Micah pulled his horse to a stop and waited for Julie to do the same. On the bluff they looked out at the wide expanse of desert before them. Far distant lay the long, irregular line of the Guadualupe Mountains. Sprawled at the foot of them lay El Paso, a jumbled collection of adobe buildings, shaded by tall, ancient cottonwoods. Even from a distance Micah noticed the occasional glint of sunlight on the Rio Grande. There were even patches of green along the curving bank of the Rio Grande, where the water was used to irrigate crops.

They'd finally made it.

He turned to see Julie staring out at her home, and he didn't like the tight anxiousness of her features.

"How far is it to your pa's ranch from town?"

"It is a a two-hour ride," she answered, her gaze still locked on the faraway town.

"Well then, I figure we should have you to home a little before nightfall." He hoped he'd managed to keep the regret from his voice.

"And then what?"

She'd lifted her chin a bit, and he realized how much that one small gesture had come to mean to him. He had to tighten his jaw before answering stiffly, "Let's just ride along for now. Get you home, then worry about what comes next, all right?"

"*Sí.* All right." She glanced over her shoulder and frowned.

"What is it, Julie?"

"Perhaps nothing." She shook her head, shrugged, and said, "It is only that . . ." Julie looked around, and Micah followed her gaze. The low-lying boulders and towers of rocks were no different than the rest of the countryside they had been riding through.

"What?"

"I can *feel* eyes on me. As if someone is watching me."

He stood in the stirrups, letting his practiced eye wander thoroughly over the land. But he saw nothing out of the ordinary. Prob'ly just nerves, he told himself. Lord knew he'd been feelin' a bit jumpy, too.

Bending his knees, he dropped abruptly back into the saddle and in the same instant felt a blinding flash of pain lance through his head. Even as he tumbled from his seat, Micah heard the gunshot echo in the stillness. Julie's scream faded away as the world went black.

Satan bolted and began a mad gallop across the desert. Julie fought to control her own mount, then stared down at her husband, spread-eagle in the sand. All breath left her body at first sight of the bright red blood streaming from his temple.

Dios Mio, Micah is dead.

She couldn't breath. Couldn't swallow. Couldn't scream.

Micah.

After an eternity-filled moment the steady drumming of a horse in full gallop finally penetrated her brain. Her chest tight with pain she hadn't time to feel, Julie picked up her horse's reins. With one last glance at Micah, she kicked the big mare's sides and raced toward El Paso.

* * *

The heavy, oak double doors swung open and crashed against the inside walls in unison. Patrick stared unblinkingly at the still, empty hallway of the Santos rancho.

He'd never planned to enter that house again. When Elena died, sixteen years ago, he'd considered his ties with the place to be severed.

And if it hadn't been for Penelope Butterworth challenging his beliefs, he might never have returned to this place, he knew. But in a few, short days Penelope'd shone a light on his cloudy vision. She'd ripped at the fragile web of half truths he'd surrounded himself with until he was left more unsure than before.

Her strength, her own determination to find the facts about her brother, her unflinching certainty in the one she loved, made his own weakness seem even more repellent to him. And in the end he'd had to return here. To the house where it had all started.

If there were answers to the doubts and questions that had plagued him the last few days . . . they were here. With her. Doña Ana.

Dear Lord, that he had come to this! Maybe, maybe, he should just leave. Leave the dead buried.

But was it? Had he ever really let go of the past? Hadn't it been haunting him for years? Not just Elena . . . but his *own* actions. And Julietta. Besides the basics of life, had he ever been able to give her anything? No. Because the past always stood between them.

It was time he faced it. No matter what.

A strangled groan choked him as his gaze settled on the wide, curving staircase that dominated the entry. His eyes followed the sweep of the polished wood banister, and in his mind he saw it as it had been on a day long past. His wedding day.

Elena'd stood poised at the top of the stairs, serenely studying the crowd waiting for her. Until her eyes locked with his. Then she'd walked down those same steps, alone. Head lifted, proud, with a white lace mantilla floating out behind her in her wake. Elena'd come to meet him. Even when Don Ricardo met her at the foot of the stairs, tucking her arm through his, she hadn't glanced at her father.

Her eyes were for Patrick alone.

He groaned quietly. And only a few short years after that, she was gone. Swiftly his brain replaced the joyous memory with another, far less pleasing.

Patrick saw Elena clearly as she lay on her deathbed. He heard himself, his voice strained, demanding a confession. Over and over he'd questioned her, badgered her until finally, exhausted, she'd given him what she thought he wanted.

Eyes dry, her tears long since used up, Elena'd thrown his own words back at him . . . admitting to everything he'd been accusing her of for the year before her final illness.

Even then there'd been no blessed relief with her confession. Even in his darkest moments he'd wanted proof that he was wrong. That she hadn't betrayed him. He could still hear her whispered pleas as she begged him for one last promise. Instead, he'd left her alone, to die with only Juana at her side.

Patrick shuddered and shook his head, dislodging the ugly memories. Squeezing his eyes shut, he swallowed heavily. God, he groaned dismally, had he been wrong all these years? Had he allowed his own jealousies and imagination to convince him of something that wasn't real.

Was the terrible crime of betrayal *his*, not Elena's?

And could he really face knowing the truth?

He opened his eyes wide again and stared into the house. Yes. Yes he could. He had to. Dear God, he owed the truth to Elena, himself, and Julietta.

Deliberately he turned away from the staircase and marched down the length of the tiled passageway. His boot heels crashed on the shining floor as he stopped at first one door, then the next, searching for Ana Santos.

If there were servants nearby, they avoided him. The only sound in the place was that of his passing. As he rushed on, his brain noted how the great house had changed. When Ricardo was alive . . . so was the rancho. Now the old building was like its present owner. Cold. Empty.

At the end of the hall, one last, closed door remained.

The rancho office. He knew that she was inside. Waiting.

Patrick stared at the brass doorknob for a long moment before reaching out and closing his fingers over the cool metal. Then he turned it firmly and threw the door wide.

She sat behind Ricardo's desk and slowly raised her black gaze to his. Her thin lips curved slightly, but didn't quite stretch into a smile. "Welcome, son-in-law."

CHAPTER
···EIGHTEEN···

MICAH GROANED, SHIFTED position, and mumbled, "Quit your shovin'."

His eyes fluttered open to see Satan giving him another nudge with his nose. The big horse shook its head impatiently and snorted.

"All right, you old hay bag. I'm awake." He raised his head and groaned at the accompanying pain. Carefully he reached up and ran his fingertips over the side of his face. Dried blood was caked along his jaw and in his hair. Micah squinted and let his fingers travel along the furrow in his scalp left by the bullet that had creased his temple.

"Hell," he mumbled and cautiously pushed himself to a sitting position. His head hurt like the devil, but Micah'd been lucky, and knew it. The shooter had probably only missed the target thanks to Micah dropping unexpectedly into his saddle. He glanced up at Satan, more pleased than ever that he'd taught the horse to always come back to him. Cautiously Micah turned his head and looked around him. The desert, splashed with deepening shadows, was empty.

Where's Julie? he asked himself. The pounding pain in his head was suddenly tempered by worry. There was no sign of her. Her horse was gone. She wasn't layin' on the ground shot, so she must have either got away or been led away.

"Sonovabitch." To get close enough to be able to *see* El Paso and then have *this* happen! Well, whoever dry-gulched him had a big surprise comin' his way. And Micah had a hunch that when he followed this trail to its end, he would find Enrique.

Slowly, unsteadily, Micah rolled over onto his knees, then clumsily got to his feet. As soon as he stood, he felt as though his head would shatter. But after a few painful moments the pounding retreated into livable throbbing.

Satan moved up to him, and Micah gratefully grabbed hold of the animal's neck.

"Steady now, boy. Don't you try no fancy jumpin' around on me today, all right?" He fought against the pain, pushing it to the back of his mind.

Right now, all he could think of was getting to El Paso as quick as he could. Someone there would be able to tell him how to find the Duffy rancho.

If he was in better shape, he knew he'd be able to find Julie just by followin' her tracks. But with his head about to split open, it'd be a lot faster to go straight to her pa's place. After all, it wasn't like he didn't know who was behind all this.

If it had been Apaches, he sure as hell wouldn't be alive right now. It *had* to be her granny again. And wherever that old bitch was, Micah was sure he'd find Julie.

As he swung into the saddle and plopped down into place, he clenched his jaw and gripped the saddle horn tightly. The world teetered dangerously for a long minute before steadying itself again.

The way Julie'd talked about her pa, Micah didn't have much hope that Patrick Duffy would be willin' to help him get her away from her granny. But at least the bastard could tell him where the old hag lived.

"And once we know that, Satan," he whispered, "we'll go fetch my wife."

The horse pranced in place, then Micah gave him a nudge with his heel. Wounded or not, Micah would ride all night if he had to.

*　　*　　*

"What do you want?"

"The truth," Patrick shot back and stepped into the room.

Late afternoon sun peeked through the heavy, maroon draperies. The room smelled stale, as if it had been closed up for too long. An oil lamp on the cluttered desktop threw a wavering light over the old woman's face, and Patrick was struck by how little she'd changed over the years.

Her sharp features had not softened with the passing of time, and those small black eyes of hers were no warmer. The only hint of her true age was the bright white of her hair and the slight hesitation in her breathing.

"Truth?" Her lips curled back like a feral animal's. "What truth? Are you here because of that gringa you have staying at your home?"

"What?"

"The woman from England. She has been telling lies about me. Is it *she* that brings you to me?" Doña Ana

265

laughed mirthlessly. "You wish to apologize on her behalf?"

"You old harridan," he whispered and was pleased when she narrowed her eyes at his insult. "Penelope Butterworth doesn't need *me* to defend her to the likes of you! I'm here for something else."

"If this is not about the English woman, I am not interested. Go away, *borracho*! You disgust me."

"I'm not drunk, Ana." He leaned his palms on the desktop and stared directly into her lifeless eyes. "Surprised? Yes, I can see you are."

"What do you want from me? Say it and go!"

"I told you, Ana. I want the truth. About Elena— me—Julietta."

A spasm of something that might have been pleasure crossed her face before she laid her pen down and leaned back in the too big chair. Lacing her fingers together on the desk, she tilted her head slightly, narrowed her eyes, and stared at him.

"Tell me, damn you!"

A sound like dry leaves crunching suddenly filled the room, and Patrick realized she was laughing. A cold chill crawled up his spine.

"You are a fool. You have always *been* a fool."

"I don't give a good goddamn for your opinion of my character."

"Character? Hah!"

"Tell me about Elena. And Julietta." He wouldn't be put off by her insults. It had taken him sixteen years to work up the nerve to hear the truth, and by God, he *would* hear it!

Suddenly Doña Ana stood up. Shaking her head at him, she walked around the edge of the desk and crossed the room to stand in front of the cold hearth. "To think that you have come to *me* to ask about your own wife and child." She glanced at him from over her shoulder. "How this must have cost you, *borracho*."

He flinched, but not from the word *borracho*— drunk. "Tell me about Elena," he repeated, forcing the words out through a closed throat.

"Hmmph! How stupid you are, gringo."

She pulled in a ragged breath. Patrick heard it catch in her throat.

"All right," she said, suddenly spinning about to face him. "I will tell you. Only because I know the truth will destroy you."

He couldn't tear his gaze away from her eyes. They bored into him like two bullets, burying themselves deep in his body.

"She *loved* you! Hah! I see your disbelief, Duffy. But it is true."

"Then why—"

"Until," she went on, louder this time, "you turned from her. *Estupido!* You believed lies. *Rumors.* You would not hear your own *wife!*" She paused for air, laying one hand across her narrow bosom. The labored sounds of her breathing filled the room until she spoke again. "I have laughed at you through the years, gringo."

Patrick inhaled sharply and tried to look away. He couldn't. He had to finish this, no matter what it cost.

"What pleasure you have given me." She lifted her chin and looked down the length of her aristocratic nose at him. "It has almost made up for Elena's marrying you in the first place. She defied me to marry you, gringo. Did you know that?"

He shook his head.

"She was as much a fool as *you*." In the flickering light of a nearby oil lamp, Ana's features twisted and shifted. "Don Vicente wanted to marry her. *Don Vicente!* She could have been rich beyond anything she had ever known. Vicente was so smitten with her he would have done anything she wanted." Ana's eyes raked up and down Patrick contemptuously. "Instead, she chose you." She took one step closer to him, wrinkling her nose in distaste. "And do you know why, gringo? Because you *loved* her."

She snorted another brittle laugh.

Jesus, Patrick groaned silently, how he'd loved her. But he didn't need this bitch to remind him of that. All he wanted from her was an answer to the question that had plagued him for years. Was Julietta really his child?

"What about Vicente?" he ground out. "Elena was . . . *with* him. She *told* me. She admitted it."

"I always wondered if she'd confided in you. Strange. I didn't think she would."

"So it *was* true." He felt the sharp stab of betrayal again, and its barb was as painful as it had been when the wound was fresh.

"Did you never wonder *why* Elena went to Vicente's bed, gringo?"

He shook his head. *Why* hadn't mattered. All that had mattered was the fact that she'd been with someone else.

Ana smiled then. A terrifying smile that stretched her lips back from her teeth, making her face look like a fleshless skull in the half light. Three steps brought her to his side. Patrick forced himself to stand still when he instinctively wanted to step back.

Looking up at him, she said in a whispered rush, "The trip you made to San Francisco?"

He remembered. He'd been gone more than two weeks. It was after he'd returned that everything had gone so wrong.

"The night before you left, Elena sent Julietta here. To us. So that the two of you could be alone on your last night at home. After you left, Elena told your servant Juana that she, too, would be staying here. With *us*." Ana sneered at him. "So no one questioned her absence during the coming week. But she never came here, gringo."

His stomach lurched. Now that he'd finally made her speak, all he wanted was to shut her up. Quickly, before he heard too much. But she wouldn't be silenced now.

"*I* knew where she was. *I* helped Vicente arrange everything. For a price. Elena was with *him* that week." She grinned into Patrick's face. "He used her in ways that most of us have never thought of, gringo. And when the week was past, she came to me for comfort."

He jerked his head at her.

"Oh, she did not know Vicente and I were 'friends.' " Ana lifted her chin. "She was humiliated. Ashamed of the things she'd done with Vicente." Tilting her head to one side, she added, "She told me of them—would you like to know what they did together, gringo? No?" She shook her head. "A pity. I, of course, advised her to say nothing to you. I told her that Vicente would only kill you, if you were to challenge him. So to protect *you*, she kept her silence."

Dear God, he thought, and swayed unsteadily. When Elena finally *did* tell him, he hadn't challenged Vicente.

She never told him she'd been abducted. He'd always assumed she'd gone with Vicente because she wanted to.

But if she *had* told him everything, he asked himself grimly, would he have believed her? Probably not, an inner voice whispered. The pain had cut too deep for rational thought.

"And do you know, gringo, the funniest part?" Ana's scratchy voice shattered his speculations. She moved her face to within a breath of his.

Her black eyes tore into his mind until he wanted to run screaming from the room. But he couldn't leave. Not yet.

"The one thing she was most concerned for during that week with Vicente? She was terrified that you would leave her and take Julietta." Ana pursed her lips. "She never guessed that you would turn your back on your child, as well."

His breath left him in a rush. She hadn't betrayed him. She'd been used, attacked, and when she'd turned to her husband, she was pushed aside. Lord, he groaned as his last defenses fell. Why hadn't he trusted her? Why had he let himself believe that their marriage had been a lie?

Of course, Julietta was his child. The girl was six years old when her mother died. And until the year before her death—the year of Vicente—he and Elena had *never* been apart. At once, memories long ignored rushed back and images of Elena laughing, smiling, filled his mind and heart until he could almost hear her voice.

How could he have turned his back on all of that? Silently he let himself recall Elena's last wish. That he promise to make Julietta happy. And he hadn't been able to do it. Because of the doubts. Because of his own stupidity. His damaged pride.

Dear God, how could he ever forgive himself?

The memories faded abruptly, and he was back in the rancho office, standing much too close to the woman behind his private hell. Doña Ana had *sold* her own child to Vicente. Even knowing her for the bitch she was, it was hard to believe any woman could do what she'd done.

"How could you do that?" he asked, not bothering to hide his disgust. "How could you hand your own daughter over to Vicente?"

She straightened abruptly, the nasty smile fading from her face. "Elena was not my daughter. She was Ricardo's *bastard* with a peasant whore. He insisted I raise her as my own." Snapping her gaze back to his, she added one last thrust. "It gave me great pleasure to see Vicente use her and you throw her away."

Patrick's brain struggled to make sense of all the new information. He felt as though he couldn't breathe, and he knew he had to get out of that house before he suffocated.

Doña Ana turned and looked up at the blank space above the hearth. "When Ricardo died, I burned his portrait here, in this fireplace." She spoke softly, more to herself than to him. "How could he have taken a *peasant* to his bed when he had *me*? His *wife*?"

Despite the pain of the last few minutes, Patrick felt liberated. Though he couldn't ask her forgiveness, he would hope that somehow Elena would know how sorry he was for not being the husband she deserved. If there were a way to make it up to her for letting her down, he would do it.

But all that was left for him now was his daughter. Julietta. He prayed he wasn't too late for her, too.

"She was a *peasant*! A whore!" Ana screamed, her voice breaking.

Patrick looked at her, and for the first time in his life he wanted to kill a woman. Instead, he settled for stabbing her with a little truth.

"Maybe she gave him love," he said, "and warm arms to lie in and a little kindness."

Doña Ana turned and glared at him.

"What did you *ever* give anyone, Ana?"

"And you, gringo! Are you any better?"

"Perhaps not," he answered softly, tugging the brim of his hat down low over his eyes. "But at least I *know* what I've done."

He turned his back on her to leave, but hadn't taken more than a step when her voice stopped him again.

"The final joke, eh, gringo? Julietta is not the bastard. Elena was."

Patrick glanced at her. A weary half smile tugged at his lips. "That's not the final joke, Ana. That's yet to come."

"What do you mean?"

"After all the damage you've done to all of us—it's going to be a stranger who will finally beat you."

"Who?" Lines of confusion faded as she remembered. "You mean the gringa from England? She is nothing."

"Don't you count on it, Ana. I do believe your time has come at last."

"She can do nothing, do you hear me?"

Patrick started walking.

"I am Doña Ana Santos!"

He stepped into the hall and didn't look back. As he left the house, Patrick heard her screams of fury and almost smiled.

* * *

Penelope dawdled over breakfast. She sipped at her second cup of coffee and lifted one hand to smooth the bodice of her riding habit.

She wasn't looking forward to climbing onto a horse again, but for the confrontation with Doña Ana she would be willing to crawl across the desert. Impatiently she checked her pendant watch for the third time in as many minutes.

For heaven's sake, she thought. Where is Patrick? She wanted to see him before she left for the Santos ranch. He'd looked so strange the night before. And he'd hardly spoken a word all evening. He'd even refused to tell her where he'd been.

Frowning slightly, Penelope reminded herself that it really was none of her business what Patrick Duffy did with his time. Then why, an inner voice asked slyly, did she spend so much energy thinking about him?

She looked up when the dining-room door opened abruptly. Patrick stood in the doorway, and it was all she could do to keep from gasping aloud.

He was a sight. He wore the same clothes he'd been wearing the night before only now they were rumpled disreputably. His hair stood on end, his cheeks were covered with dark whisker stubble, and his eyes were red.

Her mouth pursed, she told herself that he'd obviously spent the night drinking. A small curl of disappointment wormed its way through her.

"Good morning, Penelope," he said, running one hand over his face.

Eyebrows lifted, she answered stiffly, "Good morning. I see you had a late night." She let her gaze wander over him pointedly.

"Couldn't sleep." He walked to the nearest chair and dropped into it. After pouring himself a cup of coffee, he took a long drink, shuddered, and sighed.

Though it wasn't her place, Penelope couldn't stop herself from saying, "Strong drink will do that, I'm told."

He set the cup down, leaned one elbow on the lace covered tabletop, and rested his chin in his hand. "You may not believe this, Penelope ... but I didn't have a single drink last night.

"No?"

"No."

A closer look proved his point. Though his eyes looked tired and there were deep shadows beneath them, his gaze was clear, steady. And more than that, she thought with surprise, he looked ... *different*. Younger, somehow. Good heavens. What on earth was happening?

"I apologize, Patrick."

To her astonishment, he grinned.

"If not drink," she said quickly, ignoring the skip of her heart at his smile, "then why on earth do you look so—"

"I've had my eyes opened," he interrupted. "It was a painful procedure."

"Are you all right?"

"I will be." He looked down, lifted his cup, and

drained it. Pouring another cup full, he added, "After I've taken care of something."

"What?"

A long silent moment passed before he looked at her again. Nodding at her neat wool riding habit, he said, "You look ready for battle, Penelope."

Instinctively she ran her hands over her bodice and straightened her shoulders. Obviously he wasn't going to answer her question.

"May I ask, with whom?" he said.

Lifting her chin slightly, Penelope prepared herself. She realized that he would most likely try to dissuade her from going to the Santos rancho. But this time she would not be put off. It was past time that she and Doña Ana met face to face ... and nothing would be settled until they did.

"Doña Ana," she said simply and waited for his reaction. It wasn't what she'd expected.

"I see." He quickly gulped his second cup of coffee down, then held the empty cut between his palms. "You don't have to grant me this, I know ... but I'd like to ask a favor."

"A favor?"

"Yes." He set the cup back on its saucer, stood up, and walked around the edge of the table to her side. Taking her elbow firmly in his grip, he drew her to her feet.

"Patrick?" she whispered uneasily. This was *not* the man she'd become accustomed to. *This* Patrick was entirely too unsettling. "What is it?"

His face only inches from hers, Penelope's heart began to pound frantically. She watched, spellbound as his deep blue eyes moved over her face slowly, like a touch. Black hair fell across his forehead, and the whiskers on his jaws were dotted with gray. She was close enough to see the pulse point in his throat throbbing and feel his warm breath on her face.

No man had *ever* looked at her the way Patrick Duffy was now. And under that steady regard Penelope felt an unusual nervousness flutter in her abdomen. For the very first time she had no idea what to do.

He ran his tongue across his dry lips and tightened his grip on her elbows.

With a mighty effort, she managed to ask, "What is it you want, Patrick?"

A slow smile touched his features before quickly slipping away. "Many things, Penelope. Many things."

There was that flutter again.

"But first, I'd like to ask you not to go see Doña Ana yet."

Nervousness vanished. She tried to pull free of his grip. Penelope told herself she should have known there was a reason for his steady regard. He'd hoped to catch her off balance!

"Patrick, I must insist that you not interfere with this. I've come a long way to see my plan carried through, and I won't be stopped now. Furthermore—"

He kissed her.

Stunned surprise gave way to an incredible jumble of feelings that raced through Penelope's body, leaving her breathless. His warm mouth moved on hers gently at first, and then, when she began to respond, he deepened the kiss. Parting her lips, his tongue darted inside her mouth, and Penelope sagged against him.

Every inch of her body came alive. Her flesh tingled,

her breath staggered, and she thought her heart might leap from her breast.

When he pulled away, he held her tightly, supporting her weight easily. "I don't ask that you not go, Penelope. I only ask that you wait for me."

"For you?" She swallowed, blinked, and tried to focus her gaze on his face.

"Yes. There is . . . something I have to do right away." He sucked in a gulp of air and rushed on, "I don't want you going to face that old bitch alone."

"I won't have you speak for me, Patrick." Strength seeped back into her legs and she stood straight, fighting to regain control of herself. "Eustace was my brother, and I must handle his murderer as *I* see fit."

He smiled. "I know."

Stunned, she stared at him. She'd never expected him to surrender.

"I won't interfere with what happens between you and her. I simply want to be at your side." He moved one hand up to cup her cheek. "And later, when we've both finished our tasks, there's more I'd like to say."

"I, uh . . ." The warmth of his hand on her face distracted her from clear thinking.

"Please, Penelope," he whispered. "Just wait for me."

"How long?"

"A couple of hours at most."

She stared up into his eyes. "Will you tell me where you're going? And why?"

"No."

She stiffened.

"Not yet," he amended. "But I swear I'll tell you everything . . . *later.*"

"Very well, Patrick," she heard herself say. It didn't make sense, she knew. But something deep within her urged her to grant him this one favor. "I won't go alone. I'll wait."

CHAPTER
···NINETEEN···

ENRIQUE GLANCED AT her, shrugged, then looked back at the trail. "It is your own fault, Julietta. If you had curbed your harpy's tongue, this would not have been necessary."

Julietta breathed through her nose and tried once more to push the gag from her mouth. But it was no use. Her captor had tied his handkerchief tightly. It didn't give at all. She glared daggers at his back, then slumped dejectedly in the saddle.

What did it matter? What did any of it matter now? Micah was dead. Killed by this *asesino*, assassin. Her grandmother had refused to see her. Julie sighed and squeezed her eyes shut briefly. Her father, she knew wouldn't bother looking for her, once he realized that Doña Ana had won. After all, it was not for love of his daughter that he had asked the Benteens to escort her home. It was merely to best *la Patrona*.

The morning sun moved over the desert, and Julie let her gaze wander across the familiar landscape. Sand, rocks, sage, and cactus. Dry. Lonely.

For an instant she let her mind travel back to the mountains in Wyoming. To the tall trees surrounding the Benteen ranch. To the cold wind and the varied shades of green that made up their world.

Micah's image rose up before her and she swallowed, pushing her tongue against the gag in her mouth. Her eyes ached with the need to cry, but no tears would come.

She'd had such plans. She hadn't even had the chance to tell him *why* she'd insisted on being married by a priest. Julie studied her mind's image of him and tried to imagine what his reaction might have been when she told him that once married by a priest, there was no possibility of divorce.

He'd been trapped since the night of their wedding and hadn't known it. She would never have let him go.

Her eyes opened wide, and she stared malevolently at Enrique's back. And now he was lost to her forever.

Someday, she vowed silently, she would find a way to kill Enrique. Even if it meant an eternity in Hell.

* * *

Vicente wiped his damp palms with his snow white handkerchief, then tucked it away in his coat pocket. He'd waited so long.

He stood up and paced the length of his library. A glance at the clock on the mantel filled him with a growing excitement. Soon. She would be here soon.

Inhaling sharply, he walked to the closest window and pulled the heavy draperies aside. From this vantage point he could see the main road to the rancho. He would be able to watch as Julietta rode to join him.

"You sent for me, Señor?"

Dropping the deep maroon fabric, Vicente slowly turned to face the girl waiting just inside the door. Rosa stood, head bowed, poised for flight.

He could hardly credit the changes in her. In only a matter of days the plump little maid seemed to have shrunk considerably. Her thick black hair hung limply on either side of her face, and her shoulders were hunched in defeat. And yet . . . something in her stance told Vicente that there was still *some* spirit left in the girl.

Enough perhaps for one last "game" before his bride-to-be arrived.

The big man strolled to the ox-blood leather settee and sat down. Patting the cushion beside him, he said, "Come here, Rosa. We haven't much time."

She looked up through her lashes, and he thought he saw a flash of defiance before she lowered her gaze and walked to his side.

He lifted the hem of her dirty skirt and ran his palm up her leg slowly. "Soon, Rosa, my bride will arrive. And then I will have no need for you."

Her head snapped up. "I may leave then, Patron?"

She looked entirely too anxious to be away, he told himself furiously. Had she no appreciation for the honor he'd done her by allowing her into his bed? Was he to receive no respect at all from the *puta*?

His expansive mood gone, shattered by her selfishness, he said harshly, "No. You will remain here." Looking into her shadowed eyes, he added, "There will be times no doubt when I will have need of you again." Vicente pinched her buttocks and noted that she'd learned to disguise her pain.

"Sí, Don Vicente," she mumbled.

Deliberately he pinched her again, harder, determined to see pain in her eyes. This time he succeeded and smiled gently.

"Who knows, Rosa. Perhaps someday . . . if you've learned to show me gratitude for the many favors I have shown you"—he reached up and thrust his fingers inside her body—"perhaps I will allow you to leave."

She stood rigid, her face empty of emotion.

"Come, Rosa," he said, removing his hand and pulling her down beside him, "show me what you have learned."

As Rosa unbuttoned his trousers, Vicente sighed and closed his eyes. He could hardly believe that his long wait was nearly over. The message from Doña Ana had assured him that Julietta would be in his house within the hour. All that was left was to arrange for the priest to come and marry them.

But, he told himself, there would be plenty of time for that. There was no hurry, after all. Don Vicente snorted a half laugh. It wasn't as if her family would be up in arms protecting her virtue. Her own grandmother was the one who had handed her over to him. And the girl's father was not sober long enough to notice that she was gone.

Julietta would not give him any problems, he knew. Once he had taken her virginity, she would *have* to marry him.

It would all be perfect. It would be as it should have been years ago. With Elena. Vicente swallowed heavily. He felt Rosa's warm mouth close over him, and he smiled.

*   *   *

Penelope paced anxiously. She shouldn't have agreed to wait. For heaven's sake. What *had* she been thinking?

Nothing, she reminded herself sternly. As soon as Patrick kissed her, she'd stopped thinking entirely. Gingerly she raised her fingers to her lips. She'd often wondered what a kiss would be like. But nothing she'd ever imagined even came close to the reality.

A clock in the hall struck the hour, and silently she counted along. Nine o'clock. Disgusted, she marched to the front window and held the curtain aside. He'd been gone only an hour. Still another hour to wait.

In the distance a cloud of dust appeared. As she watched, it moved closer and closer until she could almost make out the fast-moving rider. Penelope squinted into the morning sun. A lone man, bent low over his horse's neck and approaching the house at a furious pace.

Intrigued, she went to the front door and opened it.

A few of the ranch hands straggled into the yard as Micah rode up, but he paid them no mind. He hadn't come to talk to the hired hands. And he didn't have time to be polite.

One overeager fella jumped out in front of him, trying to stop him. Micah urged Satan on, and the horse barreled into the thin man, knocking him end over end in the dirt. The others shouted, but Micah went on.

Just short of the courtyard, he pulled up on Satan's reins, and before the big horse had come to a stop, Micah leaped to the ground. Still slightly unsteady, he nonetheless hurried to the open doorway ahead of him.

The tall, no-nonsense woman standing there held her ground, arms crossed over her chest. "May I help you?" she asked.

"Where's Duffy?" Micah spat out and looked behind him at the men gathering around.

"He's not here at the moment, I'm afraid."

Micah cursed softly, stepped around her, and into the hall of the big house. His gaze moved quickly over the emptiness before he turned back to her. It was then the woman noticed the dried blood from his wound.

"You've been hurt!"

"Yes, ma'am, but I ain't here to talk about that. I need to find Duffy, now."

"Young man, I've already told you. He's not here. He'll be back within the hour. Won't you come inside and let me tend to your injuries?"

Dammit. Wouldn't you bloody well know it? In the next instant he told himself it didn't matter. He hadn't expected help from the man anyway. All he really needed was directions to the Santos ranch.

"No, ma'am, but thanks." He half turned away, then glanced back at her. "Would you maybe know where the Santos spread is?"

"Doña Ana Santos?"

Her face kind of froze up when she said the name, and Micah only had a moment to note that the old bag didn't have many friends. "Yes'm."

The woman stepped out of the doorway, tilted her head to look at him curiously, and asked, "What is your name, sir? I dislike speaking with strangers."

"The name's Micah Benteen, ma'am, and no offense, but I got no time to talk to you, stranger or not."

"Benteen?" She took a step closer. "Are you the young man hired to bring Julietta home?"

"Yeah." Duffy must've told her about him. "If ya don't mind my askin', who the he— heck are you?"

"Penelope Butterworth, Mr. Benteen." She held out

her hand and shook his firmly. "Is Julietta the reason you're interested in Doña Ana?"

"Yes, ma'am." Micah shifted anxiously from foot to foot. Time was slippin' by. "The old bat's hired man took a shot at me yesterday evenin', then lit out with Julietta. I'm fixin' to get her back. Now. Do you know where the Santos place is?"

"No, but I can find out." She turned around and called to the men in the yard. "Find Esteban, please. Bring him to the barn."

Micah watched one of the men hustle off, then looked down at her as Penelope Butterworth grabbed his upper arm.

"You were quite right, Mr. Benteen."

"About what, ma'am," he asked as she spun him about and started dragging him to the barn.

"We have no time for chatting. Your horse appears to be quite exhausted, Micah. May I call you Micah? Good. We shall find you another."

"We?"

"I shall, of course, accompany you on your quest."

* * *

From less than a mile off, Patrick saw the distinct outline of Don Vicente's rancho. He pulled his horse to a stop, wrapped the reins around the saddle horn, and methodically checked his guns.

He knew the vaqueros who worked for the old Don had no great love for their patron. So he wasn't expecting too much trouble getting past them and into the house. But it was best to be prepared. Sliding his pistol back into its holster, he pulled the rifle from the saddle scabbard, and cradled it in the crook of his left arm.

Patrick wasn't even sure yet just what it was he

planned to do once he was face to face with Don Vicente. He only knew it was something he had to do. For Elena's sake, he had to stare into the old man's eyes and tell him that he knew everything.

And he had to ensure that Julietta would be safe. If the only way to do that was to rid the world of Don Vicente Alvarez, then so be it.

Lifting the reins again, Patrick heeled his horse sharply and rode on.

* * *

Once across the Rio Grande the ride to Doña Ana's was a short one. Beyond noting that the Englishwoman was keeping up with him, Micah paid no attention at all.

His entire being was concentrated on Julietta. His wife.

As they rode beneath the wrought-iron arch framing the gated entrance to the Santos rancho, Micah's blood raced with expectation. The yard was surprisingly empty of life. He'd anticipated having to fight his way through loyal ranch hands, and the fact that he didn't was almost disappointing.

The unreleased rage in him intensified.

An old Mexican woman with frightened eyes opened the door to them, and Micah pushed his way past her. Fear and exhaustion gripped him tightly, and the last thing he was worried about was being polite.

Determinedly he began searching the rooms opening off the main hall. Storming down the passage, his boot-heels thundering in the silence, he threw wide one door after the other. Behind him, he vaguely heard the Englishwoman questioning the startled servant.

He grabbed another brass knob, gave it a turn, and threw it open just as Penelope sailed past him.

"Micah!" She ordered grimly, "Follow me!"

Hot on her heels he reached the last door only a breath behind her. Stepping around her, Micah threw the door wide and stepped inside. With the draperies closed, shutting out the late-morning sun, the room was in total darkness save for a bright shaft of light streaming in an open door on the far side of the room.

Micah marched across the tilted floor and stepped through the doorway to the patio beyond. An old woman in a dark green dress stood beside a water fountain. When she turned to look at him, the chill of her gaze struck him.

"You Doña Ana?" he said abruptly.

Those black eyes moved over him contemptuously, then dismissed him. "Get out."

"Lady," he shot back, taking another step toward her, "I got no time for your uppityness. Where's my wife?"

"Wife?" he heard Penelope mutter.

Doña Ana snorted. "By the look of you, Señor . . . I would look for your wife in a pigsty."

Micah sucked in air, desperately hoping to control his temper just a few more minutes. "Look here, Ana."

Her eyebrows shot straight up.

"I been shot at," he continued "chased by grizzlies, near stabbed, then shot again on account of you. And I mean to tell ya—my patience is almighty thin right now." Micah walked to within a step of her. "I want some answers, and I want 'em now. Where's my wife? Where's Julietta?"

"Wife?" The old woman's eyes narrowed perceptibly. "You say you are *married* to Julietta?"

Micah gritted his teeth. Everything he'd ever been taught his whole life about respectin' his elders and treatin' women good was about to go clean out the window.

He spared one glance at Penelope and found her staring at the old bat like Doña Ana was the Devil himself. He shook his head and turned back to his enemy.

"Listen, Granny . . ."

She flinched as if he'd struck her, then began hurling Spanish at him at an astonishing speed.

"Cut that out!" he shouted.

The old woman stopped, stunned.

"Now, Granny, I only want my wife. I'm willin' to forget about you sendin' them two ya-hoos, Enrique and Carlos, after me . . . 'cause you're old and such. But if you don't tell me where Julietta is right this damn minute"— he broke off abruptly and forced himself to pull in a deep breath of cool morning air—"I swear, Granny. I ain't never hit a woman in my life— don't know if I even can. But I'll sure as hell give 'er a try."

Doña Ana curled her lip and sneered at him. "You would not dare."

Penelope spoke up suddenly, and both Micah and the old woman turned to look at her. "Micah, if you will allow me, I have no such misgivings."

Doña Ana stared at her for a moment, then took a step back. Penelope closed the space between them immediately. Lifting her right hand, she smacked the older woman's cheek—hard.

Stunned, Doña Ana flushed beet red. Fury sparked in her black eyes, and her breath came in hard, short gasps.

"Tell him the whereabouts of his wife, you unspeakable woman!" Penelope ordered in a low, dangerous tone. "Then he can be on his way, and you and I can settle the business between us."

Her fingers curled into claws, Doña Ana struck out at the younger woman, but Penelope batted her hand away easily. Screaming in frustration, the old woman turned on Micah.

"You are too late, gringo!" She smiled at him, and Micah tightened his hands into fists at his sides. "She is gone!"

"Where?"

"To her future husband."

"*I'm* her husband."

She spat at him. "You are nothing. In Mexico it is Don Vicente who says what will be."

Micah grabbed her upper arms, felt the fragile bones beneath her dress, and released her immediately. Everything inside him called out for action, and he had to force himself to say simply, "Tell me where this fella Vicente lives."

Ana shrugged. "Why not? Vicente will have Julietta and kill you. It will be over."

Micah wasn't interested in her threats. But he paid close attention as the old bitch told him exactly how to find the Alvarez rancho. He paused only a moment to look at Penelope. "You comin'?"

"Not yet. I shall catch up with you, never fear."

"I won't be goin' slow."

"Of course not, Micah. Ride as quickly as you can."

He jerked her a nod. He hated like hell leavin' her here alone with Ana, but it couldn't be helped. If she didn't want to go, he didn't have time to *make* her.

Looking down at the evil old woman, he said, deliberately, "Thanks, *Granny*."

Ana's face flushed anew, and she clutched at her throat as she watched the man leave. Only then did she turn to Penelope.

"Get out, gringa, before I have you horsewhipped." She waved one hand at the door. "I am finished speaking."

"Not quite yet, I think."

Penelope shook her head and stared down at her nemesis. The enemy she'd come so far to crush. How strange, she thought, that this one, small woman was at the heart of so much pain.

"I want you to know one thing," she said quietly.

Doña Ana drew in several ragged breaths. Fury was evident in her rigid stance. But Penelope disregarded the woman's temper and went right on.

"Once I have assisted that nice young man in finding his *wife*," she emphasized the word, "I shall be back."

"You do not frighten me, gringa."

"That is not my intention, Señora. I *intend* to see you pay for the murder of my brother."

"*¡Loca!*" she murmured. Then in English, she said it again, "You are crazed."

"I will return again and again," Penelope went on as if the other woman hadn't spoken at all. "I will talk to everyone—from the marshal of El Paso—to the governor of Texas—to the president of Mexico."

"Be careful, gringa," Ana muttered and tugged at the neck of her dress.

Penelope moved closer, staring into the woman's eyes with all the intensity that had been built up over the last two years of struggle. "Do not *think* to threaten me. I will not be bullied or ignored. And I will *not* be silenced as easily as my brother was."

Doña Ana shook her head, gasped, and arched her neck, struggling for air.

"You see," Penelope added, "he was a man with a certain sympathy for old women ... even those who didn't deserve it. *I*, however, entertain no such sympathies. I know you for the spider you are—and I *shall* crush you!"

Satisfied for the moment, Penelope turned and regally walked away from her quarry. Composed, controlled, she swept across the patio, through the adjoining room and into the hall.

La Patrona seethed with impotent rage. Her mind a whirl of thoughts, she snatched at the most urgent one first. She must send for Enrique. He would, no doubt, after delivering Julietta into Vicente's eager hands, make for El Paso and his favorite saloon.

A small twinge of discomfort curled in her breast, snaking its tentacles along the length of her left arm. She ignored it and let herself imagine the arrogant gringa pleading Enrique for her life. As soon as she'd rested a bit, she would send one of the men for him.

Then the ugly Englishwoman would learn what it was to strike Doña Ana Santos!

The old woman slumped uneasily to the stone bench encircling the water fountain. Drops of water splashed into the pool below, and the sound seemed unusually loud.

A sharp, sudden pain shot across her chest, and she gasped aloud. Her fingers pulled at the neck of her dress, hoping for comfort, but there was none.

Trying to take steady, regular breaths, she fought for

control of the pain . . . and lost. Nothing would stop it. It grew and grew inside her body until it felt as though a boulder rested on her chest.

There was no air. Frantically she looked around at the empty patio. No one was near. And she had no breath to scream for help. Eyes wide, she felt herself slip from the bench to the stone patio.

Lying on her back, she stared up at the sky helplessly. A single tear fell from the corner of her eye and rolled down her still smooth cheek. Her throat worked convulsively, and her fingers curled uselessly at her bodice.

The pain swept on, carrying her further and further from all that was familiar.

Clouds seemed to cover the sun, and the day became dark. Another, stronger pain attacked her, and Doña Ana moaned in the stillness.

CHAPTER
···TWENTY···

JULIETTA TURNED SLOWLY around to look at the elegantly appointed bedroom. A scarlet quilt covered the extrawide bed, and there was a single oil lamp sitting on a small table beside it. A massive chest of drawers stood against one wall, and standing in a cluster on the opposite side of the room were five, full-length mirrors, facing the bed.

Five Juliettas looked back at her, and each of them wore the same, worried expression. Faced with her own fears, Julie deliberately turned her back to the mirrors and continued her inspection of the room. When her glance fell on the heavy, forest green draperies, she hurried to them, telling herself that there was still a chance. Perhaps she could escape through the window.

She pulled the fabric back and felt her hope fade. Bolted to the outside of the window were wrought-iron bars. And though they'd been twisted into the shapes of delicate birds and flowers, Julie knew they were not merely decorative.

She was trapped.

Wrapping her arms about her, Julietta turned a wary eye on the closed, locked door. Soon, surely, Don

Vicente would come to her. Perhaps even now he stood just outside that door, listening to her movements.

At the thought she straightened up and squared her shoulders. She would not surrender easily. She would tell him that she was a married woman. Perhaps he wouldn't want her since she was no longer a virgin.

Time crawled past. Why did no one come? Was there no one in the great house?

Since her arrival she hadn't seen a soul. Not even a servant in the halls or on the stairs. Enrique alone had brought her to this room, and even *he* hadn't spoken to her.

He'd simply removed the gag and untied her wrists. Then, she remembered, he'd glanced from the mirrors to her and ... smiled.

Julietta shivered and dropped to the floor, her back against the wall. Her hands curled into fists, she wished longingly for a weapon of some kind to defend herself with. But the room was carefully empty of any such item.

In the silence Julie summoned up Micah's image. She contented herself with memories of his arms around her. Even the memory of his shouting, his impatient temper was enough to comfort her. Deep in her heart, she pretended that he was not dead. She wiped from her mind the vision of him lying on the sand, blood streaming from his head. Instead, she told herself that he was even now on his way to her.

With that thought firmly planted in her brain, Julie stared at the door opposite her and waited.

El Patron pushed the girl away and stood up. He straightened the fall of his trousers and pulled at the fit of his too tight, black jacket. His sausagelike fingers tugged the edge of his deep blue satin vest over the mound of his stomach, then smoothed back his thinning gray hair.

The girl lowered her gaze and tried to make herself as small as possible.

"Go to the kitchens, Rosa," Don Vicente ordered quietly. "I will send for you later."

She backed away from him carefully.

"And for God's sake," he snapped as an afterthought, "clean yourself!"

Rosa bobbed her head and stepped into the hallway. The other servants, as always, were not to be seen. No one in the Patron's household wanted to be noticed. Her bare feet slid across the cold tile toward the kitchens, and she told herself that it didn't matter if she bathed or not. She would never be clean again. She would always be dirty. She would always feel *his* dirt on her body.

Behind her, Don Vicente began to climb the stairs, and she could not stop herself from glancing back at him. The smile on his face did not mean good things for the woman in that room.

Rosa shuddered, pushed her lank hair out of her eyes, and stopped in her tracks.

Splintered thoughts spun in her mind. When he was finished with his new woman, she knew he would send for her, Rosa, again. There would be no escape. Ever. He would never let her go.

His heavy, insistent footsteps sounded overhead, and she cocked her head to listen. Over and over again, her brain warned, he would use her. And when he was finally through with her . . . what other man would have her?

Upstairs, Don Vicente had stopped at the door of the bedroom she'd come to know so well in the last few days. She heard him thrust the key in the lock, open, and close the door.

Rosa listened, but did not hear him turn the key again.

Suddenly sure of what she must do, Rosa turned and went back down the hall to the Don's library . . . where her hell had begun.

Pure, bright sunlight spilled into the room, dappling the floor with spots of gold. A morning breeze lifted the edges of the draperies, covering the stench of Don Vicente with the fresh, clean scent of the desert.

She walked quickly, boldly. There was no reason to hide. She knew she would not be disturbed. Crossing the room, she went straight to his desk and closed her mind to the image of that first time. But it did no good. Rosa knew that she would always remember the feel of the cold wood beneath her cheek and the edge of the desk biting into her legs as he—

Enough! She tossed her head, swinging her length of hair behind her back. Pulling open the top drawer, she reached for the pistol she'd once seen. Slowly her fingers curled around the handle.

Patrick looked down at the vaquero dispassionately. The barrel of his rifle centered on the fallen man's chest, he climbed down from his horse and looked more carefully at the man who'd tried to stop him.

He'd kicked out at the cowhand when the man grabbed his horse's bridle. Now, on closer inspection, he saw the unconscious man's jaw hanging crookedly and knew he'd broken it.

Holding his rifle tightly, Patrick told himself that the man had gotten off lucky. A broken jaw was preferable to being shot. One quick glance around the empty yard reassured him that no one else had seen his arrival. Hurriedly he crossed the courtyard, opened the front door, and stepped inside Don Vicente's house.

Julietta watched the brass knob turn. When the heavy door swung open and Don Vicente entered the bedroom, her breath caught in her throat.

He was fatter, older, than she remembered. His watery brown gaze moved over her, and she shuddered.

"Julietta," he sighed and shut the door behind him. "I have so looked forward to this, our first moments together in our home."

She pushed herself flatter against the wall and didn't take her eyes off him.

"Why do you sit on the floor, my dear?" he asked. "Surely the bed would be more comfortable?"

She said nothing. He moved closer, crossing in front of the mirrors, and she saw him flick a quick glance at his own passing.

"Do you like our room?"

Julie shook her head, still not trusting her voice. All her fine notions of standing up to him, fighting him, disappeared. Her fantasy of Micah alive and coming to her died. There would be no rescue. No one to help her. She was alone.

"No?" Vicente looked about him, a wrinkle of a frown on his face. "Tell me what displeases you. I will have it changed." He smiled again, and a crawling sensation moved over her flesh.

Delay, she told herself. Put him off. Talk to him. If

he thought she was content to be there, perhaps there would be a chance for escape.

"The mirrors," she blurted out, before she could change her mind.

"Ah . . ." He nodded slowly and held out one hand to her. "It is only because you do not know *why* they are here. Come. I will show you."

She looked at his fleshy, moist hand and knew if she touched it she would be sick.

"Julietta," his voice came again, firmer this time. His eyes narrowed slightly. "I insist you stand beside me, my dear."

A glimmer of impatience shone in his small eyes, and Julie told herself that making him angry would do her no good at all. And still she couldn't bring herself to take his hand.

Pushing herself to her feet, Julie walked to his side. When his hands closed on her shoulders, she bit her tongue to keep from screaming.

Vicente guided her around to stand in front of him, facing the mirrors.

It was almost too much to bear. Five Don Vicentes stared back at her. Five sets of hands touched her. Five pairs of eyes watched her.

"Do you see now," he whispered, and she felt his breath on her ear, "how exciting it is to be able to watch as well as *do*?"

He dipped his head to plant a kiss on her shoulder, and Julie's eyes squeezed into slits. And still she watched the mirrored Don bend to her flesh.

"You are frightened, I know," he said softly, "but no woman remains a virgin forever."

Virgin. Here it was, she thought wildly. Her chance.

She caught the reflection of her own eyes and said quickly, "I am not a virgin, Don Vicente."

He stopped. Raising his head slightly, he looked into the mirrors and met her gaze. "What did you say?"

"I said I am no longer virgin." She swallowed heavily. His fingers on her arms tightened. "I am married."

"What?" His round, sweaty face suffused with color, he glared at her mirrored image. "When? Who?"

She winced at the strength of his grip, but lifted her chin as she answered, "In Vacio, a few days ago, the priest there married me to Micah Benteen."

"No." He shook his head firmly, refusing to believe. "You are promised to *me!*"

Suddenly terrified, Julie watched his reflection as rage swept through him. His fingers dug into her shoulders, and he shook her until she felt as though her head would snap off her neck.

Furious, he pushed her from him. Unwilling to turn and face him, Julie watched him in the glass before her. He cursed her, Doña Ana, and the mysterious gringo husband. His eyes wild, he flung his hands out wide in frustration, and in the mirrors, behind him, Julie saw five reflections of the door swing open.

A young woman with shadowed eyes stood on the threshold, a pistol in one hand. Slowly the five girls lifted their guns, pointing them at Don Vicente's broad back.

Julie screamed and dropped to the floor. She peered up at the mirrors through half-shut eyes and watched as the Don turned to face the girl.

He took a single step, held out his hands, and shouted, "Rosa!"

But his voice was lost in the deafening roar of the

gun. He staggered and lowered his head to look at his chest. Before the sound had faded completely, there was another shot, and Julie saw Don Vicente's body crumple lifelessly.

In the almost painful silence that followed, Julie cautiously raised her head. She watched the girl with the haunted expression drop the pistol, turn, and walk out of the room.

It was over.

She turned her head and risked a glance at the man lying so near her on the floor. His lifeless eyes stared back at her, and Julie felt tremors engulf her body.

Vaguely she heard someone running. A man's heavy steps thundered through the quiet house. Then a voice she thought she recognized shouted her name.

In a bewildered daze she stared at the empty doorway across the room. It couldn't be, she knew. She wanted to get up. She wanted to run from that place. From . . . him, but her legs wouldn't move.

Helplessly, she waited. When Patrick Duffy entered the room, his gaze frantically searching for her, Julie swallowed back a sudden rush of tears and said softly, "Papa?"

Patrick hesitated only a moment, then rushed toward his daughter. Still grasping his rifle with one hand, with the other, he pulled Julietta from the floor and clasped her to him.

Her knees weak, she wobbled unsteadily and buried her face in his chest. As she cried, he held her tightly and sent a silent, thankful prayer heavenward.

He hadn't expected to find her here. But when he heard that terrified scream, he'd known it was Julietta. And for one brief, hideous moment, Patrick had thought sure that he'd been too late. That he'd missed his last chance with his daughter as surely as he'd lost Elena.

To whatever gods protected fools, he owed a debt he could never repay.

"Are you all right?" he whispered, suddenly thinking of all that might have happened to her in that room.

"*Sí*, Papa," she answered softly, her fingers tight on the lapels of his brown leather coat. "I am fine."

Patrick sighed in relief. Through some stroke of good fortune, he'd gone to Don Vicente's rancho on the very day he was most needed.

Memories of the last few minutes crowded his brain. At Julietta's scream he'd instinctively raced for the stairs. And when the gunshots sounded out, he'd thought his heart would stop. Reluctantly he remembered the face of the girl he'd passed at the head of the stairs. Patrick had realized at once that *she* was the one who'd fired the gun, simply from the emptiness in her eyes.

Now, glancing down at what had once been Don Vicente, Patrick grimly told himself that but for that girl, Julietta might have come to be like her.

Slowly he guided his daughter from the room, turning his back on his old enemy. In the hall he leaned against the wall, cradling Julietta close. He felt her trembling as his own and wished heartily that he knew what to say to her.

What words could he offer her to atone for the years of inattention, neglect? How could he expect her to forgive him when he knew he would never forgive himself?

"Papa?"

Julietta spoke, and his eyes snapped down to hers.

He stared into deep blue eyes, so much like his own. Tears hovered on her lashes, but her trembling had almost ceased.

He leaned down and placed a gentle kiss on her forehead. His eyes squeezed shut as he fought for control of the overpowering feelings rushing through him. For the first time in years, he felt truly, wholly alive. Pulling his head back, he looked directly into her eyes and tried to speak past the knot in his throat.

"Julietta, I'm so sorry." Even as he said it, he knew it wasn't enough. That one tiny phrase couldn't begin to explain how deeply he regretted the time and years lost. And yet it was all he could say. "I am so bloody sorry for everything. How I've hurt you. I . . ." His gaze moved over her face, and his right hand patted her shoulder awkwardly. "There aren't enough words, Julietta, but—"

"No, Papa," she said gently and laid her head on his chest, "no more words. It is enough that you're here. Holding me."

His heart stopped, lurched, and beat again more steadily. It was more than he deserved, he knew. And somehow he would find a way to earn the love he'd treated so carelessly for too long.

People moving and whispering belowstairs caught his attention, and Patrick reluctantly straightened up, drawing Julietta with him. His arm around her shoulders, he started downstairs. A flush of pride swept him as he watched his daughter's chin lift.

At the foot of the wide steps an old woman waited, anxiety etched in her eyes. "*¿El Patron?*" she asked.

In Spanish, Patrick said quickly, "There was an accident. Don Vicente is dead."

"Dios mio," the woman muttered and crossed herself. Then she cast one quick glance out the open front door.

Patrick followed her gaze and saw the nameless girl who'd delivered his daughter from danger. She was walking toward the wide drive, away from the rancho. Quickly he said, "Don Vicente was showing me his pistol, and the gun went off. My daughter was very upset by the terrible accident."

The old woman's eyes narrowed, and she looked from one to the other of them.

She would have her suspicions, Patrick knew, but she wouldn't do anything about them. His and Julietta's word would be enough to quiet any official trouble. And he would not allow that poor girl to suffer any more than she obviously already had.

Deliberately he walked past the housekeeper. He and Julietta stepped outside into the morning air, and he felt his daughter's limbs go limp.

Patrick supported her weight and guided her to his horse. There would be time to talk later. Now he wanted to get her home. Where she could rest.

From not far away, the thunder of a horse in full gallop roared into the stillness. Patrick turned to see a wild-eyed man with reddish brown hair and blood covering one side of his face ride full tilt into the courtyard.

The young man leaped from his still-moving horse and shouted, "Julie!"

She straightened and spun about in her father's arms. "Micah?" she said unbelievingly. Her jaw dropped, her eyes rolled back in her head, and she fainted.

Patrick didn't have time to do more than catch his

daughter before another horse and rider entered the yard.

"Penelope?"

The stranger was beside him trying to pull Julietta out of his grasp. "What the hell happened to her?" he shouted.

Penelope Butterworth was sliding from her saddle, despite her efforts to stay seated. Her soft brown hair had fallen from its ever-present knot. A tumble of curls covered one eye and hung down over her ear, and her ridiculous wool riding clothes were blanketed in dirt.

He'd never seen her look lovelier.

"Let go of my wife, mister," the young man snapped and tugged at Julietta.

"What?" Patrick asked, tearing his gaze away from Penelope.

"I *said*—"

"Patrick," Penelope interrupted, tilting even farther to one side of her horse, "this is Micah Benteen. Julietta's *husband*."

"Husband?"

"That's right," Micah answered and scooped his wife into his arms. Cradling her close, he kissed her forehead and began talking in a frantic undertone.

"But how? When?"

"Patrick . . . if you wouldn't mind," Penelope called and slipped another inch or two, "perhaps you could lend me a little assistance, and we could discuss their nuptials back at the rancho?"

Confused, Patrick hurried toward the tall woman who'd given him back his life. His hands at her waist, he helped her down, then glanced back at his daughter and, it appeared, his son-in-law.

"Benteen, you said?"

"Yes." She tugged at her little jacket and pushed her hair back from her face.

"Strange . . ."

"Patrick?"

"Hmmm?"

"Is everything all right now?"

He tore his gaze away and stared down into the gentle brown eyes looking up at him. A smile tugged at the corner of his lips, and he carefully smoothed her hair back from her forehead. "Yes, Penelope. Everything is just fine. Or will be."

"Will be?" She tilted her head and asked, "What does that mean?"

"It means, Miss Butterworth, that everything will be just fine the minute you agree to marry me."

Eyes wide with shock, Penelope's mouth opened and closed and opened again.

Patrick grinned. "Does that mean yes?"

Still staring speechlessly, she nodded.

"Good." He bent down and covered her mouth with his.

"Julie?" Micah whispered between kisses feverishly dropped on her brow, her eyes, her cheeks. "Julie darlin', wake up. C'mon, girl, open your eyes!"

Her eyelids fluttered, then slowly opened.

"Lord, woman! You scared me to death, keelin' over like that."

"Micah? It is you?"

"Hell, o'course it's me! Who the hell else calls you *darlin'*?" His relieved smile took the sting from his words.

"No one," she answered and reached up to touch his bloodied cheek. "Oh, Micah . . ."

"Don't you worry. It ain't bad."

"I thought you were dead."

He glanced over his shoulder to make sure the other couple couldn't hear him. But they were far too caught up in each other to notice a thing.

Leaning down, Micah whispered, "I not only am *not* dead—you wait till I get you alone . . . I'll show you just how alive I am."

Julie reached up and wrapped her arms around his neck. Pursing her lips slightly, she said, "Kiss me, husband, and then take me home. I think you must prove to me that you are indeed alive."

His lips met hers briefly, then he pulled back and looked down at her. His smile gone, Micah said quietly, "Don't you never go off without me again, wife. You hear me?"

"I love you, Micah." She laid her head on his chest and listened to the wonderful, glorious pounding of his heart.

Micah's arms closed around her, and he squeezed her as though he would never let go of her. "Hell, Julie, I love you, too."

···EPILOGUE···

Benteen Ranch, Wyoming

"Read that last part again."

"Nah ... I want to hear about the bear again."

"Why don't y'all shut your fool mouths for a minute." Trib glared at his brothers.

"Hallie," Ritter said and leaned over his wife's shoulders, "why don't you read the whole thing one more time?"

Hallie Benteen Sloane looked around the table. Shadrack, Jericho, and Trib stared at her, obviously waiting.

"All right," she finally agreed, "but we've already read the damn thing two times. The dang telegram don't get any longer the more ya read it, y'know!"

Ritter kissed her cheek. "Once more?"

She smiled up at him and heard Jericho say softly, "Now why didn't we never think of soft talkin' her into doin' things? Would've saved a helluvalot of fightin' over the years."

"Wouldn't have worked," Shadrack answered. "You ain't near as pretty as that husband of hers."

Trib laughed, Ritter chuckled, and Jericho took a

swing at Shadrack. But as soon as Hallie began to read the telegram again, everyone settled down and listened.

DEAR FOLKS STOP HELL OF A TRIP STOP SHOT AT STOP MET A GRIZZLY STOP SHOT IN THE HEAD STOP GOT MARRIED STOP JULIE KIDNAPPED STOP GOT HER BACK STOP GRANNY DEAD STOP VICENTE TOO STOP BUSTED HAND ON ENRIQUES FACE STOP ME AND WIFE HOME SOON STOP STAYING HERE FOR DUFFY'S WEDDING STOP MISS YOU ALL STOP [SIGNED] MICAH AND JULIETTA BENTEEN STOP

"If that don't beat all," Trib muttered for the third time.

"Never thought I'd see the day ol' Micah'd get himself hitched." Jericho shook his head sadly.

"*I* never thought I'd live to see the woman who'd have him!" Hallie mused, propping her chin in her hand. "Though I'll admit, I'll be pleased to have another female around here ... 'specially with the baby comin'."

"Wonder what happened to that bear?" Ritter wondered aloud and dropped onto the bench beside Hallie. She leaned against his chest and handed him the well-read telegram. His free hand moved over the small swell of her abdomen gently.

"Hell with the bear," Trib spoke up, staring at the ceiling. "Who the hell did Duffy marry?"

"And who killed Granny?" Shad asked.

"And that Vincent fella?" Jericho added.

"And how in the devil did Micah get shot in the head?" Hallie wondered.

Jericho laughed and punched Shad's arm. "Good

thing whoever shot him got him in a spot where it won't do no harm!"

"Dammit," Trib said firmly, rubbing his splinted leg, "none of us is gonna get any answers at all till Micah and Julietta get back here." He inhaled slowly, raised one eyebrow, and asked his sister, "So, how about we have us some more of that cake of yours and start in plannin' Micah's new sleepin' quarters?"

"Good idea!" Shad said and jumped up to help.

Ritter laid the telegram in the middle of the table and poured everyone another cup of coffee.

Diamond Wildflower Romance

A breathtaking new line of spectacular novels set in the untamed
frontier of the American West. Every month, Diamond Wildflower
brings you new adventures where passionate men and women
dare to embrace their boldest dreams. Finally, romances that
capture the very spirit and passion of the wild frontier.

__TEXAS JEWEL by Shannon Willow
    1-55773-923-4/$4.99
__REBELLIOUS BRIDE by Donna Fletcher
    1-55773-942-0/$4.99
__RENEGADE FLAME by Catherine Palmer
    1-55773-952-8/$4.99
__SHOTGUN BRIDE by Ann Carberry
    1-55773-959-5/$4.99
__WILD WINDS by Peggy Stoks
    1-55773-965-X/$4.99
__HOSTAGE HEART by Lisa Hendrix
    1-55773-974-9/$4.99
__FORBIDDEN FIRE by Bonnie K. Winn
    1-55773-979-X/$4.99
__WARRIOR'S TOUCH by Deborah James
    1-55773-988-9/$4.99
__RUNAWAY BRIDE by Ann Carberry
    0-7865-0002-6/$4.99
__TEXAS ANGEL by Linda Francis Lee
    0-7865-0007-7/$4.99 (May)

FREE
Romance
(a $4.50 value)

Send in the Coupon Below

To get your FREE historical romance and start saving, fill out the coupon below and mail it today. As soon as we receive it we'll send you your FREE Book along with your first month's selections.

Mail To: **True Value Home Subscription Services, Inc. P.O. Box 5235**
120 Brighton Road, Clifton, New Jersey 07015-5235

YES! I want to start previewing the very best historical romances being published today. Send me my FREE book along with the first month's selections. I understand that I may look them over FREE for 10 days. If I'm not absolutely delighted I may return them and owe nothing. Otherwise I will pay the low price of just $4.00 each; a total $16.00 (at *least* an $18.00 value) and save at least $2.00. Then each month I will receive four brand new novels to preview as soon as they are published for the same low price. I can always return a shipment and I may cancel this subscription at any time with no obligation to buy even a single book. In any event the FREE book is mine to keep regardless.

Name _____

Street Address _____ Apt. No. _____

City _____ State _____ Zip Code _____

Telephone _____

Signature _____
(if under 18 parent or guardian must sign)

Terms and prices subject to change. Orders subject
to acceptance by True Value Home Subscription
Services, Inc.